# HANDS OF
# THE MORRI

Visit us at www.boldstrokesbooks.com

## By the Author


Transitioning Home

The Hands of the Morri

# HANDS OF THE MORRI

*by*

## Heather K O'Malley

2023

# HANDS OF THE MORRI

ISBN 13: 978-1-63679-465-5

THIS TRADE PAPERBACK ORIGINAL IS PUBLISHED BY
BOLD STROKES BOOKS, INC.
P.O. BOX 249
VALLEY FALLS, NY 12185

FIRST EDITION: OCTOBER 2023

---

**CREDITS**
EDITOR: CINDY CRESAP
PRODUCTION DESIGN: SUSAN RAMUNDO
COVER DESIGN BY TAMMY SEIDICK AND CHARIOT LOWERY

# Dedication

To all the amazing female fighters and warriors I have known, you are an inspiration, especially Sarah, Jennifer, Gwen, Emma, Jacqui, Alania, Nancy, and countless more.

And, as always, to Kaye

# CHAPTER ONE

Nibs drifted his way over the barren field, hanging on to a breeze that helped him stay aloft. As he flew, he scanned the few stalks of last year's crop that showed a wet tan through the melting snow, to see if there was anything to eat. He spotted nothing. The village he headed toward was part of his normal range and was usually a good source of food. There was a wooden palisade with a ditch round it, the bottom of which still had a decent amount of snow cover on the bramble, which would have plump berries come fall. Thin rivulets of smoke twisted into the cool morning air from numerous chimneys from the various wooden buildings. A few spots of light green, signs of the forthcoming spring, showed here and there in the fields, along with the buds of leaves on branches and new sprouts of grass.

With a steep turn toward the village, he noted others up and about; scents from the baker's oven wafted in the breeze, brought up in the flavorful smoke. The somewhat burned loaves were tasty when he had a chance to get some. Chores were being done by people, various farm animals were tended to, compost was being turned, and bodies were moving through the darkened slush of the dirt streets. Cats sauntered through the morning, hoping to find a bold rat or mouse. Dogs followed their humans, ghosting their chores. Despite these signs of life, the early morning was bereft of the usual noise of the day, mostly.

One of the larger walled households that abutted the palisade was quite busy. Numerous women wearing similar black clothes, with a black padded coat over it all, moved about in the busy act of packing and loading gear onto both animals and carts. The pack animals stood passively, and the two small carts were laden with various trunks and foodstuffs. One was covered tightly with a tarpaulin, the other wasn't. Perhaps there might be a morsel of food in easy reach? The bustle was far more action than in any other place in the village, and he was unsure if the payoff would be worth the grief, despite this location usually being good pickings.

Nibs landed at the gate of the walled household to get a better assessment. He watched the people in the courtyard briefly and then something behind him on the ground moved in his peripheral vision and caught his attention. Heading toward his perch was a familiar human, the boy who was kind to him, shared food, and the occasional shiney, though he was not in his usual place. His usual place was on the other side of the village, in a building that smelled of leather. This required more attention.

Nibs looked toward the oncoming friendly face. Something was wrong with his friend. The boy's hands were clenched white in nervousness, and he had a burlap sack over one shoulder, as he limped forward to the closed gate. His normally shoulder-length hair looked wrong and one eye was swollen shut. Nibs let out an interrogative gronk the young man did not respond to. This concerned him even more.

In front of the gate, one of the armored women noted the young man's approach. Cocking his head, Nibs watched as the young man drew closer and asked in a shaking voice, "Pardon me, but I would like to speak with your kaitan."

The woman wore a padded coat under a vest of black canvas with silver-looking rivets all about it. Over the right breast was an embroidered heraldic crest, black with a silver anvil in the center, a silver and brown hammer at an angle with little flecks of gold, like sparks. She wore a padded coif, and a kettle helm sat on her head; the strap was done up under her chin. A halberd in hand, the guard looked at Nibs's human and nodded before she knocked once on the gate.

The small wooden door set toward the center of the larger gate opened and a flushed-faced woman in a similar outfit looked out. "Yeah?"

The woman gave a jerk of the head toward the young man standing there, who shifted awkwardly. "Wants to talk with Kaitan Tanrei."

Nibs cocked his head and noted how the other woman's eyes widened a little when she faced the young man standing there, before turning back to the other. "Really now?"

"Aye."

With a slight shrug, the woman gestured the boy forward and turned, leading them through the busy yard. Murmured thank ye's trailed them, as they moved through the organized chaos of the company preparing to leave. Nibs flitted closer, hopping into the air and flapping toward the building they were heading to. He wondered what his favorite person was doing and how he had gotten hurt.

In the eye of this whirlwind of preparations to leave stood an older woman with white-streaked dark hair, a nose that had been previously broken, and well-kept armor similar to the guard's. She had a war hammer at her hip and was watching the process unfold around her. People came up to her, received orders, and hustled off. As the guard and his person drew closer, she turned and noted their approach. "Yes?"

"Kaitan, this local wanted to speak with you," said the escort. The kaitan turned her gaze on him, a clear order to start talking.

"Uhm…Kaitan Tanrei, I…" The young man swallowed heavily, even more nervous with those piercing eyes on him. "I'm the cobbler's son and I…I mean…was wondering if I could…uh…join your company?" He stumbled over the words and struggled to get the request out under the gimlet eye of the kaitan.

Nibs watched Kaitan Tanrei scan his person, likely noting everything Nibs had already seen, such as the slight indication of healing bruises on the face and the uneven sack over one shoulder, even the detail that his shoes also looked a little worse for wear. The woman's eyebrow quirked at this detail, given that he had just said he was the cobbler's son. "I see. You do know we're an all-female company, correct?"

"Yes, Kaitan." He did not raise his head, so it looked like the kaitan was speaking to a mop of mousy hair with an awkward knife cut shaping it. Nibs would usually find it funny but nothing about his person looked comfortable.

"There are no men who serve in our company."

"Yes, Kaitan."

"And you want to travel with us when we leave, Oxlen, your town?"

"Yes, Kaitan. I...I don't want to be here anymore."

Tanrei was silent a few moments, looking over the young man some more. Nibs was trying to figure out what she was seeing and the way his person was standing reminded him more of a whipped cur than the usual nervous but fine young man he was familiar with. The kaitan sighed, nodding. "I see. You're likely a lost sister. Fanlis!"

A slight woman exited the building that housed the company. Her dark hair was in a braid, and she wore the same black gambeson the others wore. Her coif was down, she had an inwardly curved sword at her hip and was sliding a rolled-up map into a leather capped tube. She drew closer and said, "Yes, Kaitan?"

Tanrei gestured over to the nervous young man who fidgeted awkwardly. "We may have a lost sister wanting to join our company. Either way, they want to leave with us. Can you take charge of them?"

"Certs. You, come along." Fanlis turned back to the building, waving the young man to follow them. Nibs grumbled that he could no longer see his person.

Once inside, Fanlis stopped and gestured at her travel desk and ordered, "Get those files sorted and put away in the leather satchel sitting on top. Someone will be by to fold the desk for travel shortly. Then I'll drop you with the chiurgeon to get looked at. Toss your bag by the door for now."

He complied quickly and got to work under the watchful eyes of Fanlis. Though he had little idea what she was doing, the work progressed and the travel desk was fully packed and closed up. Fanlis took the satchel of paperwork from him and slung it over her shoulder. She then indicated he should place the collapsed desk by the door. Moving to the altar, which looked like an anvil with a hammer lying atop, Fanlis waved another person inside. "Lynarra, prepare for the rite and get the altar ready for travel."

"Yes, ma'am." This woman was on the short side, with blond hair in a braid, dressed in the same black and silver uniform.

Fanlis turned to face him with a focused look on her face. "Come on, let's have the chiurgeon take a look at you. If it's only bruises, those heal."

As they walked from the building and toward another area, Fanlis asked, "So you want to run away to war do you?"

He grumbled under his breath about his father before he said, "I don't want to run to war, but better war than dying slowly by seasons here."

Fanlis looked at him directly. "So, you would rather leave your village and your known for an unknown that will likely take your life?"

He lowered his head and grumbled just loudly enough to be audible. "If I can be me while doing so, yes."

Fanlis smiled faintly and nodded. "Well, that's enough for a start. We can talk more on the road. Regardless, the Morri will be the one to make the decision about you. Will anyone miss you?"

"Probably, but who cares. They've made it clear to me all I'm good for and I want no part of it. One way or another, I want to leave."

"Eldest?" Fanlis asked.

"Yes. But I don't want to spend my life shearing sheep, processing leather, or making shoes. My da refused to let me continue my schooling or go to one of the monasteries when I asked. I just want to be away. Away from this town and away from him. This isn't my life. I just want to go where I feel…" Words failed him in that moment, so he shrugged, scuffling the ground.

Fanlis looked at him, seeming to assess the truth of his words. "Right, well then, Recruit, once we're sure of your resolve, you'll be inducted into the Hands. Until then, you'll do scut work, run errands, and anything else we can think of to keep you busy. It's only until we reach Turling."

"Thank you." Some of the tension he was holding drained.

Fanlis waved a hand airily as she started walking again. "Yes, yes, well, you came to us, so there is that. Let's get you to the chiurgeon so she can look at your wounds. Afterward, you can take some of those bundles outside. The kaitan or one of the sarnts will show you what horses they get strapped to. For now, since you might be a lost sister, we'll just call you Recruit. If the goddess determines you are indeed a lost sister, you'll earn a name from her."

Recruit nodded and went in through the doorway Fanlis directed him toward. Nibs watched him go with some concern, but the young man did look more hopeful and less stressed overall. That pleased him. He watched as Tanrei came over to Fanlis a short while later. "Well?"

Fanlis smiled slightly and faced her commanding officer. "There are hints he's indeed a lost sister but no outright confession or anything. It's clear he hasn't been treated well, given the wounds, and couldn't care less about this village. Regardless of what happens, he wants out of here."

"Hopefully, before next winter they'll have gotten over things. It's doubtful the people here will recognize him after nearly a year. And that's only if we get stationed here again." Tanrei shrugged. "They do like to rotate us from hold to hold. And we could use another recruit or two to help fill in the gaps. I'm hoping the spring gather will help with that."

Fanlis nodded. "True enough. I was thinking I would have Canli watch him. Her platoon is a bit understrength and it's likely he would need to go there anyway if he's confirmed as a lost sister. I can also have Flit see if she can ferret anything else out from him. Besides, if nothing else, we'll know more when the dedication and the Rite of the Lost Sister is done."

"Indeed. Do that. It's almost time to take down the altar. Do you want the Recruit?"

"No, let him pack the horses once he's done with the chiurgeon. He'll meet the Morri soon enough, and then all things will be decided. Anyway, Lynarra is almost done with that task."

Nibs ruffled his feathers against the chill spring air as he watched the activity. He cocked his head and made an interrogatory tok noise to see if his human noticed as the young man passed near his perch. All he was doing now was work, which was just boring. He tried the sharp and metallic sound again but did not get the response he wanted.

Kaitan Tanrei headed back outside to supervise the last of the packing and the formation of the company. She turned and stared at Nibs sitting on the main beam of a roof. Nibs noted that the woman scanned the courtyard, tracing his line of sight until she spotted the Recruit hefting things onto the back of one of the pack animals under the directions of Sarnt Canli. The woman nodded to herself before walking with purpose toward one of the horses.

Slowly, the company finished their take down. Business wound down as they began to line up in a loose formation. After a short while, the work was complete, save the altar to the Morri. Kaitan Tanrei walked up in front of the troops, all dressed in their black gambeson as well as their black cloth-covered armor with silver rivets, and snapped out, "Hands, attention!"

The company snapped to attention, which surprised Nibs enough that he hopped to the side and ruffled his feathers. Kaitan Tanrei stepped forward. "Blessed Morri, Lady of the Forge, women, and warriors, we thank you for the safety of this winter's rest, here in Oxlen. Bless us as we travel and help us to always improve our steel. May we all be forged anew and unto completion. Morri bless."

Many of the others replied with, "Morri bless."

The Recruit followed along with the ritual awkwardly, doing up the black gambeson he had been given to better blend in and stay warm in the chill, unsure as to what his role could be in the faith of the Morri. He knew she existed, but Father Tombol, the local priest of the Triad, had not gone into any detail about the other divines in the pantheon. The names were familiar, but he knew none of their sacred lore.

Once the prayer was complete, Fanlis and Lynarra took the altar down and carried it to one of the carts. As the box containing the components and the altar were secured in the cart, Kaitan Tanrei nodded and ordered, "Mount up!"

Those few who had mules to ride mounted, while others took up the reins of pack horses, or got onto the cart. The rest slung their packs and settled them into place. The Recruit was amongst the pack train, tasked with trying to lead a rather stubborn mule. While he was busy coaxing it forward, on either side of him were other members of the Hands who masked his presence. They moved from the walled building. The path of their journey took them out of the wooden palisade, on past the farm fields and the pastures for the herd of sheep, and onto the trail under the trees.

As they moved from the walled household to march through the village, Nibs ruffled his feathers again to ward off the slight cold, watching his person walking with a laden mule away from his usual place. That behavior was rather odd, and he was concerned. After a quick scan where he spotted nothing particularly tasty lying about the now abandoned yard, Nibs launched himself into the air. It was clear his person was going away and he did not like that. The gathering needed to be consulted.

Nibs flew back to the forest, toward where the eldest and wisest of the flock roosted. He spotted the gathering of elders sitting on several branches and flew to a lower branch respectfully. Once settled, he hopped forward, kraaing to get attention. The elders turned to face him. He bobbed his head and said, "Elders, my human goes with the women warriors."

The gathering of raven elders shared a look before turning back to him. "And?"

He cocked his head and struggled to find words to express what he was feeling. "He is my friend and I don't want him to go. He shared food and gave shinies. I was comfortable near him. What should I do?"

"What do you want to do?" croaked out the eldest, a raven whose feathers were no longer as lustrous and were shaggier in places, and most heavily tinged with grey.

Nibs thought a moment. What did he want to do? His friend had departed the village and that made him unhappy. Little else in this area made him happy to that degree. He already had been thinking about leaving here to find a mate, but hadn't departed yet as he was concerned for his friend. "I wish to follow."

The eldest nodded. "You said he travels with the women warriors? The Hands, as that flock of humans call themselves, are friends to many raven and crow flocks as well. It is unlikely they will do you harm if you follow. Do as you must, to watch over your human and to find your happiness." The other elders nodded in agreement with that pronouncement and wished him well.

Nibs bowed his head in thanks, grateful that the advice matched his heart, then dropped from the branch and flew off. Flying across the cleared fields of the village, he banked to follow the group's passage into the forest along one of the roads. He was doing what he wanted, going on a journey, and looking after his human. What's more, the elders had agreed, or at least not argued against doing this. This was a good sign and he was going to find his own flock somewhere else. He easily spotted his favorite person, as he was the only person not wearing a black coif as cover for his head. Nibs swooped down from the sky and landed on the Recruit's shoulder. The Recruit started in surprise, and squawked out, "Nibs!"

Nibs ran his beak through the young man's hair, nuzzling and making small noises to soothe his person. It was clear he had suffered some to be here and moved as if he was injured. The young man reached up gently and ran the back of a finger down Nibs's breastbone. "I'm leaving, Nibs. I'm tired of being beaten. If you don't want to leave here with me, then feel free to stay. I'll understand if you do that and I'll miss you."

The gurgling awk in response made the Recruit nod. "Okay, if you feel that way. Just so you know, you're free to do what you want."

A brief croak was the response before Nibs went back to nuzzling his hair, trying to soothe the troubled young man. Nibs could not have cared less for the stares; he was with his human again and his human was calming down from the agitated state he had been in this morning. And who knew, this could just be the sort of adventure Nibs had been craving.

The Recruit looked around and noticed several of the other Hands around him had noticed the interaction. Many of them simply stared at him, some grinning. Blushing, he lowered his head and moved on, hoping to attract less attention.

The Recruit noticed that Fanlis slowed her horse to eventually come alongside the mule he guided. She rode silently and just observed the interactions of both Nibs and him for a bit. She neither said anything nor commented, simply watched. The Recruit squirmed under this further scrutiny which caused Nibs to flap forward to perch on the tailgate of a cart before chiding the Recruit with an ahhk. Fanlis took this all in before riding back to the front. He had no idea what that had been about.

The Recruit simply kept his head down and moved on, trying to not focus on the whys and whats as opposed to walking at the pace the riders set while he guided the laden mule. It wasn't difficult work, and the mule was rather well behaved based on his experience with such animals, but the pace was faster than he expected. All he had to do was occasionally pull the animal's head up higher so it could not crop the early grass on the sides of the trail as they puffed along.

He looked up at Nibs on the back of the cart, thinking it was nice to travel without having to work for it. The cart was a nice and stable place, despite the rocking from the ruts in the road. Nibs said gwah. He repeated the sound as best as he could manage. The Recruit just walked on, working to stay to the pace, but he smiled at the silly sounds Nibs made. Sarnt Canli came alongside and asked, "How're you doing?"

"Do you always go this fast?" he puffed, looking over at Canli, who was dressed fully with armor, weapons, and a backpack.

She looked at him with some evident amusement. "We're going slow right now to build ourselves back up after the winter. It's hard to do the training we prefer with all the snow, but we do what we can. The pace will only get faster. For all the work you've done in your village, you've never marched all day or trained like we do. Training for this takes time, and you'll grow stronger. Eventually, you'll add armor, weapons, and ruck if you stay with us."

He groaned and Canli laughed as she smacked him on the shoulder. "Don't worry. It gets easier. We'll be training and doing exercises to get you where you need to be. If your steel is ready for this, we can refine you and made you stronger, if that is the Morri's choice."

"So, I'll really be one of you?" He perked up slightly. Anything would be better than repairing shoes or herding sheep.

"That's the plan. Before that, we need to get to the temple in Turling and you have to go through the dedication."

"What's that?"

"There is a ritual, overseen by priestesses of the Morri, where you commune with the Lady and she tests your steel and determines where you'll best fit. With lost sisters there is more to it, as that dedication includes the Rite of the Lost Sister. You get a new name, and…other changes." Canli smirked at the end.

"I get a new name and the goddess tells me what I'm to do?" He squinted in confusion, trying to work that out. From what Father Tombol taught, that was not the way things usually went.

Canli looked past the cart and up the column of troops. "That's basically it. There is a lot more to it of course, some of which I can't go into. But during the dedication, some of the women, now and again, speak with the Morri, but there's no rhyme or reason to it. The ways of the divines are not our ways. The Morri was not what I expected, that's for certain."

He turned his head to face her. "Did you see her?"

"In my dedication? Yes. When I saw her I had expected to see her in her aspect as warrior, but what I got was smith."

"Smith?" He had been vaguely aware of the Morri as goddess of smiths but not with the different aspects she apparently had.

"Yeah, the Morri is goddess of smiths, crafters, mothers, and warriors. One of the priestesses told me she was more accurately…" Sarnt Canli looked up as if recalling the exact wording. "Goddess of that which is made or forged, and we interpret it in those ways. I don't know. Not a priestess."

The Recruit was quiet for a bit as they walked. Canli pushed her pace and moved up to check on some of the other people leading pack animals. He continued to march and let his thoughts travel. Nibs made several toks and the Recruit turned and offered a weak smile when seeing Nibs on the cart. "Am I doing the right thing, Nibs?"

Nibs chuckled. His human always seemed to fret about things like a chick before its first flight, all trepidation and feather ruffling. Nibs went gwah and flew to his shoulder, and proceeded to nuzzle through his hair once he had settled. The boy needed to calm himself. Every raven knew that in flight, you had to commit or you would fall. Right now, the young human needed to get his wings under him and flap.

When the caravan stopped for midday, Nibs could tell how welcomed it was by the Recruit, who stood hunched by the mule panting as sweat trickled down his body. Canli showed up and guided him through a few stretches the others were already doing. The Hands who rode were doing a different set of stretches. The meal was handed out from the back of one of the carts; each person given a hunk of cheese with a wax rind on the back plus a small loaf filled with a savory mix of herbs, vegetables, and meat. Waterskins were refilled from a cask on the side of a cart, and in a short while the company continued on.

Nibs flew off to find something to eat, keeping one eye on the group and his human, as there had not been enough obviously dropped food for him to be satisfied. He could tell some of the riders and walkers had switched, though his human was still walking as he led the mule. Hopefully, the boy wouldn't wander off while he tried to rustle up some food. When the group moved off, Nibs noted there were plenty of bits lying about he had not been able to see. He chased off the smaller birds and was able to get his pick of the leavings. A hunk of cheese was a particularly enjoyable find, and he made plenty of pleased noises as he ate. Nibs returned to the cart quite sated and perched on the tailgate, to supervise as well as take a short nap.

Another woman marched up from the back of the column and kept pace with the boy. Nibs cocked his head, ruffled his feathers, and tucked his head back down, sure his human was being taken care of by this new flock. It wasn't common for ravens to move from flock to flock, but it did happen. Humans seemed to do that even less, but there were times. Clearly his human felt a need to go from the safety of the nest and spread their wings to find something better. He understood, as that was why he was here, traveling away from his flock, as well. Nibs would watch over them and do what he could to keep this one safe.

The Recruit smiled to himself seeing that. The woman just walked alongside for a while before asking, "So ye want to join the Hands or do ye just want to get out of your village?"

The Recruit started a bit, as he had been brooding. "Uhm…I… uh…yes?"

The new person chuckled. "Both…right. Who gave ye the shiner?"

"Father." He lowered his head and kicked a clump of loose dirt.

"He often give ye shiners?"

There was a lull, filled with the sound of plodding feet and the creak of the cart wheels. He finally spoke toward the ground. "Yes."

The woman nodded. "I understand. Me da hit me when I objected to his idea o' a good marriage with a man his age. When the swelling went down enough to open me eyes, I fled to one o' the shrines and got sanctuary. Me da chased me there, but the Hands had…words with him."

"You got better?" He looked up briefly into her face.

"Bodies heal. Ye get better over time, that's just life. The real pain has nothing to do with the fists." She looked off into the distance.

The Recruit nodded, kicking another clod of dirt, this time into the bottom of the cart. "Yeah."

"And hey, ye're already gone and it isn't likely your da will come after ye, e'en if ye are eldest. And we're here. No one screws with the Hands." She clapped the Recruit on the shoulder. "'Sides, at the dedication who knows what the Morri'll say. Ye might not even become one o' the Hands. Or she may not welcome ye and send ye on your way. The Morri has opinions and nothing we do changes that."

He nodded then tugged on the reins to keep the mule from cropping grass. "I just...I don't want to be a farmer or a cobbler anymore. I feel like I'm supposed to be something else, something different, something more, not be trapped in something wrong."

The woman nodded. "Many o' us felt the same, ye know. All ye have to do is stand at the dedication and be true. She'll take the measure o' your mettle and decide. She'll know your truth."

"The goddess really gets involved?" This fascinated him, as nothing he had ever learned from the local priest ever hinted at this.

"Not all o' us see herself then, but she does let the priestesses know what your steel be good for. She can tell what best to forge ye into, more than anyone else. Ye just need to be yourself. Name's Flit."

"Uh...I'm..." He was unsure what to say based on what Fanlis had told him.

"The Recruit, aye that's obvious. You're on your way, so don't fret." Flit beamed at him. "'Sides, I'm sure ye be wanting the extra energy your frettin' is burning for something else, like say, this march."

The Recruit laughed a little and kept moving forward.

# CHAPTER TWO

Nibs flew ahead of the group and followed the human pathway the Hands traveled along. The past two days had been first a cold rain turning to a cold drizzle with bits of frost in the morning. Today the weather was a touch nicer, since the front had passed and there was no rime on any of the gear or wagons. Flights above the treetops had allowed him to see the retreating front and the clear blue behind it. Two days had been spent mostly sitting on the cart or flying when the rain lightened and being somewhat miserable. His person was clearly far more uncomfortable than he was, as he plodded through the mud that must have been worse than perching on the tailgate of a cart. Humans really seemed to enjoy walking through things that looked unpleasant for the feet.

Nibs realized this had to be the human condition, walking around with a sort of numb or dumb look on their faces through whatever was in their path. To be fair, his human had that look a lot, and honestly, he had not made a definitive study on the weirdness of humans. Maybe he should observe more of these Hands, to see if that truth fit them as well. He had been well fed during this trip, from scraps tossed to him, to stolen cheese, and other morsels he had been able to find, so there was a good bit of contentment on his end. Perfect for thinking deep thoughts.

Since he flew in the branch-free space over the roadway, he spotted the large open area ahead. Rising up a small thermal to get a better look, he spotted what had to be the destination. In the center of a large cleared area on a raised section of land was a walled town with farm fields about. It had stout walls made of stone, and inside was a good-sized human community. There was a wooden palisade connected to the side of the stone, as other humans had built against this place, and around everything was a ditch with a few small bridges over them. From within the stone fort there was the clear sound of metal hitting metal. This was certainly larger than the village his human had come from and larger than some of the smaller hamlets they passed along the roadway that were little more than several families banded together by their isolated fields.

He drifted closer and spotted numerous people working in the fields, turning the earth with plows pulled by oxen. There were several smaller flocks of various other birds following behind the plow who picked over the newly exposed dirt for whatever food it turned up. The town had people moving about; one group herded a group of cows toward one of the fallow fields to graze. There were banners flying about the stone fort, and he recognized the anvil and hammer of the Morri. This had to be the place they were heading to.

As he circled the town taking in the differences from the village he had left, a kraa caught his attention. He turned toward the source of the sound and spotted a group of ravens calling out to him. They were roosted on one of the taller and more centralized buildings of the stone fort. He spiraled down and landed before them, hopping a few times on the slanted tile roof. Several of the ravens gathered here were clearly elders, so he bowed his head in recognition.

One of the elders spoke. "You are new to this area, not one of the flock."

"Yes, honored elder, I have come following a human who is a friend. He is with a group coming down that trail. They have the same symbol that is on the flags." Nibs gestured with his head.

The eldest bobbed his head in understanding and looked to the other elders. "I see. They are here to speak with the ones inside, to spend time here."

"Are they?" Nibs seemed surprised by that statement. Where his human was going had been a bit of a mystery.

"Every spring, humans gather here to speak with the ones who stay here. They are called the Hands. There is a presence here, like that of the Green Lady or the Feathered One, may her blessings be upon us, and it is a raven friend. Do not be surprised if you feel or hear their voice, especially if your human is coming here. We have an accord with them and it benefits both us and the humans."

"You assist them?"

"At times. The head speaker of the presence here has one of our eldest as friend. She sits in on things from time to time, watching what these humans do. Several of us have learned to speak as they do."

Nibs gave a quick ahk of surprise. He had never heard of such a thing. Something in the distance caught his eye, and as he turned he spotted movement heading this way. The group of humans came around a bend at the edge of the fields and were now in sight of the stone fort and the town. He bowed to the gathering of elders. "My human is here. I need to check on him."

Nibs flew across the fields and to the cart to check on his human, who still trudged along leading the mule. His landing was awkward as the cart hit a pothole just as he was ready to land, so there was a good bit of extra flapping and he gave a slight waaw of surprise.

Nibs turned his eye onto his human. It was clear the walking was doing him some good. The boy did not seem as tired as he had been the first few days of this journey. That was encouraging. Maybe his human would be able to do more things? He also seemed happier the farther they moved from the old village.

The Recruit walked along, gazing at the stone fort they moved toward as well as the walled town. The hammer and anvil flag of the Morri fluttered in the slight breeze and he noted the local town built itself against the more secure fort and had expanded over time, including a section outside the palisade. He had to admit they would be fools not to move close to safety as there were occasional bandit raids and attacks by beasts. They marched along the hard-packed earth road through open fields, where various groups tilled the earth with teams of oxen to prepare for the spring planting.

As they moved farther on, he spotted with some awe, a priestess of the Arndor, dressed in their colors of tan and brown with a light green sash about her waist and a crown of woven wheat on her head. Next to her, a member of their faith stood, holding a standard with their sheaves of grain symbol. The priestess was giving a blessing to the fields for a better growing season. Oxlen was too small a village to house such an important priestess or priest. All they really had was Father Tombol, the old priest of the Triad who did not care for the other divines, and rarely shared any of their stories or rituals.

This town, Turling, was far larger than his old village of Oxlen, being perhaps four times larger with more noise and scents competing, and that was discounting the stone fort. Moving closer to the town's main gate, it was clear there was, in addition to the larger stone fort with the banners of the Morri flying, a smaller keep with the ducal flag of Tivas flying, and the walled city had been built in sections, showing how a hamlet had grown into a village, then town by the expanding walls. Clearly, the temple to the Morri had been here first and all other growth started from there.

There was not a straight line through Turling from the main gate to the temple. The road wound from one side across to the other and passed through two internal gates before it reached the stone fort. He could tell the town had certain areas focused on certain things, but development was a work in progress as the sharp smell of leather being treated cut the air when the wind shifted and obliterated the scent of food they had been moving through. He had seen numerous tradesmen of different specialties as they had marched up through the town. It was enough to make his head spin.

After a winding march, they passed between the stout, metal banded wooden gate and into the courtyard of this temple complex that seemed larger than his village. There were a large number of other people here, as if several different companies of Hands had gathered. It was more people in one space than the Recruit had ever seen before. Additionally, there were numerous knots of young women not in the distinctive black and silver of the Hands but rather regular clothes, nervously grouped to one side of the courtyard. Numerous Hands whose faces that had become familiar over the last few days headed out to speak with others once they had been dismissed. Canli waved him down and he started to assist with unloading the carts and storing the gear in the section assigned to their company.

Once that task was dealt with, Canli waved him over. He nodded and moved to where she waited with Flit. "Recruit, right now you need to go join the other recruits who are here for their dedications. I was informed the priestess said they will begin with that tomorrow as no other companies are headed here. It looks like there's a good-sized group of you so it might take a few days to get through you all."

"Days?" His eyes widened in surprise. He had not expected this to take that long. What exactly went into this dedication?

Canli nodded. "Each person goes through this ceremony on their own, and the time it takes varies. Some people go through it quick and others take a while. The Morri makes her decision about you in her own sweet time. When I did my dedication, there was a woman who took two days, not waiting mind you, but in ritual, so yeah, it can take a while."

He goggled at that. Two days? For a ceremony? For one person!

Flit chuckled and patted him on the back. "You're gonna be fine. Once this is done, the training, so ye learn the basics of being a Hand. 'Sides, I'm sure Nibs will look after ye while ye wait."

They all smiled at Nibs who cawed out laughter from the back of the cart. With a quick flap, he perched himself on the Recruit's shoulder and ran his beak through his hair.

Flit led the way toward a small wooden barracks attached to one side of the wall near the large central building that was the temple of the Morri. There were several other wooden barracks a good bit larger than the one he was being led to. A stable was near the gate by another large building where he had helped store things that Flit said was the quartermistress. Near the temple was a stone building, clearly a large forge. That building was larger than any forge he had ever seen, bigger than the tavern back in Oxlen, but the stone looked more worn than even the temple. The whole keep was well laid out, and he could figure out the placement of things just by looking about.

As they neared the small barracks, several groups of young women stood in small, tight, anxious cliques trying to talk their way past nerves. Stationed by the door was one of the Hands in the distinctive black and silver uniform, a woman who reminded the

Recruit of one of the women back in his village. This woman was a sarnt like Canli, as evidenced by the silver stripes on her sleeves. She looked at Flit. "New recruit?"

"Lost sister," replied Flit, resting her hand on his arm. "Kaitan Tanrei vouches."

"Does she...very well." She wrote something down on the clipboard with a bit of graphite. "I have a bunk near me where you can rest. There are several other lost sisters in this year's dedications, so you won't be alone. We'll know more about the order you're going through in the morning after the priestesses go over the lists." The woman looked up from her list and looked over the Recruit and Nibs. "And who's this?"

Flit chuckled. "This is Nibs. Watch raven for this one. They're basically a pair."

The sarnt snorted and made another note. "Not the strangest thing to happen during dedications. Hello, Nibs."

Nibs bobbed his head and looked around curiously. Several of the other young women in the surrounding groups had stopped and stared at his human, eyes wide, bodies shrinking back, like they were watching a predator appear in their midst. Nibs even turned his head some to check behind them, verifying there was nothing sneaking up. These women were afraid of his human because it was male. Glaring at them coldly, Nibs croaked and spread his wings, making the others turn away. He then ran his beak through his human's hair comfortingly.

The sarnt noted what occurred and turned back. "That's why I want you to bunk near me, with the other lost sisters. It's not you they're scared of, not really. Some of these recruits had it bad before they joined up and haven't healed enough to see that lost sisters are in the same boat as them. It's just their fear gets the better of their thinking."

His human nodded. "That's fair."

Flit patted him on his shoulder. "It's not, but don't worry about it right now. You're a lost sister. We know ye've had it rough. I'm sure the Morri will see to ye finding your proper place, should your steel be right. And if that's the case, they need to shut up."

"Thank you, Flit." He actually managed a faint smile.

"T'will be okay. Either Sarnt Canli or I will check up on ye tomorrow, likely me though. Ye just relax, listen to the sarnt here and do as I said, be your truth."

The Recruit nodded and watched as Flit headed off.

"If anyone gives you grief about not being a real woman after the ritual, tell any of the Hands. They'll set them straight quick enough. If you're lost, you will be found. If you're not, you'll be sent to the town. That's all. Being lost is not a bad thing and is easily correctable. Now off with you." The sarnt gestured to a nearby Hand and they escorted him back to a bunk and to where he should put his stuff.

Once accomplished, he sat on his bunk and ran a finger down Nibs's breastbone. He looked about the room, seeing some of the young women staring at him as if he were diseased or dangerous. The whole thing made him feel so out of place. "What am I even doing here, Nibs?"

Nibs replied with a kleeklop, which made him feel somewhat better. Unsure what else to do, he headed outside again. The Hands within the dorms chivvied the others out as well. The sarnt looked over the assembled young women, which looked to be around a hundred all told, and said, "Right, all of you, listen up! You are all here for dedication to the Morri. Everyone. This means each and every one of you are going to stand before the Morri and have your mettle tested. Some of you will go on to become Hands, others priestesses, and some of you will either head home or move into the village to start your new life. Every one of you faces this. The lost sisters among us have an extra level of this, as their truth gets measured and then their steel. The Ritual of the lost sister will find them and make them their truth. All of us are in this together so try not to be afraid of each other. Now we're all going to go to the refectory for supper. It's not going to be heavy because the last thing you want is to be too full when you stand before the Morri. Some people have vomited due to overeating, and that is not the first impression you want to give the Morri. Trust me, if you do, you will be the one cleaning it up. Are we clear?"

The group of them replied with, "Yes, Sarnt."

They moved in more of a gaggle than line as they headed toward another building which looked like a large, low barn. As they walked across the courtyard, Nibs flew off and headed toward the roof of the temple where other ravens were congregated. The group tromped through the doors and stopped.

Inside the building were various tables with benches, and on one side a large open space that looked into the attached kitchen filled with people working. Under the directions of the sarnt, they filled three different tables. The sarnt sent them off to grab food and return to their seats in what passed for an orderly fashion. He tried to stay out of the way and not crowd anyone, which he noticed other lost sisters doing as well. Part of him wanted to talk to them, to maybe find out about this thing they had in common, but he felt awkward and embarrassed, unsure as to how to even begin a conversation on this topic. Thus, each lost sister sat at the outer edges of the tables in uncomfortable silence.

He sat and looked at his food, a bowl of some sort of stew with a rich mushroom gravy. There were small hand loaves of bread on the table with butter available. He grabbed a loaf and split it open and spread some butter on it with a knife. One of the other women decided to sit across from him, keeping him from isolation. She was a large-boned girl, both taller and broader of shoulder than he, and skin the color of rich loam, with long dark hair. After she grabbed up her own loaf, she grinned and asked, "So, hoping to be a Hand?"

He nodded, looking back down at his bowl. "That would be nice. But anything to get out of my village would have worked. I just couldn't stay there any longer."

"I hear that." The woman chuckled and had a big spoonful of the stew. "I left after a boy tried to take liberties with me, despite knowing I wasn't interested. Broke his arm and I took off because I didn't want to deal with my father's response or the city elders. I was already in trouble and leaving, but he just had to add to things. Found a company of Hands heading here and joined. Better than my other options. Name's Elsif."

"They told me to go by Recruit right now, that I would be given a new name once I went through the dedication. Something to do with being a lost sister and getting a new start." He shrugged uncomfortably, focusing on his own meal. He dipped a chunk of buttered bread in to sop up some of the gravy. "That part I'm less sure of, honestly."

Elsif raised an eyebrow. "Less sure if you're a lost sister?"

"Yeah, I mean, I think I know what that means, but how do I know it's real? The local priest of the Triad never said anything about that and no one else ever talked about it as a possibility. I do know things never felt right and I've always felt sort of...sideways in my own skin, but what does that even mean? I'm just not sure what to think about all of this. Maybe the Morri can tell me?" His skin flushed hot as he peered into the murky depths of his stew.

Elsif regarded him over her bowl, piece of bread paused on its way to her mouth. "You think the Morri can tell you who you are?"

"Well, yeah. I mean if I don't know, shouldn't she?" he replied, looking at Elsif as if it were obvious.

Elsif paused, working this over in her head. "I guess. The Morri knows mettle. She can tell you what you're made of, what you can become, what can be forged and shaped from your steel. Isn't who you work to become more important than who you are? Who you are is your past. It's the steps you've already taken. Becoming is your future."

The Recruit paused and blinked a few times, trying to make sense of what Elsif just said, as it was a point of view he had never encountered. The Morri could set him on a path to be forged into whatever his steel could handle. All he needed to do was acknowledge what his mettle was and that he wanted to become better. The smith of the gods would work out what was best for him, so yeah, maybe becoming was more important. He took a few breaths, heart racing a little at the thought. "I never thought of it that way. I guess I'll find out."

Elsif smirked at him, lifting her mug of water in a bit of a toast. "I guess you will."

# CHAPTER THREE

The next day began far earlier than he had been prepared for. Once everyone was awake and dressed, they headed over to the refectory for breakfast in the faint light of the morning. Remembering the admonition to eat light, he did exactly that. Given his own nerves and anxiety, it was not that difficult. He managed a bit of porridge and some bread. Even that was in smaller portions than he usually ate because of how his stomach jumped. There were so many unknowns about this dedication and no one who knew more was talking.

Once the meal was finished, the group was led to a different building where large copper kettles hung over low-burning fires with pipes coming from them to stop in front of large bathing tubs. Inside, there was a ritual bath of blessed water filled with various herbs. Whisps of steam filled the air with a scented haziness. Toward the back of the room was a curtained off bath where the lost sisters were guided by a priestess. The water in this area gave off a slightly different herbal scent. He couldn't identify it, but it was rich and fragrant.

After his turn in the tub, his body tingled, and all the potential recruits were dressed in white robes tied shut with blood-red sashes. The courtyard was mostly quiet as the group followed a priestess across the open space and into the temple. They walked barefoot over freshly strewn straw that kept their walk from being too muddy. Once inside the main temple, acolytes motioned for them to sit on the available benches.

The sarnt moved to stand in front of the altar upon which was a larger-than-life statue to the Morri. She caught the eyes of each candidate before speaking. "The priestesses have an order they will call you in. The order is based on how difficult to judge your mettle will be, so the more difficult you will be to sort, the later you will be. That means the more complex or discordant your steel is, the longer you will have to wait. Until you are called you will wait here. That means no eating, though there is water and an herb tea if you need some. My suggestion is that you pray to the Morri to help ease your judgment. If you need the outhouse, let one of the acolytes know and they will escort you."

The recruits shifted uneasily at that. The sarnt continued. "When you are called up, you will be taken into the inner sanctum. There you will be given a sacred tisane to drink and an herbal salve shall be rubbed into your body. This is needed to help you connect to the Morri. The priestess will chant a prayer to the Morri to dedicate you to her service. After that, the Morri will judge your steel and determine where you can best serve, as either a priestess, Hand, or helper. You may be told your service is not required, in which case you will be escorted into the town by the quartermistress's assistants to help you get settled with a good job. You may or may not remember anything of your meeting with the Morri, though those of you later in the list will likely recall more than others. Pray and prepare yourselves."

The sarnt walked behind a curtain to one side of the altar, leaving the rest of them to study the altar and the statue of the Morri in front of them. The surface of the altar was covered in baskets with various offerings, such as the last of the winter apples, a few loaves of bread, skeins of yarn, carded wool, a few hides turned to leather, beads and baubles, precious stones, thin wire, and the tools of various crafts. There were also candles about and cones of incense sending up thin streams of bluish smoke that gathered about the roof in pools. The statue was tall, stretching nearly to the ceiling of this three-storied stone building, carved of some black stone that caught the flickering light and made things appear to be in motion.

The sculpture of the Morri showed a strongly built woman at an anvil, working something into shape, with a shield on her back and a raven on her shoulder. The Recruit just stood there, eyes dancing between specific parts of the sculpture and the whole. He had never seen a sculpture that size before, and it was hard to take it in all at once. The shrine in the village had several wooden sculptures of the Triad, but they were only a foot high at most, apparently carved by Father Tombol. This…this towered above them, and the light trickling in from windows at the top to the walls as well as from numerous candles almost seemed to make the muscles move of their own accord.

The Morri had not been popular in the village. The only person who had a sculpture of the Morri was the blacksmith, who had one near where his forge had been placed, and it was far simpler. There were larger and more elaborate sculptures of Father Sun, Mother Earth, and Lady Moon, the Triad. There were a few others, though the shrine priest focused his teachings on those three, and how all things submitted to the will of Father Sun. The unit of Hands that stayed in the village over the winter months brought their own shrine and held rituals by themselves, because, for all they protected the village from dangers, they were not actually welcome by many of the village elders.

As the first person was called, one of the other lost sisters, he just stood there trying to find his center. This whole situation was overwhelming and he was at a loss for what to do. All that made sense in the moment was to keep moving forward as, if nothing else, the Morri would say who he was. At some point during his musings, Elsif came and stood next to him, also taking in the sight of the goddess. "That really is something," she said.

He turned to her. "Huh?

"I've never seen a statue of a woman built like me or anything. It's not common, so to see this…? All the boys, they said my size was unnatural, that real women were smaller and dainty. Honestly, seeing this makes me want to learn more about the Lady. And it assures me that this was the right choice."

"It makes me want to learn about her as well," he admitted with a nod, before turning back to the statue. After a few moments of silent contemplation he said, "I'm nervous."

"Why?"

"I…I just don't know what's going to happen. I had to get out of my village and would agree to pretty much anything to accomplish that…but this lost sister stuff…I mean, I'm just me. How can I be a lost sister?"

Elsif put a hand on his shoulder. "You are here now, in this place, soon to stand before the goddess herself, where she will test your mettle and state where you belong. You said you were hoping she could tell you who you are; now is not the time to back out. Besides, the worst would be if it's decided you're not a lost sister and are sent away, maybe to live in this town away from your old village. The rest…who knows?"

"Fair point." He smiled and tried to calm himself more. Elsif was right. He really was away from his old village and the abuse he had endured. The worst that could happen now was being let free into the town to try to find an apprenticeship or something in a place where that life would not haunt him. In every way he could figure, his life was already so much better. Elsif's name was called and she strode forward, head held high, certain of her place in the world. He wished he could have that kind of surety.

The light turned from one side of the temple to the other as the day passed, the group constantly thinning. When the outside showed the reddish glow of sunset, the sarnt came back into the temple. "Right, you all, let's go. The priestesses are done for the night. We'll start again in the morning. Hopefully, we can get through the rest of you tomorrow."

The sarnt led the way to the refectory, where the group barely spilled onto a second table. He sat at the second table with the only other lost sister left and two other girls. No one was in the mood for talking and everyone simply pushed food around their plates, this time with some sort of meatloaf with a mushroom and onion gravy. He tore into it, no longer holding back the hunger as it overcame the anxiety of the day. A quick glance showed he was not the only one eating like that.

His sleep was fitful with lots of vague dreams that created more disquiet in his mind than anything comforting. At some point, he woke in the dark and just lay there, staring at the ceiling. As dawn started to creep through the windows, he finally sat up. Hopefully, today would be it.

They again had sacred baths, again ate lightly, and again returned to the temple where they sat in silence, as if all the conversation from yesterday had dried up. Most of his time was spent staring up at the large sculpture of the Morri, wondering what she was like and how this would take place, what in his life would change. It did help his nerves some, but it only took the edge off.

There were only two others left in the temple chamber with him when he was finally called forth. By that point, he had expected to be the last one called, but clearly there were other ideas. All other lost sisters had been called earlier, and now by the looks the other two were giving him, they had expected him to be last as well. The sarnt held open the curtain, waving him forward. He was not as successful as Elsif had been in striding forward with purpose as his nerves and anxiety returned in full force.

The day was moving into evening, and the inner sanctum was lit by candles and the glow of a small forge. The bare earth in front of the forge looked dark and wet in this flickering light. By the forge stood an old woman with her gray hair bound in a bun. Numerous wisps of hair had broken free over the course of the day. Her strong hands had a few dark spots on their backs and the skin looked a mass of wrinkles. Her attire was similar to the outfit the sculpture of the Morri wore, including the leather apron. While old, she was standing solidly and seemed more in place in the world than he was. A raven, one far older than Nibs, stood next to her on a rough wooden perch. They both watched him intently as he entered the smaller room and drew closer. Her smile was kindly. "Greetings, young one."

The raven croaked out, "Greetings."

That startled the Recruit. He heard stories that some birds could speak with human voices, but he never expected to experience that himself, certainly not before being dedicated to a goddess. Unsure what else to do, he nodded respectfully. "Greetings, holy ones."

Her eyes crinkling, she said, "It is finally your turn before the forge. Time for your dedication to the service of the Morri and your

Rite of the Lost Sister. Thus begins your journey with the goddess. Before we get started, the Morri also requested a few others be present for your dedication, if that is acceptable."

Blinking a few times in surprise, he blurted, "I get a say?"

"Of course. That is vital to everything the Morri believes in. None undergo this rite if it is not of their own free will."

He nodded, heart racing faster. This was it, the moment where everything was to take shape and he would see what there was to see. He swallowed hard. "I consent."

She nodded. "Very well."

She waved a hand in summons, and from the side, behind another curtain came Kaitan Tanrei and Fanlis, who had Nibs perched on her arm. The raven had been shifting uncomfortably until he spotted her and let out a loud gwah. The Recruit blinked a few times before asking, "Uhm…hi. Hi, Nibs. Holy one, why?"

"This is who the Lady requested be present for your dedication. Instead of having a missive sent with you, she wanted the results of your dedication spoken directly to them. I believe it is clear you are likely to join this kaitan's company. As I work the Morri's will, it was done and they are here. Now, come stand forth on this patch of earth and prepare yourself."

Swallowing rather hard, he stepped forth and stood on the wet dirt, bits squishing between his toes. The heat from the forge made him start to flush and sweat. The coals brightened, as someone was working the bellows, making the heat more intense and the glow brighter. Two acolytes came over and undressed him, working his arms out of the sleeves and allowing the dress to pool on the floor, leaving him naked before the forge. The bellows warmed the fire more and he seemed entranced, gazing at the glow as it brightened and darkened. When handed a chalice, he drank down the slightly bitter herbal mix which was not even remotely soothing in the heat. He tongued a piece of herb free from his teeth and swallowed it. The acolytes began to rub the salve the sarnt had mentioned into his body, starting with the bottoms of his feet and working slowly upward.

There was a faint murmuring in the air, possible prayers, or words spoken just at the edge of his ability to hear. The distinct sound of the elder raven's voice joined in, making the whole experience seem more dreamlike and otherworldly. Nibs joined in off and on, adding noises to the mix, his voice unlike any other. As they rubbed the last of the salve into his scalp, the world…loosened, shifted, colors deepened, the glow of coals intensified, and tones in the chanting became discrete though the words were no clearer, swirling into a growing crescendo that had little to do with sound and more to do with rhythm and feel. The old woman stepped forward with another chalice, one that smelled warm, of different herbs, and honeycomb. There was another scent as well, underneath, but he could not figure it out. It made him think of freedom and movement. She placed the chalice against his lips. "Drink this and be found."

Once the chalice was empty, his head fuzzed more, he grew dizzier. The world vibrated at the corner of his eyes, sounds began to slur together, and words became clearer but less differentiated from music. When the coals brightened again, fire and earth breathing right before him, he stood spellbound, breath matching the pulse of the coals, teetering, wobbling, and he ultimately tumbled forward into the light.

When he was no longer drowning in pure sensation; a faint sound grew in strength, hammer ringing on steel, pulling his attention. As he rubbed the distortion from his eyes, the first thing he focused on was the large woman standing by a huge forge, looking very much like her sculpture. A scarred and scorched leather apron was over her clothes, and her boots had burn marks along the shank. Sweat covered her dark skin, plastering her hair to her head; muscles moved as she hammered a rhythm into a billet of steel she held by tongs, red hot on the anvil, sparks and flakes of impurities flying. After a few more hits, the billet went back into the coke to reheat. The Morri turned, dark eyes with traces of forge glow in them traced over his body. He could feel the weight of her gaze upon his skin and knew she was seeing more than mortal eyes ever could. She finished up and nodded. "Good, you're here."

Not having a clue what to say to an actual goddess, he stood there and nodded, then noticed his body did not look as it had before. It now was somewhat diffuse. Before he could put more attention toward that, the Morri turned and worked the bellows with one hand, turning the billet in the coke with tongs held in the other hand. "Come over here and pick up a hammer."

He complied, holding the forge hammer awkwardly. The shoe hammer was something he was far more familiar with, yet that seemed similar to this particular forging hammer. There were others about the room, but this was the one that sat most naturally. When she turned back to him, the Morri glanced down and corrected his hand placement. She smiled at him and took up the tongs. The billet was again a bright cherry red. Placing the billet on the anvil, the Morri ordered, "I'll tap a rhythm, you follow with your hammer on the steel."

She began with a tap, tap, strike, tap, tap, strike. The work was odd, and he lost himself in the simple rhythm of it, as the billet lengthened and thinned, folded back onto itself, as there were repeated cycles of heating the metal and working it. Little flakes of impurities came free, knocked off with the rhythm. With careful supervision, he drew the steel, scattering ash over the heated metal and folding it carefully over. The pattern of hammering drew him in, and time stretched. His body grew more solid, more present, less diffuse. After an unknown period of time, the Morri called a halt and scrutinized the billet before setting it to the side. "Nicely done, Asche."

She looked the now-named Asche over. The examination was unnerving as he could almost feel the weight of the Morri's gaze on him as an actual physical presence. His body felt weird, almost in flux, though that was settling down. The Morri nodded after the scan. "Good. Yes, good. Your truth is being revealed and imperfections are being worked free and will continue to work themselves out. Lost sisters have such good steel at their core, though it requires a delicate hand to forge properly. To be forged of such steel is a gift, however, there is always a cost."

The Morri lifted the drawn-out steel billet they had been working on, inspecting the metal for any serious flaws. "Your childhood, your missing girlhood, is the cost of your steel, as time lost can never be regained. You may feel those parts of you, those experiences, that do not match your steel are a deep loss, but it is up to you to determine if it is a fair price for being found. Those lost moments can build up your strength or turn into pockets of fragility causing your steel to fail. To be forged into your truth is not easy, nor is it meant to be."

"To shape steel takes knowledge, patience, skill, and good materials. If the core material is wrong, the steel breaks. If not refined properly, it breaks. If you draw out the blade poorly, it breaks. If you do not anneal it, the steel becomes strong but brittle. If you do not work the steel, fold it, you cannot work out the imperfections. If you work it too much, you can ruin the steel and it will not take a proper shape. If you temper it wrong, it twists or breaks. Your steel is good, strong even, at its core, so we can work together to shape you to your best, to make the most of your steel. Events do not always play out that way, but if you stick to the process, we shall see what kind of steel you are made of. That is, if you want to go through the work?"

She placed the steel billet back into the fire, using the bellows to heat the blade again back to a cherry red. The Morri looked over at her. "Shall we?"

Asche picked up the hammer, hefting its weight more comfortably with her now solid form, and joined the Morri at the anvil. Time to get to work.

## CHAPTER FOUR

The first sound that registered upon awakening was Nibs's croak. He was either grumbling or talking to himself. This happened a few times during the rare naps Asche had managed to steal. She opened her eyes slightly, trying to hold back the brightness. "Ugh…not so loud, Nibs."

The sound of her voice froze her in place, and her eyes snapped open. "Nibs?"

The raven chuckled at her, sort of a cr-ur-ur-ur-kk, and she could understand why. She sat up and looked at her hands, at the way her robe pushed out near the top, at the way she looked smaller yet the same. She wasn't even sure what she was seeing, just that this wasn't how she looked at the start of the ritual, though in almost every way that mattered, she felt more right than ever. "Wha…?"

One of the healers walked up to her bed, surprising her. "Ah, good. You're awake."

She looked at the woman with wide eyes and shrank back. "Eep!"

"Shhh…breathe…it's okay. You're safe and in the healing house." Asche calmed some and sagged against the pillow. "The Rite of the Lost Sister can be rough to those who undergo it, and to combine it with the dedication exhausts most everyone. You may be clumsy for a while, but you'll be fine once you reconnect with your body. Here." The healer handed over a wooden cup.

As she drank, the cool water helped her center herself and wake more fully. She looked up at the healer for some sort of explanation. "I changed?"

"Of course you did. That is the purpose of the rite after all, to return to you the body you should have had. This is the you your mother should have birthed had your essence not gotten lost. It happens more often than you think, so this is a common event yearly. You are now found and made whole, blessings upon the Morri."

Asche tried to make sense of it. While she had been unsure about the whole lost sister thing, there was no denying the truth of what her body had become. This new form felt correct in a way the previous one had not, like her skin finally fit her straight. She turned her arms back and forth, taking in what felt like a great thinness but wasn't much changed from how she had been before. She rotated and flexed her hands. "This is me? This is really me?"

"Yes." The healer patted her on the back comfortingly. "This is really you."

She looked down again at her hands, which looked familiar yet different. There was the slight scar on her right hand from where he had punched a barn wall in frustration just last year. The nails on the hands were the same length and slightly ragged from where he had bit them a little in nervousness while awaiting his turn at the dedication. As she ran a hand through her hair Asche felt like the same rough knife cut her father had given her was still there. Nothing and everything had changed.

"I…" Words failed.

The healer smiled in understanding. "Things will fall back into place in a few days, you'll see. The training you will undergo as a Hand will acquaint you with your proper body, so you will learn what new things it has to tell you. This has always been the way with finding the lost. Now, so you know, there is a guest here to see you."

"There is?" Asche looked about in surprise. Who would come to see her?

With another pat on the arm and a smile, the healer walked off. Shortly, Elsif came up and grinned at her. "Ah, good. You're awake."

Given how her body was aching, Asche asked, "How long was I asleep?"

"All of yesterday, and after the ritual. Sarnt Canli told me that was to be expected after the Rite of the Lost Sister."

"Wait, Sarnt Canli?"

Elsif beamed at her. "Yep, I got transferred to your company. Apparently, they needed more heavy infantry, and since that's what I'm good for, there you go. Canli is my sarnt and responsible for training me. I've been getting my gear and stuff, and I start training tomorrow."

Asche felt her cheeks warm, and she smiled, pleased by this development. "Wow. I'm glad. I hadn't really expected to make any friends yet. The Hands sort of kept their distance on our way here."

"So, do you have a name, because I'm sure your old one doesn't fit anymore. And you mentioned you would get one at your dedication." Elsif snickered a little.

"Asche."

"Asche. Not a bad name. There are two girls in my village named that. So, want me to bug the healer to get you some grub? You've not eaten in over two days, and you went through a... significant change. I'm positive you're rather hungry."

Asche was about to say yes, when her stomach gurgled rather loudly, confirming the statement. Elsif laughed and stood. "I'll be back to feed that beast."

As Elsif left, the healer returned. "While your friend is gathering your meal, do you need assistance getting to the privy?"

Asche blinked a few times, trying to process that question, when the pressure in her bladder made itself known. "Uhm…"

Standing showed another difference she had not been consciously aware of. She was shorter than before. Not by a great deal, but enough the world looked slightly different from this lower angle. Her balance was off, as she had never walked in this body, so there was an adjustment that came quickly. Another new thing to become aware of, she grumbled to herself as the healer helped her to the chamber pot, explaining the changes she needed to be aware of in terms of her body. The whole period thing sounded odd, but she knew her mother went through something monthly, though her father said it was not fit conversation material.

Once she returned to the bed, Asche sat down, trying to think about how different something like going to the bathroom now was. While it was fundamentally different because of the changes, it was essentially the same thing. The healer stayed there and kept explaining things she should have been taught with her first moon time when she had been younger. The healer also explained that the company's chiurgeon would be able to help her as well to remind her of these details. Asche was pleased to see Elsif headed toward her carrying a tray laden with food, a bowl of something, a hunk of cheese, and a mini loaf of bread. There was also a mug on the tray. It looked like there was a little bit of steam rising from the bowl.

The healer took the cue and left. Elsif came up and held out a tray. "Here you go. I wasn't sure what you might want, but the refectory had an idea. I also told Sarnt Canli you're awake, so someone should be by shortly to collect you. I think they know your specific assignment, because I did hear you're still assigned to them."

"So, I'm a Hand." She was unsure how this was now her life. The smell of food hit her, and her stomach growled in need. Asche blushed a little and began eating, starting with the chicken stew that was thick with vegetables and herbs.

Elsif nodded. "Yeah, a number of people made it into the Hands. Of the last two, one is to be a priestess and the other turned out to be a lost brother, who is going to train with the smiths. There was a lot of commotion over that one."

Asche looked up. "Oh. That is a surprise. I mean, both of those other girls were so feminine. Whoa…but I'm definitely a Hand?"

"Yes." Elsif chuckled. "Canli asked me to keep an eye on you and let them know when you woke up, since she heard we had hung out before the dedication. I think Officer Fanlis has your assignment, but I haven't met her. I'm going to be in the heavy unit. Yesterday, I ran around and got all sorts of equipment. They're already making me a suit of armor, which is pretty neat. I've never heard of brigandine but apparently, it's a type of armor only the Hands use.

It's like a big coat with a lot of metal plates in it. The blacksmith said it was about as good as the plate armor the nobility use, so that'll be nice. I still have to decide what weapon I want to focus on, either the war axe or war hammer. Kind of thinking hammer. It just feels more right in my hand than the axe, and things make a nice crunching sound when I hit them."

Elsif looked so excited and pleased by the notion that Asche had to struggle to keep from chuckling at her. It reminded her that she was now a Hand and had a job and a weapon she might be good at. But what did she know besides cobbling and herding sheep? Well, there was mucking out stalls, but what sort of combat application that might have was beyond her. "I have no idea what sort of weapon I might be good with or what job I could do. All I ever had happen in my life in terms of fighting was wrestling and some fistfights." The next admission came out with a bit more pain. "More often than not, I lost. I won a few of the fights, but not most, or my father beat me for not being enough of a man in his opinion."

Elsif scoffed, shaking her head slowly. "He's an idiot."

Asche looked at herself and the shift she was wearing, then smiled, thinking about her father and how he reacted to catching her wearing that shift a little over a week ago. His face had been puce. "True. He would hate this."

"Good." Elsif looked over at Asche. "You doing all right?"

Asche smiled. "Still getting used to all this. Having a new body is not what I expected when I left my village, or even while I stood before the high priestess. I just wanted a way out."

"How could you expect this? I mean, I know my local priest mentioned lost sisters and brothers a few times, but never the Rite of Finding, that you went through. You seem like you had no real idea about any of that, so it would be even more of a surprise. And you've been awake only a little bit, so it's still huge, new, and overwhelming. After a few months, it'll just be your body and life, the past mostly forgotten. It'll become your new normal."

Asche felt her eyes relax and her shoulders lowered a little. She looked up at Elsif, giving her a hesitant smile. "Very wise. Are you sure you shouldn't have become a priestess?"

Elsif smirked at her in response.

Before the conversation continued, the healer came over, noted the emptying food bowl. She checked her over once more before standing up. "You seem fine and the transformation is complete. Head back to your unit once you have finished your meal. They'll make sure the quartermistress gets you supplied with clothes that fit. Don't worry about the shift. Keep it."

Asche focused on the last of her meal, sneaking bits of cheese and stuff to Nibs, who had flown in from the open window and been eying the tray with some desire. Nibs stood on the foot of the bed and looked around when not sneaking pieces of Asche's lunch.

It didn't take long for her to finish the tray, to practically the last crumb. Elsif put it to the side, where the healer indicated it should go. The clothes she arrived in looked larger now than they did before. It wasn't as bad as she feared, but she was smaller than before, by several inches. The boots were loose and would be a pain to walk in. That needed a fix as soon as she could manage.

Asche left the healer's building in the shift they had given her and some basic woven shoes. They walked through the large open courtyard, where others were training with lots of activity by the smithy and another building. Nibs leapt from her shoulder and flew off toward the tops of the temple. Asche watched him go and called out, "Have fun, Nibs!"

Elsif led her to a building near the external wall of the temple grounds. This was the barracks for Kaitan Tanrei's unit, now her unit. Sarnt Canli was seated at a desk near the entrance, talking with some people and spotted them coming closer. When they neared, Canli raised her voice and said, "Elsif, the armorer needs you to help fit your armor. She knew you were busy so she wanted to see you as soon as you were free. It's probably the chainmail rather than the brig. Go."

Elsif said her good-byes and hustled out while Sarnt Canli walked over to Asche. She patted her shoulder. "Glad to see you made it through everything in one piece, and welcome to the Hands, Asche. Fanlis wanted to see you, and you'll get assigned to your team, who works under her command."

It was a short walk down the hall to the intelligence officer's room/office, where Fanlis was going over paperwork in two different stacks. She looked up only when Canli knocked on the doorframe. She peered up at them and then smiled. "Ah, good. You're here. Thank you, Sarnt."

Canli nodded and headed back to her desk. This left Asche again under intense scrutiny, as Fanlis looked her over and then gestured to a chair. "I take it the Morri decided on a name for you then?"

"Asche."

Fanlis nodded. "Good. That matches what we were told during the ritual, but you're the only one who could verify that. Well, Asche, the dedication let us know what position you would be best suited for and the priestess let us know. I'll be upfront with you. The position you were assigned is not easy. You're going to be in my ranger unit. We do several things, such as reconnaissance and infiltration, as well as support all the others as light infantry and backup archers. In addition to that, I was told you need to assist with the shrine."

"Told?"

"Yes. While you were communing with the Morri, the high priestess passed on what the Morri decided would be best for your steel, as I said. I don't know why we needed to be told directly, but we did. Anyway, ranger is not an easy role. We occasionally have to go into places unarmored and without weapons to get an accurate assessment of our enemy. We are also the ones chosen to go on special missions, such as breaking into keeps to open a gate during battle, or to travel behind enemy lines. We scout both in front of and behind our unit to make sure no one is going to surprise us. We need to be skilled at the bow, spear, dagger, and raven's head sword. It's a great deal of training to become good at those weapons and sneaking about, which we do a lot of." Fanlis held her eyes as she spoke.

"Okay." Asche wasn't exactly sure what else to say. The whole position of ranger sounded like more than she wanted to deal with.

However, if the Morri thought this fit her steel, who was she to question it? Maybe it would help her become more her?

Fanlis smiled at Asche. "Now that I've worried you, let me explain it's not a bad job, but not one everyone is suited for. Besides, if Nibs stays with you, we should be able to use his help as well, if he wants to. It is known that ravens help wolves hunt and are exceptionally clever. I would never turn down any aid that can keep us all aware and alive when we reach a battlefield. That's a question we will definitely be looking into later. Right! You're in just a shift and we need to get you settled. Your sarnt is Terris, and she's in charge of the rangers when I'm not there. She'll get you to the quartermistress and introduce you to the others in our squad. You'll get clothes there. Welcome to the Hands."

Asche left, following Fanlis's directions. After a brief search of the area, she found Sarnt Terris. Terris was a lithe woman, with dark hair and eyes, who carried herself a bit like a stalking cat. After a quick scan of Asche from head to toe, Terris said in an accent Asche had not heard before, "So, you are new one, eh?"

"Yes."

"Good. Have not had new one in several years. Nice." She slapped Asche on the back, the force of it making her stumble forward. "Come. We get gear now. Training starts tonight."

Asche followed the sarnt out of the building, almost needing to jog to keep up with her long-legged stride. As they headed across the yard, Nibs cawed and glided down to land a little roughly on Asche's shoulder. With a quick smile, Asche said, "Hey, Nibs. You sticking around?"

Nibs cawed and ran his beak through Asche's hair. Asche reached up and gently scratched the breastbone, knowing this was something Nibs enjoyed. Sarnt Terris watched this from the corner of her eyes as they neared a building. Once inside, Asche was left with a priestess who looked her over before returning her gaze to Terris. "What exactly does she need, Terris?"

"Whole kit, extra clothes, shoulder reinforcement for claws, weapons, armor. Lost sister. Here." She handed over a piece of slate with things written on it.

The priestess looked it over and then back to the sarnt. "Right. You don't have to stay, Terris. I'm sure the two of us can handle this. After she's done here, I'll send her over to get her weapons sorted and get the measurements for her armor."

"Good." Sarnt Terris slapped Asche on the opposite shoulder, gauging her strength so as not to dislodge Nibs. "Do as she says. Over soon. Then back to barracks."

As Terris left, the priestess turned to face Asche. "Right, we have some clothes for you, including small clothes. That should help right off and should fit better than what you currently have. Since you're a Hand, you won't often need a shift or a dress of some fashion, and normally you'll be wearing tunic and braies. Right now, we have to take measurements to make your binder, as well as your boots. Those will take a few days to make, so you'll have to make do with the new clothes I've given you until then. I can get you a better pair of slippers if the boots are too large."

It was weird being naked in a new body. The chill air caused her new nipples to crinkle and tighten. Gooseflesh ran up and down her limbs. The process was handled very quickly, as a cord was stretched and knotted at certain intervals with a bit of colored cloth incorporated into the knot. The priestess was able to explain the few pieces of new clothes and their care. The small clothes needed for moon time was a bit more than Asche expected, but having a new body had to come with unexpected difficulties. The herbal tisanes available to help treat those pains and prevent pregnancy were also new surprises.

"Here is a rucksack. You need to store your gear here. Try to get things in there efficiently, but it's okay if it's a mess. Terris or your specific trainer will show you how to properly pack your gear, bedroll, and anything else. Let's get started."

What followed was a blur of clothes and various bits of equipment she wasn't even sure what they were, as they were items she had never seen in her old life. The clothing items were uniformly black with silver or gray threads through them. Most of the tunics had patches over the left breast with the anvil crests of the Hands. Asche awkwardly carried her poorly stuffed rucksack, the blankets of her bedroll draped over her shoulder, to the next place. All this equipment was heavier than she expected, and when she realized she would be getting even more gear she was more disheartened. Nibs laughed from his perch on the edge of a building, and Asche could agree she certainly looked ridiculous lugging all this around. The weapon master was next.

The woman was well muscled and clearly worked as a smith. Several other women and a few men worked busily at different forges about the large smithy. She looked at the slate Asche was carrying and said, "Ranger, eh…not too hard a kit. Do you have any experience with weapons?"

Asche shook her head. "Some with a pitchfork, more with a broom."

The woman grinned. "So, none. Right. Here's a dagger and a backup knife. And all get a raven's head."

At Asche's confused look, the weapon master turned and grabbed both a dagger and knife from a small collection on a shelf. Then she headed across the smithy to a rack containing a number of weapons. She picked up a blade that was curved inward, with a knuckle guard that was literally carved to look like a raven's head and beak. She wrapped the sheathed blade in a leather belt dyed black like the weapon scabbards. That would make the carrying a bit easier. "This is your sword. It's not the longest, but it's better up close. Design is almost a mix of sword and axe, for fighting purposes. Hits hard but it's not the best against heavily armored foes. The armor tends to stop the blows from causing damage. But the curve throws most sword fighters, which can help, as they're more used to the kind of straight blades the nobility wield. You'll learn."

That saw her moving next to the armorers, who took measurements and sent her on her way with very little conversation after handing her a black padded gambeson that she had seen the other Hands wearing on the march here from Oxlen, and had worn one herself. Given how overladen she felt, it was a blessing she hadn't been piled under a large collection of actual armor pieces. On her way out of the armorer's, Terris intercepted her. The sarnt took one look at the armful of gear and shook her head. "Come along, Asche. You have bed with others. I'm pairing you with Flit and she will show how to pack all of this. Once you in uniform, then to work. There is much training to get you ready for fighting."

As she waddled her way back to the barracks, following behind the sarnt, she realized the idea of fighting was not as unwelcome as it had been before. Maybe with this training she would be better able to defend herself. Back home in Oxlen, she hadn't done very well at that, to be honest.

# CHAPTER FIVE

S weat dripped in her eyes, which burned as she leapt as high as she could and then landed as quietly as possible with her knees bending deep, almost to the point of her butt touching the ground. There were three more repetitions before she was allowed to stop. All of the new members of the company were training together in the early morning, doing the basic exercises that would build them into the warriors the Hands wanted.

Elsif looked over and smirked at her, almost making Asche laugh. Everyone in their group was equally worn out and sopping with sweat by this point. The sarnt leading them was still breathing easily and only glistened, grinning at their discomfort. "Right! First, we cool down and then break out to your units for more specialized training."

Asche dragged herself upright. The majority of the other new girls were with either of the two infantry units or archers. Even the supply team had gained at least two people. She was the only person heading off to work with the ranger team, which was common, as those spots were rarely added to. Each day the exercises were some sort of variation of archery, sword, spear, or sneaking. Flit called them the four s's, which everyone thought was a bad joke. Asche usually just stared at her when it came up.

Nibs watched Asche trudge off. She was some wet smelly thing he didn't want to be near, and based on the last few days, that was only going to get worse. Staying at a distance certainly smelled better, as there was a slight miasma of sweaty human funkiness that tended to stick to his feathers and took forever to clean. Watching from half the courtyard away was better than being nearby. Another of the local ravens landed next to him on the branch he perched on and ruffled her feathers a bit before turning to face Nibs. "Come, the elders have said we must train."

Nibs turned his head, looking quizzically at the newcomer. She was a fit female raven maybe a season or year older. Her feathers had a pleasant shagginess to them that he liked. "Train?"

This new raven bobbed her head. "Yes. If you are to stay with your human, you will need the skills to do so. She will be in battle, in danger, so knowing more about how humans do this will make you both safer. That is, if you still want to help?"

She launched herself from the branch and headed for a covered section of the temple. Those were points Nibs considered but had been unable to problem-solve himself. He wanted to do more to help Asche but was at a bit of a loss, given that the human could not understand the language of ravens. Though, from what he gleaned from what she had said, it sounded like occasional raven assistance was something the flock had worked through already. Maybe they had answers to his question. Nibs followed; powerful wing strokes brought him alongside her. "Now what?"

"We work on the hardest first." She turned to land on a section of temple roof that was protected from wind and weather. "Counting and human speech. If you can say simple things to your human charge, you can more easily keep them safe and help the Hands."

"I know how to count," Nibs replied, a touch affronted. He had been educated by his parents and flock like any self-respecting raven.

"In human numbers?" she asked, cocking her head in a manner that drove home her point.

Nibs grumbled in annoyance. She chuckled. "First thing, speaking to humans. With a bit of practice, we can mimic their voices, so we can use that to tell them things. Humans make a bunch of similar sounds they call words, which is how they speak, since sometimes they cannot convey a whole idea with a sound. They have a lot of different words, but we don't need to know all of them to help. They don't really have a lot of sound options they can make, something in the area of sixty different sounds, so we have to make do with their limited selection. But once we can talk like them, we can work with them. Like with our brother wolves, we scout out the area, find prey, give warnings of hunters, the same sort of things with the same sets of rewards, ease of food access, safety from predators, and such. So, we have learned how to speak human words to train them to understand what we have been trying to tell them."

Nibs sighed heavily. "Will it take long?"

"Maybe. You have to learn what the human sound chains mean, so you can talk to them. Knowing the ideas they are trying to convey makes it easier to learn the words. So first we learn the ideas, then the words. Also pay attention. Slight changes in sounds can convey different words and ideas, almost like we can, but not as well done."

Nibs began learning the basics of life amongst the Hands, what a team, platoon, unit, company, and more were. What archers were, what cavalry was, all sorts of human military ideas that were things ravens never dealt with. Humans had a lot of words for some odd things that did not make any sense and took a good bit of explaining to get the idea. This was especially tricky when it came to numbers. After eight things, wouldn't "many" work just as well? Did they really need to know the specific count of large numbers? His trainer simply pointed out that humans were odd and allowances had to be made for their strangeness.

That night, Nibs slept heavily. He had worked harder than ever before, both physically and mentally. Whenever he checked in on Asche she was also engaged in some sort of activity. Thus began the pattern for the next several weeks: Asche working with weapons and doing exercises to grow stronger, and Nibs learning about how human armies worked and how to speak to humans, as well as getting shown a few new flying tricks by ravens who had followed different Hand companies before. They didn't really do more than say hello to each other during that time, which was nice and reassuring, but far too brief. Since the training was intense, they were both too tired to do more than keep each other company at the end of the day when they could. Nibs flew for hours each day to let the new information settle, as they covered a great deal. Each day as the sun set, the elders spoke to Nibs about what working with the Morri meant, and who the goddess was to them.

After a week or so of constantly learning something, during one of the rare free moments, Asche felt emboldened enough to ask Flit why they were training so hard.

Flit looked at her a second, assessing what her answer should be. "Our task is to protect others. Many of the aggressors are men. What ye need to realize, Asche, is that men are generally stronger and more aggressive than women. When the Hands were formed, the Morri knew this and taught us that in order to counter that particular advantage we needed several things. The most important of which was training. Most levies have people who have been taught the basics of the spear and naught else. Most guardsmen have been taught a bit more than that. We train harder than knights, harder than anyone, and that gives us a skill to counter the strength, the reach, and the aggressiveness of most foes we'll face. Training like this is a huge advantage."

Asche pondered this, and realized something was missing. "You said there were other things that helped?"

Flit nodded. "Aye, our weapons and armor. None else have armor like us. Only knights have better armor, and then only occasionally. And the Morri is the goddess of smiths before aught else. The steel that makes our weapons and armor is stronger and lighter than others. And if you're lucky enough to have blessed steel...well, that can change any fight. The Morri makes sure we are as prepared as can be to face any challenge we come across. In order to protect what needs protecting, we have to work smarter and longer which is why we train so hard."

When the new recruits' armor was ready after a week or so, it was distributed and any adjustments that were needed to make the fit better were taken care of. After that was accomplished, wearing the armor was incorporated into training. Asche had thought she was tired before, but that next week, with running in her new brigandine armor, weapons practice with dagger and raven head, doing even more exercises, and learning about basic first aid and how to care for her gear, Asche was drained to the point where all she could usually manage was to stumble to her cot and fall in at the end of a day.

There was so much work going on Asche was fairly numb, exhaustion creating a blanket that muffled her thoughts and actions. She made friends in her unit, especially with Flit as they worked together most often. She and Elsif were growing into closer friends as they talked after supper most nights for a short bit before Asche went to bed or joined in on whatever entertainment was happening that evening, music mostly, as there were a number of Hands who played instruments.

Asche admitted this was not a bad time. She ate more food than she ever had, and much of it of a better quality, but there was very little weight gain as her body grew leaner and stronger. She was even aware she had gained some height back, almost to where she had been. What's more, the initial awkwardness of movement she felt since the Rite of the Lost Sister faded over time to where her body felt like it had always been hers. Even back at Oxlen she had never worked so hard and had to admit the majority of what she was learning and doing was interesting. There was so much more to life than making shoes, shearing sheep, or tilling a field. Learning all this made her feel more alive than ever before.

There were also drills on how to move silently, which were more akin to a game than other training they did. The platoon went out from the temple compound, through the town, and out to the woods. While there, Asche was tasked with sneaking up on Terris in various situations. Needless to say, there was much to learn. Going slowly and working on foot placement did not seem like it would be difficult, but there was no denying she was not nearly sneaky enough in Sarnt Terris's mind. Two of the other Hands, Tigh and Elles, were scary invisible in the woods and gave her several bits of advice. Flit helped most of all, spending time explaining how she could better move about stealthily.

Working with the other rangers, Asche realized just how good the rest of them were at not just stealth but everything else. When the others moved, there was a slight rustle of old leaves and branches rather than the discordant crunching and snapping she made as she plowed through the forest's undergrowth. The advice given by the various women helped her learn how to move quietly, though she was aware that until she could get her body to follow that advice, she would still move like a pregnant sow. Sarnt Terris informed her they would continue to work on her skills until Terris thought she was ready. It was remarkably not comforting.

One of the new tasks Asche found engaging was when she worked with Fanlis and Lynarra in the care of the company's altar and learning the liturgy of the Morri. Being guided through morning prayers and offerings was different from anything she had done back in Oxlen. Back then, Father Tombol dominated all such activities, keeping the specifics of the worship of the Triad a bit of a mystery, probably hoping it would make the Triad seem even greater than they already were.

Here with the Hands, things were a lot more open and clearer as to how one would go about worshiping the Morri. Little offerings of food, raw ore, wool roving, or coin were easy to understand as gifts. These were practical things. The use of incense before the prayers was also easy to grasp, as Father Tombol had taught that the thin smoke carried prayers to the divines. It was obvious the Morri had little use for ostentatious displays of faith and far preferred simplicity over pomp, more the opposite of Father Tombol's approach to be honest.

The Morri's focus on crafts, on the forge, on protecting others called to Asche. Having been a victim, she wanted to protect others from that. Training to be better made more sense than just simply being good at something and remaining happy with that level of skill. Even the work of cobbling shoes had a learning curve that took time and practice to become good at. Learning new skills and crafts was something Asche enjoyed.

Over the next several weeks, other companies left the temple to start their missions for the late spring and early summer. Asche learned that various city-states and smaller countries paid well for the services of the Hands to supplement their forces. The Hands were never in the vanguard of armies, but worked to protect the people, to aid in the defense of towns and villages near battlefields. Some of the companies went off to check the security of other shrines and even some of the few temples to the Morri in different lands, which made sense to Asche as she had heard about different military units dedicated to the protection of the different faiths. The primary role of the Hands seemed to be protection against minor threats and to help people if they were in need. It seemed a better use of her life than fighting for the desires of some noble.

After another day of heavy weapons training and the basics of how to fight in formation where the whole company worked as a unit, Asche and Elsif sat under a tree to eat their evening meal of a rich stew and small loaves of rye bread with a hunk of white cheese. They also talked about their different training between the heavy infantry and the rangers. Nibs flew past and landed on a branch overhead, giving a soft gwah to get Asche's attention. Asche looked up and beamed at him. "There you are, Nibs. I was wondering where you'd gotten off to."

Nibs croaked and said, "Busy learn speak."

Asche's and Elsif's eyes widened in surprise. "Nibs! You can talk!"

"Cr-ru-ru-ruk," said Nibs. "Always talk, just learn speak human."

Asche was having a bit of trouble wrapping her head about this. Nibs could talk to her in words she could understand? This changed so many things. "Wow! Who taught you?"

Nibs glided down from the branch to land near Asche's small loaf of bread. "Elders. Friend to Hands. Think speak human help keep Asche safe."

Nibs leaned out and took a bite of the bread loaf, making Asche chuckle. She grabbed a bit of cheese and offered that as well, before reaching out carefully to stroke a finger down Nibs's breastbone. "You are a very clever raven."

With an odd croaking chuckle, Nibs replied, "All raven clever."

Elsif closed her mouth and snickered. "That's very true."

Nibs cocked his head to the side, considered Elsif a moment, then he straightened and looked right in Asche's eyes. Asche could tell this was more serious than before, and she paid close attention. "I help. I learn speak so I help."

Asche started at this. There was no way to expect this sort of development. This was after all just a raven that liked her. "You want to help me, I mean, help us, the Hands?"

Nibs bobbed his head a few times in response.

Asche looked over at Elsif, to see if she had any guidance. "Don't look at me, he's your friend."

"Thank you so much, Nibs," Asche said. "I'm glad you're willing to help out and stay with me."

"Nibs good bird."

"Nibs best bird," Asche said. This was more than she ever expected to have happen with her friend. Now when she opened her heart to Nibs he might be able to give her advice or guidance. It was such a wonderful development, and she hoped Nibs was pleased with it as well. She looked over at Elsif. "Well, I guess I should go let Sarnt Terris know we're going to have some more help with recon."

Nibs took that moment of inattention to reach into the stew bowl to grab out a piece of beef and promptly hopped away with it. At Asche's wordless protest, Elsif snorted, and said, "You better eat your food first, before the raven gets it all."

Sarnt Terris was quite pleased at the news about Nibs, and thanked Nibs directly, speaking to the raven as if he was one of the other Hands. She then led Asche and Nibs over to the building the company was billeted in so they could see Fanlis. Fanlis looked up from her near-constant paperwork, one eyebrow quirked in question. "What brings three of you here?"

The sarnt gestured with her head toward Nibs perched on Asche's shoulder. "Seems we have a new recruit."

Fanlis put down the quill she had been writing with and steepled her fingers. She considered Nibs intently. Nibs stared back, unfazed by the theatrics. "Nibs, is it? Did the other ravens here at the temple convince you to work with us?"

A quick bob of the head was the answer.

"And you're willing to help Asche here with her work as a ranger?"

Another bob was the answer.

Fanlis sat back in her chair and smiled at both Asche and Nibs. "I have to admit, I hoped something like this would happen when I first saw the two of you together. Being able to get a look down on things, to let us know who's moving where, with what units, will certainly help a great deal to make sure we're as safe as possible in combat. This can really make a difference in any conflict we run into."

"Nibs help Asche, help Hands," said Nibs.

"Excellent. You're not the first raven to help the Hands, just the first to come work with a company rather than help out a temple or shrine. I'll let the kaitan know, so we can best work out how you can help. I'll look in the records and see what ideas are in there. Thank you very much for this, Nibs. We'll make sure you're fed and taken care of as best we can, despite you not being a Hand. Sarnt Terris, start working to integrate Nibs into ranger patrols and teach him how to report what he finds and to whom. Let's get to work."

Asche left the office and went to the back of the first floor where the other rangers were staying. Sarnt Terris called everyone together. "We have new member of team. Nibs here will work with Asche on scouting duties. I am sure he can talk to rest of us as he wants, but he'll be working with Asche primarily. Any questions?"

Flit smirked when she heard that and joked, "Ye got us a two-for-one deal on recruits? That's new."

The others laughed, and Asche snickered a little. Everyone took the time to say hello to Nibs and get to know him. The next day, Sarnt Terris and Flit helped Asche and Nibs learn how to report what they saw while scouting. The sarnt combined all this with stealth practice, setting up several tasks Asche had to complete without getting caught. Nibs helped, as he was able to tell Asche what was out there without her getting too exposed. However some of things were set in such a way that only Asche could spot them from the ground. What took most of the practice time was learning what was and wasn't important to report, something neither was very good at.

"Remember, Asche," the sarnt explained after a few runs, while the others changed parts of the course about. "Just knowing how many in group is not enough. There is difference in what ten archers can do compared to ten heavy infantry or ten light cavalry troops, not to mention ten levy troops. Being able to tell those details at glance will come with time and practice. You'll get there."

Asche noticed when Nibs spotted someone rapidly headed down the nearest road near to where they were training. He closed the distance and noticed it seemed to be a regular person riding hard down the road. He returned to the training area and swooped down to land on a branch, croaking out, "Rider!"

The rangers looked in the direction Nibs had turned and spotted a message rider headed toward the town, his horse in a bit of a lather. He was dirty and had flashes of a brownish red that might be blood on his tunic. The sarnt gathered everyone with a call and they hustled back to the temple.

The runner was already out of the courtyard and speaking with someone when they arrived. Noting this, the sarnt ordered, "Make sure gear is ready! We might head out soon."

Asche glanced at Flit questioningly. Just because there was a runner, was there really any reason to do more than wait? Flit shrugged. "Ye get a feel when a thing concerns ye. I'd get ready if I were ye."

## Chapter Six

Kaitan Tanrei looked over the assembled company with Fanlis to one side and a priestess of Morri on the other. "A rider reached the temple with news that a group of bandits has attacked one of the smaller shrines and the village attached to it, Gehrlen. A runner set out before the entire place was surrounded and they headed straight to a shrine a day away, despite being wounded. With no farspeaker on site, a rider was dispatched and they reached here after a day and a half of travel. We do not have a full assessment of what we will face when we get there, but we head out now to rescue our sisters, the villagers, and if necessary, assist in rebuilding. Gear up! We're moving out."

Thanks to the sarnt's foresight, the ranger unit ran into the barracks and swiftly returned with their gear. Flit and the others rushed off to help get horses in tack and get wagons ready, and assist the supply unit in having the supplies loaded. Asche followed along to help Fanlis and Lynarra packing up the altar in preparation of loading it into one of the wagons. Once Fanlis and Lynarra placed it into the carry box, Asche stepped forward to help Lynarra carry it to the wagon.

In short order, the company was assembled and ready to move. A few of the Hands from other companies rushed out with the last of the provisions to load in the wagons, including some prepared foods to tide them over for the several days needed to race to Gherlen and its shrine. The kaitan looked over the company, catching the eyes of her lieutenants and sarnts in turn, before she mounted her horse. "May the Morri bless us on this mission. Move out!"

Members of the ranger unit trotted ahead on horses, with Nibs overhead. The set pace was rather quick, however, thanks to the weeks of training, Asche was able to keep up without too much panting. Even the wagons were moving faster than usual, as they wanted to get to the besieged shrine as quickly as possible. The damage would already be done, they just hoped to deal with the raiders, whoever they were, if they were foolish enough to linger.

Asche's heart raced, though not from the pace. This was it; the Hands were marching off to fight for the first time since she joined. Asche found this whole situation exhilarating, aware that she was going to go out and hopefully rescue someone. And yet, Asche was also well aware that in going off to rescue someone it likely meant she would have to fight, have to kill, and have the possibility of being killed. All the training done so far only made her more comfortable holding her dagger or swinging the raven's head as if she could fight, but to use it on someone? That was another issue entirely.

From what some of the others said, the bandits could either have attacked and tried to make off with food and whatever easy wealth they could snatch from the people who lived there, or they might have tried to capture as many of the villagers as possible in order to sell them. All the stories she had heard about bandits back at her village talked about those being the usual reasons for such raids. What they were moving into did not make her feel very comfortable. Either parts of the village would be destroyed, or maybe they would need to chase slavers down to save the villagers. Neither sounded like fun.

Flit marched alongside Asche, and Asche was sure her partner noted the stress she was feeling. "Asche, 'tis going to be okay. The odds are likely that we're going to get there and have to help the shrine and village rebuild. Sadly, we do a lot of that, and so in a few seasons ye'll be a skilled carpenter and builder. After that? If nothin' else, we're gonna hunt the bastards down. The Morri wants us to punish those who attack her shrines and people under her protection."

Asche smiled weakly, looking over at Flit. "I just, I mean, I never…"

Flit patted her shoulder. "I know. I was so scared in me first fight I peed meself and then vomited all over me gambeson after I stabbed someone and they spurted blood back out at me. Fighting people isn't glamorous like in some bard's songs. 'Tis bloody, smelly, and hurts even if ye win. The Hands fight to protect, fight to avenge, fight to make sure others are safe. We don't fight to make ourselves heroes. That's who we are, not heroes of song, but warriors for the Morri."

"I'm just a kid from a farm village. I don't know anything about being a warrior," said Asche. She rolled her shoulders forward, feeling not only the weight of her rucksack, but also of her thoughts. "I mean, I still have issues with the weapons."

"That's most everyone who's a warrior, Asche. It's easy to be a soldier, to fight simply for pay, or to be one of the levy troops, who have no idea what they're doing and just follow the orders of the nobility. 'Tis even easy to be one of the nobility, raised to this life of battle by trainin' and tales. The Hands are different. We take untested people, and after the Morri examines their steel, they begin the process of learning how to do this." Flit looked off into the distance, her thoughts on something. "The Morri takes our raw ore and turns us into weapons and tools. Basically, she shapes each of us to be what best suits us."

Asche swallowed hard and shook a bit, her gear rattling slightly. While that may be true and might be what was actually happening, it still did not address her real concern. "To tell you the truth, I'm not sure I want to kill anyone."

Flit scoffed and shook her head before she looked over at Asche. "Who does? Ye're new to all this, and we all know that. All ye really have to do is follow orders and stay alive. If it turns out ye can't kill in the heat of battle, then I'm sure something else can be found for ye to do. It has happened, though rarely. Though, the Morri doesn't make mistakes in judging steel."

The conversation turned over and over in Asche's head as they marched into the late afternoon. It made sense that a divine would not make a mistake in judging her steel, but she did not want to end someone's life. Weren't brigands like these little more than bullies with weapons? However, the Hands had better weapons and armor, so wouldn't they be the bullies? That did not seem right to her, but her thoughts were in a knot.

Camp setup was a quick affair, as the company stopped in a clearing alongside the road normally used by merchant caravans who brought various goods to the villages. People busied themselves with setting camp in the fading light of sunset and the cooks bustled about, preparing that night's simple dinner. The meal was pasties heated quickly over a fire with hunks of a sharp white cheese. The bits of gravy in the pasty really added to everything. The cool water was actually rather nice after that forced march.

Afterward, Sarnt Terris informed the rangers they were not on evening watch rotation, which pleased all of them. Flit got a flute from her bag and began to play a few light tunes the others added beats to with clapping and slapping their thighs. Asche held herself back from the others, as her thoughts still roiled over the need to kill, the need to fight others. When she had left her village, she had not thought this might be the cost of her freedom from her father.

The Morri had given her more than she ever dreamt possible. This change and the time spent becoming her new self had broken free long forgotten memories as a little, running about the village, trying on a friend's dress and declaring she was a girl. The memory, and fear of that beating after her father found her also returned. No wonder she had not thought about being a girl after that, but had swallowed all that inside. It had been days of needing to stay inside and heal so the neighbors would not talk, which had also irritated her father. And there was little wonder her father, so determined to have a son follow in his footsteps, had done all he could to wipe that incident, and those urges, from reality.

But she was found now, in the skin she should have always worn, more whole by the day. It was an unlooked for gift, and maybe she did owe the Morri for this miracle. She drew her raven head from its scabbard and held the blade in front of her, twisting her wrist from side to side, gazing across the odd patterned steel of the blade that was a hallmark of Morri smith-wrought items. The weapon had a weight and a presence she had not really understood from stories, until she had first hefted it. This was not a toy, like the sticks used in play fights by littles, this weapon was a tool of death. Bands of light from the different fires reflected off the steel and flared along the edge as she raised and lowered the tip. Did she owe the goddess this?

Not killing others had been driven home in what Father Tombol taught to all in her village. It wasn't death per se, as death was a part of the cycle of life, but rather the act of killing another person. The triad frowned on that. Killing in defense of others or self-defense was okay, but from what she understood, not all their fights would be purely defense. Would a goddess lead her astray, especially against her parents? There had to be something she missed.

It wasn't difficult to find Fanlis, as she shared the tent that housed the shrine. When Ashe found her she was looking over a map and taking notes. It was odd how much writing was part of her job. Weren't the Hands a military order rather than armed scribes? Fanlis looked up as she entered. "Can I help you, Asche?"

"I had a question, and since you're the one in charge of the shrine, I thought you could help." Asche shifted nervously under the gaze of her superior. Authority figures generally made her uncomfortable.

"Certainly. What is it?" Fanlis set down her quill and sat back in her chair, never taking her eyes off Asche.

"Well, it's about fighting and killing, the things I've been trained to do, and how the triad is against that."

"Wasn't expecting that," said Fanlis, who sat back in her chair. "But let's see if I can help. Are you looking for justifications for killing, for the reasons why we have to kill sometimes, the purpose of violence, or something else?"

"If killing is wrong, why do we do it?" asked Asche, feeling her cheeks burn. She had not thought it would be quite this mortifying to ask this.

Fanlis sat there a moment, organizing her thoughts, clearly taking the question seriously. "Let me ask you a question. If a person is stronger than others, does that mean others should listen to them?"

"No."

"But if they're a bully and threaten you, using their strength to dominate things, what can you do?"

"You can fight back," answered Asche, unsure where this was going.

"Okay, let's say you and your friends beat them. Won't they come back and retaliate, maybe hurt someone in trying to force you to do what they want?"

Asche was aware Fanlis was leading her somewhere with this, she just wasn't sure where or how this connected to killing, but the point had to be conceded. "They could."

"Then how can you truly stop them?" asked Fanlis.

"Uhm…maybe jail, if you have one. Banish them."

"All good responses. But how can you stop them if they are actively hurting people in front of you?"

"I guess you have to attack them."

"Yes. And if you're a woman, the bully is likely stronger and larger than you, so you'll need a weapon to make things fairer. If you are using weapons, there is always a risk of hurting someone so bad they die. If you are physically strong enough, you can do the same. That death isn't a murder. It's simply killing someone, or in some cases, akin to putting down a rabid animal." Fanlis held Asche's eyes as she spoke. "I believe the deaths the triad are talking about are murders, where you plot and plan to kill someone, or hit someone really hard and kill them on purpose. Or if you're a bully attacking others and you kill one of them. If you are trying to force others to do as you say and you kill them, that's not good, and is what I believe the triad is against. But killing a bully who is hurting others and won't stop, killing someone who is attacking you, killing to protect others, I think those are valid reasons for that act. Using your strength in arms to fight for others, you are not hurting people to glorify yourself but rather to protect the larger community. That's what the Hands are trying to teach you. We fight for the betterment of all, not accolades. Does that help?"

"I guess. At least it gives me something new to think about." Asche stood.

"If you come to the decision you cannot fight, let me know. We will hold you out of combat and you can join a temple or shrine as a priestess or in some other fashion with no shame. You have to do what is true to your steel, not what anyone else thinks. This is more an issue between you and the Morri than anyone else."

"Thank you." Asche left the tent and wandered about the camp, pausing to stare into the dark trees at the few hints of stars above the greenery. As she moved by an area, Elsif came over and laid a hand on Asche's shoulder. "Hey, you feeling okay?"

Asche smiled at her. "Not great, honestly, but it's not physical. I'm nervous and unsure what to do, and my thoughts are all jumbled."

Elsif moved to better look into Asche's face. "Jumbled about what?"

"The priest at my village preached all the time about how violence was bad and that killing was one of the worst things you could do. Said the triad was against that and it was a sure way to earn suffering in the afterlife. So, while I'm excited to go off and start my new life with the Hands, I'm not sure I can hurt people or kill them."

Elsif looked thoughtful, turning her face to the sky for a second. "You ever fight with your brothers or anyone else in your village when you were younger?"

"Yeah."

"I know it isn't exactly the same, but it is kind of like that, this whole fighting thing we're going to be doing," said Elsif.

"How the hell is fighting bandits with swords and spears like wrestling with your brothers?" Asche stared at Elsif in some confusion.

"Well, obviously it's not exactly the same," Elsif replied with a slight huff. "But those fights were almost always about something, right?"

"Yeah? Almost always something stupid."

Elsif rolled her eyes. "Like kids fight over something sensible. Anyway, did you ever get into a fight to break one up?"

Asche nodded, remembering a number of tiffs and flat-out brawls she had waded into. "Oh yeah. I was eldest, so it fell to me to keep the peace amongst the others, not that it helped."

"Well, that's what we're doing." Elsif beamed at her. "We're going to keep the peace. And sometimes the only way to keep the peace is to thump harder than they can. If we can do it without killing them, great, they can be put under the lord's justice. But sometimes keeping the peace meant really thumping someone hard enough they would stay down and stop causing trouble. I've been on both sides of that situation and it usually worked, at least until the next spat. Weapons just make the thumps more dangerous."

Asche thought about that, about keeping the peace. It made sense and fit what she knew about the Morri. The warriors who worshiped her were all known to be protectors or defenders. They were ones who protected villages from raiders or angry beasts, hunted bandits or slavers. And the occasional need to thump harder than the other person was something she had experience with. The way Elsif put it was now meshed with what Fanlis and Flit said and made a whole lot more sense in her head. Maybe this wasn't going to be as bad as she feared, especially if they weren't the aggressors. She could fight to help others. "I should be able to do that."

Elsif smiled and opened her arms for a hug. Asche moved into her arms and sank into the embrace. It felt wonderful and helped her worry settle. It gave her a sense of peace and security she had missed a good deal of her life. Since she had been taught the Morri was a goddess of protectors rather than fighters, maybe keeping the peace was more in line with that than basically killing anyone who got in your way. There were a few rough lads back in Oxlen who thought that way, that the ends justified the means, and were not headed toward a good end. She was still wary of killing, but Elsif was right, sometimes you had to really thump someone to stop them in a fight.

# Chapter Seven

The pace the company set as they traveled was no issue for Nibs. Flight was easier than traveling afoot and he was able to make good time. The last several days, all they had done was move quickly from spot to spot, almost a forced march pace for the majority of the day, as the Hands raced to help the small town. Various members of the Hands were starting to get exhausted due to the pace, so they trudged with long faces and slumped shoulders. Nibs noted Asche was tired more often than not and generally in some sort of mental fugue state as if she marched and slept at the same time. While it was admittedly interesting to watch, he was not sure how much longer the group would be able to keep this pace.

Ahead, he spotted the walls of a shrine to the Morri, with a small village attached. This could be the place they were headed toward. They had passed several other small walled villages and even another shrine to the triad on this journey, but not one dedicated to the Morri specifically. Mostly, the supply people with the wagons went in and bought fresh bread and other foodstuffs before using the horses to catch up with the rest of the force on foot.

As Nibs drifted closer to the village, he noted a few faint whisps of darker smoke that rose from several of the buildings which smelled more of unconstrained fire rather than cooking or a forge. He remembered what he had been taught by the elders, and understood something was likely wrong. Nibs circled the area, scanning to see what was there. It did not look like any village that he had flown over before.

One of the first things he noted were the armed and armored men who moved about, both in the shrine area and village, giving people threatening looks. There were a few unarmored people who scurried about doing human chores, and they seemed scared, like rabbits reacting to any noise. Some of the armored humans yelled, and the unarmored flinched, then hurried to comply. Another thing that caught his eye was the pile of dead dumped in the courtyard of the shrine. There were several priestesses in the pile based off clothing, and Hands, as well as other women and a few men who were likely townspeople from what Nibs could make out. This did seem like the place they were headed toward. This also seemed to be exactly the kind of information he had been taught to pass on.

He winged over and headed back toward the road the company traveled along. Nibs made good time in his return, flapping to build speed. Even with steady progress, it took a while, as he had flown a good bit ahead, even farther ahead than the forward scouts who tended to have a few field lengths or more of distance from the main formation. The black clothing was not that easy to spot through the trees, but the silver thread and steel weapons were shiny enough to draw his attention. He did not circle down as he felt this was urgent, instead he dove down fairly quickly before he braked hard to land on a branch in front of the group. Nibs sat on the branch and scanned the area before he spotted Fanlis. Nibs gave a loud kraa that immediately drew all eyes to him, and Kaitan Tanrei ordered the company to stop. Nibs gave a powerful wing stroke and landed on the shoulder of Fanlis with some difficulty, as the woman shied away a little. The information officer started a bit and turned her head toward him. "Yes?"

"Enemy at shrine. Dead priestesses, other women, some men. Scared people," said Nibs.

"Were there a lot of them?"

Nibs thought back. He had not counted the enemy but had a rough estimate. "Over fifteen?"

This seemed to surprise Fanlis. "Over fifteen and they're still in the town?"

Nibs bobbed his head. "Guarding."

This seemed to concern Fanlis, and she frowned. "Thank you, Nibs."

Fanlis rode quickly to Tanrei to pass along Nibs's report as Nibs headed back toward where Asche marched.

Asche dug out a piece of cheese when she saw Nibs approaching. After he landed, she let Nibs grab a few chunks. The pace of the march changed to where they were going slower, though still along the road, to try to keep from making as much noise as they usually made on a march. Instead of reaching the village a little after noon, they were more likely to arrive closer to dusk. After a short while, the company was under the cover of the trees a short distance from the cleared area around the town.

Fanlis gathered her troops to pass along the new order. "Right, so Nibs noted there are armed and armored forces in the town we're supposed to go help. That's unusual behavior for bandits. And there are apparently at least fifteen of them in the town and shrine, possibly more as I guess Nibs didn't count. That's also unusual, as that is a larger number of bandits than we usually see. Something odd is going on and we need to find out what."

Fanlis turned and asked, "Nibs, can you go fly and see if there are more people anywhere near us? We don't want an armed force stumbling onto us as we work. I'll have something tasty for you when you get back."

After having his breastbone rubbed by Asche, Nibs took off and headed back toward the village. Fanlis continued on as Nibs spiraled his way higher. "Right, so I want a count done as soon as possible. Try to get the best info you can without too much danger to ourselves. I'm looking at you, Tigh and Elles. I want safety over risk. That info will help the kaitan plan for the assault. Be safe out there."

The small platoon of rangers, under the command of Sarnt Terris, began making their way forward through the trees toward the town and the shrine. They had quickly stripped off their armor and gambesons to appear more like regular farmers though their tunics and braies were also black. Their armor would have given away too much if it was spotted. Same with weapons, they were restricted to dagger and knife, as they were easier to hide and easier to explain if caught.

Asche winced at every branch break, but honestly, no one noticed as the other daytime noise of the forest swallowed the sound. That was not even taking into consideration the fact that the town was surrounded by open land where the fields were. The noise would not travel that far. They still moved through dense woodlands, though she began to see hints of brightness where the edge of the woods was and the bracken thinned. After giving a good scan of the area, Terris made a hand signal indicating a change of direction and pointed off toward a clump of bushes.

Moving cautiously, it took them a bit to get over there and form up into a semicircle completely blocked from view. Hidden by the bushes, Terris low-crawled along the periphery of the bush until she reached the edge of the fields.

After a short while, she crawled back then she took a seat, looking over the other rangers. "Alright. Thaw has happened here, but something must have distracted the farmers. This field has not yet been cleared of last year's growth, which makes me think this was fallow field last year, which is in our favor. We use shaggies to get closer to walls without being obvious, then we need an accurate count of hostiles. There is rise over there which looks to have good-sized trees and overlooks town. Flit, take Asche and look. You make the count. The rest, with me. We shall move closer and see what we can."

The shaggies were outfits made with burlap strips and netting that the wearer attached foliage to in the field to appear like whatever groundcover there was. Asche had been taught to wear and disguise it with plants and sticks on one of the stealth training days. Skilled use allowed a ranger to look like nothing more than a tuft of grass or some sort of bracken as they slowly worked their way closer to their target. Asche had to admit she was nowhere near as skilled as several of the others at either the stealth or making the shaggies look good. Yet another area where more training and practice was needed.

Asche moved around the boundary of the fields with Flit in the lead. The two of them stayed at least twenty feet from the edge of the woods, well out of sight of anyone in the town and deep in shadow. Sarnt Terris had been right. This side of the fields was higher than where the rest of the team was going in, though they had moved into a field that was not nearly as overgrown as the fallow one as they neared the palisade. Flit pulled free a spyglass and looked from where they were situated toward the town and frowned. "We don't have enough elevation. Time to climb a tree."

The lowest branch on this hardwood tree was high enough that Asche needed to give Flit a boost, enabling her to reach one of the lower branches and pull herself up. She climbed higher, staying out of sight of the fortified town. Once she was at least halfway up, she wedged herself into a nook, and pulled free the spyglass to take another look into the village. She called out softly, "Ready for note taking?"

Asche had the scrap paper she was to write on resting on her palm, graphite at the ready. "Go."

Flit scanned the area carefully. "I see twelve armed men in the town. Three on the walls. The rest seem to be collecting people or something. Not really patrolling, so much as watching. There's also a large group of people in the center of town, by the well."

Asche took down the highlights of what Flit was reporting. She was sure all that was important, but she did not have enough experience to understand why.

"Four on walls of the shrine. Same behavior but watching inward, not out. Can't see in there from this angle. Looks to be a similar number of armed men on the shrine grounds. I guess maybe twenty men I can see, so maybe thirty all told. Basic equipment. No metal armor. No signs of siege, but some signs of a few fires, mostly by the stables. I guess they entered by stealth somehow, though 'tis a lot of bandits for one group. People on the far wall are scanning more than others. They're looking outward, toward the road so maybe they're waiting on others?"

"Will getting higher help?"

Flit paused, thinking about her answer. "No. The trunk gets thinner if I go much higher, so t'will be easier to spot me and the wood might bend under me weight. No spyglass seen on anyone so possibly not."

Asche nodded, not thinking about Flit being unable to see her. What she said did seem sensible. What was obvious from where she was standing was probably harder to see from the town. They were supposed to be unseen after all. "The others have reached the base of the wall."

Asche's breath held at that. She was worried for the others she had been growing closer to. In the month or more she trained and lived with the rangers, she had started becoming friends. It was yet another new thing for Asche, and she did not want to lose anyone.

"Tigh is over in a blind spot for the guards. Elles is in. No response. They are too busy looking inside the shrine grounds to notice them. The rest are moving back." Flit was quiet after that as she scanned the town for any sign the two who had made it inside had been spotted or caused a disturbance. Asche was tense, worried about her friends, and looked toward the wooden palisade of the town and shrine, as if she could make out any details from this distance. After a while, Flit called down, "The others are clear of the field. Elles has made it out of the shrine. She passed a signal that she has information."

Flit climbed down at that point, taking the same care she had on the way up. After dangling briefly from the last branch, she dropped to the ground. When she landed Flit crouched deeply, nearly silent, just like one of the exercises Asche had done. "Let's go. Slow and steady."

"But there is someone still in there," said Asche. "Don't we need to watch to see if they need help?"

"'Tis fine, Asche. This is how we do things. Besides, Elles gave me the okay. Give me the paper." Flit took the scrap paper from Asche and the graphite, then proceeded to draw a rough sketch of the town, plus where the watchers were stationed, and scribbled a few notes in the margins. After she had completed the sketch, the two of them set off to where they had split from the rest of the rangers.

After a short while, they rejoined the rest of the platoon, seated by a tree drinking water, well into the line of the forest. Terris looked up at the two of them approaching. "You got map?"

Flit nodded. "And the count."

"Good. Have water, and then let's return to company."

Flit and Asche both had some water. Asche noted Tigh was not there with them and asked Elles, "Where's Tigh?"

"She's back there in the village. She hopes to provide cover for trapped Hands and priestesses if things go sideways. She's also trying to figure out a way to free and arm them if she can."

Asche stared at Elles. "Without backup?"

Flit patted Asche on the arm. "'Tis okay. Tigh does this. She's brave to the point of foolhardy, but she wants to be a Sword. To that, she throws herself into things like this to prove she is ready to become one of the Morri's chosen."

Asche shook her head, trying to wrap her thoughts around those ideas, of putting your life on the line for the good of others and that curious notion of trying to become one of the Morri's chosen. Hadn't she already been chosen by the Morri during her dedication? How was this different?

Terris stood. "Anything else?"

No one had anything to add so they headed back toward the company at a good pace as the light began to fail. They moved back faster than they had come out, but they had neither seen nor heard any signs of scouts out here in the forest. Once back at the encampment, Terris led them to the shrine tent that doubled as Fanlis's work space. After the rangers all crowded in, Fanlis looked up from what she had been writing and scrutinized them one by one. She leaned forward, hands steepled. "Report."

Terris handed over the scrap of paper with the map and notes. "Town has good cleared area around it, though one or two fields have yet to be cleared for spring planting. Most growth is mid-shin to knee in height, a bit higher in fallow field. Flit counted roughly twenty-four, with basic gear split between sections, none wearing metal armor. Her assessment of thirty overall seems likely, assuming there were others in buildings and such, maybe sleeping guards. There are seven guards on walls, with two facing northern road looking like they expecting others. Tigh and Elles went over palisade by shrine, where guards mostly were watching inward. Tigh decided to stay undercover but ready to protect priestesses if it comes to it. Elles reported Hands bound back-to-back. They are being held in courtyard and under guard, isolated from those in town with an armed contingent around them. Whoever got in knows who we are, how we act, and our reputation. They are taking no chances with any Hands. Tigh mentioned to Elles she was going to see if she could do something about that. From what Flit reported, farmers are being gathered up in center of town, though under less guard."

Fanlis sat back, tapping her chin. "That is odd behavior. It's almost as if the people of the village have been captured and are being held for transport. We have no other sign of wagons or what not in the village itself?"

Sarnt Terris shook her head. "None."

Fanlis gazed down at the map of the region and at the map of the town and shrine. As her eyes danced over the maps, she frowned. "Thirty bandits in one group? That seems unusually high for this duchy in particular. This doesn't feel right. What is going on?" She was quiet a moment, still looking down at the map. "Tigh's in there you say?"

"Yes, ma'am."

"I hope she finds someone in command we can capture. There has got to be some sort of story that could explain all of this. Anything else?" Sarnt Terris shook her head. "Right. I'll take this to the kaitan. The rest of you, get some rest. You'll likely be sent in to get the gates open tonight. That seems our most likely response. Terris, you know what that entails, so let Asche know what goes into that."

The sarnt nodded and led the team out. "Right! Get food, take nap. Whatever battleplan, we will be part of it. Likely getting in there and opening things up like she said. So, night work it is. Flit, set Asche straight on what she needs for tonight."

Asche sat at her bedroll, unsure how to process it all. Maybe she just needed to sleep and let the people in command make decisions. There was no way Flit, Terris, or even Fanlis would set her up for failure. The Hands talked a great deal about how important working as a team and a unit was. She just didn't want to disappoint.

## CHAPTER EIGHT

Asche and the other rangers stood there as Kaitan Tanrei looked over the map of the town Flit had sketched. Tanrei half talked to herself and half talked to Fanlis. "If the count is right then we outnumber the enemy by a significant margin. Terris, are you sure we have significantly better equipment?"

The sarnt nodded.

"That will help. A nighttime assault would be best, though that's hard on the troops and increases the likelihood there would be casualties due to mistakes. Going in without light will make it far too easy for the attackers to mistake their own people for enemies once they got stuck inside."

Fanlis nodded. "The same is true for our troops, though the uniforms help with that. The watchers looking out along that one trail for further support is concerning. So we go sooner rather than later because there's no way to know when their support would arrive. If we lay siege to the town, there's no telling if the bandits would yield or kill the villagers. Getting up the walls would be the difficult part, as even starlight might be enough to spot movement in an open field, but at least a few of you rangers have already done that in daylight, and gone undetected as well."

The Kaitan looked at the map a bit longer before she nodded. "It's clear the rangers have to go in and open the gates, especially for the heavy and medium infantry units to move in and clean things up. The weight of their armor would make it tricky to get up and over the walls in silence, so that needs to be considered. Archers might be of some use, especially if these bandits are stupid enough to have a torch or lantern with them to provide a viable target. While they help you see in the dark, it makes an easy target to shoot at." Tanrei rubbed her eyes as she went over things to work out what would and would not work in this battle plan. "And all of this will last exactly as long as it takes to get stuck in combat, when all the surprises tend to come out. After that, training will tell, and our troops are unmatched."

Asche and the others watched Tanrei going over the map, trying to visualize the space. To Asche it sounded like the battle before them was fundamentally simple, and the enemy being bandits rather than hardened troops was a large part of why it should be easy, but that could also be the reason the kaitan was trying to do this right. Fanlis spoke up. "If the plan is strong enough, we might be able to get out of this with only a few injuries and no deaths among the Hands."

The kaitan looked over at Fanlis. "If not, then we'll sing the funeral rites tomorrow for sure. Thirty bandits who likely snuck into the town in small numbers is a sizable force, even with all our advantages. They have weapons and armor, and Elles said she was sure some of them had taken the equipment from the Hands at the shrine to improve their gear. No, in this situation it's the training that truly made the differences between them. I hope they have repurposed the armor, and that the leaders and the strongest have the gear, because they're the ones with answers and it's impossible to question the dead.

Asche stood ready to answer any questions Kaitan Tanrei had about the enemy, but doubted she would be asked anything. Further questions to Flit and Elles expanded her understanding of the situation. "Fanlis, there are parts of the explanation missing, so prisoners are a must. We need more of the blank spaces filled in to understand why this attack happened and of course, who is behind it."

As she waited, the sound of wings caught her ear and Asche turned to see a raven headed their way, likely Nibs. The wingbeats also seemed harder, as if the bird were tired.

Nibs landed awkwardly near Fanlis on the ground. He walked in a small circle, moving his wings a bit, stretching. Fanlis set down a mug of water and a bit of pasty for him. She just waited for the bird. Rushing him to speak faster than he was ready was a sure way to get him to ignore her forever. The potential value he represented made her wait. Nibs drank and then cawed some, almost like clearing his throat. By this time, Tanrei was aware of Nibs's presence and turned to face him.

Nibs croaked out, "Away from shrine, up road, people with chains, cage wagons. Armed like others. Smell off."

Fanlis started a little. "Slavers? But we're not close to the border. It's incongruous for that threat to be here, this deep into the duchy. Are you sure the wagons had cages on them?"

Nibs bobbed his head before he returned to drinking from the mug.

Fanlis cursed under her breath and turned to the kaitan. "Slavers incoming from the north apparently. They have wagons for the villagers plus chains. This was a damn slave raid."

Tanrei turned back to the table and traced her finger along the road on the map on the duchy. "How far?"

Nibs cocked his head. "Some movement of sun."

Asche groaned at how not helpful that was. She tried to extrapolate from what she did know, which was how far they were from the village. "Longer than from here to the shrine?"

Nibs bobbed his head. "This twice and half again. Almost turned back before I saw as light was fading. Was setting camp."

Fanlis gave a slight sigh, letting out some worry the battle might have shifted against them. "Far enough. If that's the case, they'll likely show up tomorrow rather than tonight."

Tanrei grunted. "There's no guarantee of that. How many slavers?"

Nibs bobbed his head. "Twenty."

"Okay. This changes some things. Fanlis, I need an idea what the weather will be like pre-dawn." Fanlis moved away to the shrine to try to commune with the divine. From what Asche had been taught, it wasn't the best way to get information and sometimes did not even remotely work, but it was what they had.

Nibs hopped up near Asche, who smiled at him. "Long flight?" Nibs nodded. "Tired."

Picking Nibs up, Asche and the other rangers headed out and to get some food. Once she had eaten her fill, Asche moved her plate with the remains of a meal and shared bits of cold meats, cheese, and bread with him. Nibs preferred to gather his own food, but human food would do in a pinch. Especially cheese. That stuff was so tasty. The trick was to not eat it exclusively, which he had been taught as a fledgling would make a raven ill if he over-indulged. A sick raven was often a dead one, so it was a concern. Asche was quiet, and Nibs croaked in question.

Asche just shook her head. "Sorry, Nibs, been thinking. Gonna be fighting tomorrow."

Nibs bobbed his head. That much seemed obvious.

"You've been busy. I was sure you were going to come by while we were out reconnoitering the town, but there was no sign of you."

"Scout," croaked Nibs proudly, then ruffled his feathers.

"Just like me." She smiled at him and rubbed his breastbone. "I'm sure you have been doing a great job."

"Saw bad guys." Nibs then bobbed his head and cocked it, looking at Asche expectantly.

She ran a finger down his breastbone a few more times before scratching behind his head a bit, which got Nibs rolling his head back and forth in pleasure. "More bad guys then?" Asche yawned broadly. "Sorry, Nibs. I think I need to get some sleep."

With a quick caw, Nibs said, "Me too."

Asche curled up in her bed roll while Nibs flew to a branch above her, to be close when morning came.

❖

Asche was shaken awake by Flit. "Come on, lass."

Asche worked herself out of her bedroll with a yawn, wishing she could get more sleep. The canopy of trees was dark, with an occasional glint of starlight peeking through. There was a faint silvery glow from what moonlight there was, making it light enough to make out outlines and some details. After a short stretch, she followed Flit toward a faint glow of candlelight over by the command tent. Fanlis was there, waiting. Once the rangers arrived, Fanlis started her briefing.

"Okay, here's what we're going to do. Two teams are going to head into the village. Terris, you're leading the one going into the village proper and Elles will lead the one going into the shrine. Primary target is to open those gates for our heavy and medium infantry to barrel through. Once the gates are opened, move in and try to secure the prisoners. Elles, if you can manage it, free the Hands with Tigh, since more help in this kind of fight would be nice. More swords would be good, so if you can get them weapons it would be even better. Hopefully, Tigh is ready to make that happen."

Fanlis paused and looked them all over, as if assessing their readiness. "We get to the walls using shaggies. Remove those, and then over the palisade. The plan is to do this in the dark, as there is supposed to be fog this morning, which will limit their vision. Then once successfully inside, we shift to the next part of the plan, which is opening the gates. That is straightforward. The third phase of the plan deals with ambushing a group of slavers headed toward the town that Nibs spotted. I'll brief you after the town has been secured on that plan. No need to put the cart before the horse."

Flit tapped Asche on her shoulder. "You're with me. We're gonna go for the town gate while the others take out sentries. Remember, ye fight only after the gate is open. That is our first job."

"Right." Her stomach roiled a little at the notion. This was actual combat, not fisticuffs and scuffles with others but actually using sword and dagger against people. She had been given a light task, open the gate, but to do that, they had to scale a wall and move in silence past a collection of bandits who would no doubt love to take her or any of them captive. It was entirely possible she would have to take a life or lose her own in the course of this mission and that realization was daunting. The tales sung by traveling minstrels at the tavern never hinted at the grind, the training, the fear, and the absolute difference between a hero's tale and being a military order of a goddess. Maybe her own saga might be worth something in the end, but who would want to hear about pre-combat jitters?

They were again going in without their brigandine. The regular black braies and tunic with the black gambeson were all they were wearing. The quilted gambeson was some comfort, but Asche had to admit she was unsure how well the fabric and padding would deal with blades. She checked the placement of her gear one more time, tightening the belt with her weapons a bit more to ensure nothing slipped.

The rangers moved out first as they headed into the foggy darkness toward the captured town. They covered the distance to the edge of the woods quickly, following the route they had taken earlier. There had donned their shaggies and began the slow process of moving crouched over across the field. Flit and Asche split off midway through the farm fields, heading toward a section of the wall closer to the town's gate. As they began to draw closer, they lowered to a high crawl so as to appear more like bracken in the dark. Several times, she and Flit froze. The sounds of two guards on the wall talking seemed loud. The edges of their torchlight hit them, but there was no reaction from those guards. Asche's heart raced as they resumed their patrol, only slower than before. The fog was thick enough they trusted it to protect them from being seen and identified as anything but a shrub.

Asche felt a spot between her shoulder blades itch and half expected a spear or a lucky bow shot to find her. There was a guard up on the palisade looking out into the darkness, the fog glowing ruddily from the flickering torch. Finally, he turned and continued on. Each movement forward took forever, longer than their patrol earlier. She swallowed heavily, trying to wish herself invisible.

Once they reached the walls, they stood there, backs against the wood, ears straining for sounds, to figure out if the patrolling guards were nearby. They were not positive it was utterly clear, but after not hearing anything that indicated a problem, Flit helped Asche up the wall, making a cup with her hands to boost her up. After grabbing the top of the wall at a spot between sharpened logs, she scrabbled over with some effort and looked both directions on the palisade.

The fog was still rather thick, and bits of it glowed orange from flickering torchlight, but none of it was close.

Asche leaned over the palisade and stretched a hand down. Flit took a few steps back before she ran toward the wall and leaped partially up it. Asche clasped hands with Flit and was able to haul her over without making very much noise. Flit was far more comfortable with this particular move than Asche had been.

Drawing their daggers, the two of them looked both directions on the walls before they turned their sight toward the town and the gate they had been tasked with opening. There were no visible swirls in the fog that could indicate movement, nothing to outline an enemy, the patches of light undisturbed. Flit gave a gesture to indicate their movement and led the way down a nearby ladder. Asche was tight on her heels, her palm sweaty on the dagger.

They clung tight to the darker shadows as they moved between buildings; the wattle and daub walls were rough when they leaned against them. The hints of the gate were barely visible in the warm glow of two torches on the top of the wall. They watched closely, as the glow could impede their ability to see anyone beyond the pools of light. Asche heard a sound that made her turn away from her primary objective and look at the building she was against. It was the sound of sex and someone crying. While Flit headed across toward the gate, Asche turned and moved to the door of the house.

The sound disturbed her. The distress and discomfort of those sounds gnawed at something visceral inside her, something that reminded her of too many nights back home, lying on his pallet, surrounded by straw, listening to where her father would slap his mother into submission before...Asche felt the muscles of her face firm as she slowly opened the door. It was a blessing when the door did not squeak. There was a deep guffaw and she heard, "Quit your snivvelin', you're good at this, so good I'll keep ye as me own when we sell the others. Won't that be nice?"

Her eyes adjusted to the stub of a candle guttering in the room, providing shadows that moved about that cast this scene in an even more morbid tableau. The sounds continued, the sobs quieter and weaker, grunts louder. Sliding through the shadows was suddenly easier, and she moved with more purpose, as all her lessons snapped into sudden focus. This was what the Hands were for after all, not to help glorify nations, but to fight for the protection of the common folk against those who thought might made right. With a slight shift of position, Asche was behind the man.

Almost moving without thought, her left hand went around the head, over the mouth, and pulled his head sharply backward as the dagger's blade slammed home into his back, in and up, driving the air out of the man's lungs. After pulling the man back further and away from the woman, she turned the body and rode it down to the floor. The man collapsed heavily with her additional weight, and he thrashed about weakly. That stopped when she dragged her dagger across his throat and blood splashed against the dirt and straw. The body shook then stilled.

Asche looked up and over toward the pallet where the woman lying on her back with her skirts shoved up had raised her head and was staring at her in wide-eyed disbelief. Asche nodded and held a finger over her mouth. The woman nodded dumbly and pressed herself to the back of her bed.

Asche moved back outside. She heard muted sounds of a fight and rushed over. She spotted Flit rolling around a thrust from a spear and ramming her dagger through a man's throat. The man dropped his spear and scrabbled for the blade. With a wrench, Flit tore the dagger to the side, cutting the man's strings in a rush of blood. As Flit wiped her blade clean on the bandit's tunic and started to drag the body out of the way, Asche raced up and helped. Flit glared at her.

That was when Asche noticed the blood on Flit's forearm and the gash in her gambeson. Asche was about to offer apologies when the glare intensified. Asche felt it was better to keep her mouth shut and just followed Flit. They moved back to the gate in uncomfortable, tense silence. As one, they lifted the beam that held the gates closed. They put it down against the wall carefully before Flit moved back to the gate and pulled it open. As the gate swung open, the heavy and medium infantry swarmed in, followed by the others assigned to the action. Asche thought she saw Elsif head deeper into the buildings, war hammer and shield at the ready.

Where the troops spread, the sounds of battle erupted, though it was not much of a fight overall. While people streamed in, Flit spun on Asche and hissed. "Where the fuck were ye?"

"I…uh…" Asche shifted uncomfortably, feeling put on the spot.

"That bastard nearly skewered me. I needed me backup."

"Uh…there was a woman, uh…rape…" Asche thought she had done the right thing when she had gone in to save that woman. Hadn't she?

Flit groaned and ran her hand down her face. She sighed and looked at Asche sternly. "There are always women being raped, Asche, or worse. We know that. Some of us have lived that before we escaped to the Hands. We hate that and we'd kill them all if we could. But we canna stop them all. That is why we follow orders. She would still be just as raped in the short time difference between us opening the gate and some heavy getting to them. Following orders and accomplishing the mission gets us support and then those bastards die like the scum they are. Suddenly, I had no backup, just me with me dagger and an ass with a spear. What if they got smart and raised the alarm instead of attacking me? They could have foiled the mission and put all the rangers in jeopardy."

Asche had no response as words stuck in her throat. Her cheeks burned and her stomach roiled with an acid taste in the back of her mouth. This was not what she thought would happen when she went to save that woman.

Flit sighed; her shoulders slumped forward, and she shook her head. "Come on. Wrap up me arm. We need to help with cleanup."

After binding Flit's arm with a strip of cloth bandage, they refocused on the task at hand and moved out to look for any bandits the assault forces had missed. When Flit went in to check on a sound from a small building, out of the fog, a bandit rushed Asche. His face was dark with anger, and he was hefting a large axe one-handed. He started to howl in rage at the sight of her. The man came down with an overhead slash, getting his second hand onto the shaft during the swing and treating her as wood to be split.

Freezing briefly, Asche shifted to her left to avoid the attack and swung her dagger at the man's exposed side. The man drew the axe handle into a block but twisted his body to do so. Asche drew back her arm for another attack when the man lunged with the axe. The blunt top slammed into Asche's chest and knocked her out of position.

With a gasp of surprise, Asche awkwardly brought up her blade to deflect another downward chop. She used her other hand on the spine of her dagger for greater support. With a turn of her wrist, the axe slid to the side and Asche kneed the man in the stomach. Folding more over the surprise of the blow than the force, Asche brought her dagger into position and down into the base of the man's neck. She stabbed downward with all her strength. The strike severed the spine and continued through the neck, to stick out the other side. There was a little blood sprayed, some hitting her. The man dropped with a whump, and Asche stood there and blinked at the body. The dagger was pulled from her hands by the weight of the corpse.

Flit rushed out and witnessed the end. "Ye okay?"

Her hand on Asche's shoulder broke her from her reverie, as she stared at the bandit's remains. Her body twitched a little with the adrenaline still flooding her system, urging her to move. Her eyes were trapped by the bandit's eyes, as the man's head had turned to face her as he fell. Asche pivoted toward Flit and vomited. The surprise was enough that Flit got splashed on her boots even as she tried to dodge backward. Asche fell to her knees, still heaving, her dagger forgotten in the body.

Flit groaned and looked about to see if there was any danger close at hand. There was not, thanks mostly to the fog. Shouts of all clear begin sounding throughout the village. Flit sheathed her dagger and helped Asche to her feet. She took the few steps to the bandit and twisted Asche's dagger a few times so she could pull it free. "Come on, let's get to the well. We need to get ye clean."

Asche was numb, feeling a weight in her mind that muffled everything. Killing a person was not like slaughtering a pig. The sounds and smells might be familiar, but the reality was very different. And when she had killed the man raping that woman she had not had this response, but then again she had moved almost without thought. She shuddered as she walked with Flit, the dagger hanging forgotten in her hand; her eyes were open but not registering what they saw as her mind kept replaying both deaths. The sluice of cold water from the bucket brought her more to the here and now as she sputtered.

Flit was also wet, though thankfully her gaze was more sympathetic than angry. "Good, you're back with us. Take care of your weapon. Just pour some water over it for now. The other rangers are over there. We can sit and rest for a bit."

Asche followed Flit's gesture to where other members of the rangers were questioning villagers and some of the priestesses. She nodded acceptance then began to clean her dagger, trying not to remember what she had just done with it. Once her blade was cleaned and sheathed, she moved to join the other members of the rangers to learn more about their job, following Flit's orders instantly as her mind was still dazed by all that had happened.

# CHAPTER NINE

Sarnt Terris finished her report to Fanlis. "Assault in shrine area was easier as Tigh managed to free other Hands and get them weapons. When it was clear battle had started, they leapt up and engaged bandits. There were no further injuries or deaths amongst shrine personnel. From reports, only deaths were village guards killed in initial assault and the farspeaker. Apparently, bandits started filtering into town over course of day, with a bunch arriving in traveling merchant's wagon. They stormed out and main focus was shrine. They mostly cowed villagers with violence and surprise."

"Was any paperwork found on them or in that wagon?" asked Fanlis as she looked up at the sarnt and Asche who was standing behind Terris.

"None found yet."

"Okay, head back to the others. We have to regain focus to get ready for the next phase of the attack. Hopefully, the slavers will have more information than the brigands. I'd really like to know what they were doing here and what they were hoping to accomplish."

Terris nodded and headed out with Asche at her heels. Already, the other platoons were preparing for the next phase, the ambush of the slavers. The archers were finding positions along the wall and next to buildings to allow them the most effective area of fire. The heavy and medium infantry were positioned in places out of sight, ready to rush in and overwhelm them. The rangers had more of a support role in this and weren't supposed to do anything major until the battle stopped, when they would get to work trying to trace the slavers back to their market.

Terris stopped near where the rest of her platoon was, resting against the wall of a building after they recovered the rest of their gear from the wagon. Asche had ensured that Flit's wound had been seen to by one of the chirurgeons, and she should be healed in a week or so. The others had escaped injury in the short battle. Flit had talked to her, but apparently Terris needed to make sure Asche understood such action was not going to be tolerated.

"You know what you did wrong?" Terris said, turning to face Asche.

"Yes, Sarnt." Asche hung her head.

"Do you know why it was wrong?"

"Flit explained."

"That's not what I asked. Do you know?" The last three words came out in a sharp staccato.

Asche paused and thought things over like she had been doing since Flit chastised her. It was all she had thought about since. "I think so. We all have parts to play in the plan and to deviate from them can ruin the entire plan."

"Yes, especially as rangers. We are given most tasks, most difficult tasks, and given least guidelines for what we do. When we have specific task, we need to accomplish that before we go off and do something else. We are eyes and ears of company. We are questing fingers of Hands. If you and Flit had delayed together to rescue woman, it would have been better than doing that alone. We cover each other's back."

"Yes, Sarnt."

"You fought without backup. Did you like it?"

"No, Sarnt."

"Will you do again?"

"No, Sarnt."

Terris nodded. "Good. Get back to others."

Asche hurried back and asked if Flit needed anything. She just shook her head. "Relax. Rest. Ye were yelled at, now we're good. Don't be an idiot again, okay?"

"I'll try."

"Good, that's all anyone can ask."

❖

Nibs had woken as dawn broke and was now gliding over a section of trail to the northeast. He searched for the bad people he spotted yesterday. They should be rather close to where he was, if he remembered yesterday's flight. Ahead, he heard the creak of wagons and the weird smell that lingered about them, fear and unwashed human bodies, with undertones of rot. Strong wing flaps gained him a bit more altitude allowing, him to spot movement through the trees. From what he could see from this vantage point, they were acting like they had been yesterday when he spotted them, casually riding along. Their brash voices made a few ribald jokes Nibs had little context for, so he ignored them.

He landed on a branch in front of them and watched them pass under his position, getting a more accurate count and trying to note anything else that might be important. The humans cared about the oddest details.

Nibs took off from his perch and winged his way back to the shrine at a very good speed, foregoing the usual aerial play he preferred in order to let Asche and the Hands know what was on the way. With the better numbers he was sure Fanlis could come up with something clever. Besides, he wanted to check on Asche. This morning he woke to a nearly empty camp, the last few people filling the wagons with gear to head to the shrine. When he reached the shrine, he searched for Asche and found her off to one side, looking sad. Fanlis had called for him. Nibs was concerned for his human and wanted to return quickly in order to comfort her.

When he was halfway back to the shrine, he was joined by a few other ravens, who drifted down to him from behind and higher.

He had been so focused on moving quickly he had forgotten basic flight safety. "Greetings," one of them said.

"Greetings," Nibs replied, casting glances at the others.

"Heading to the shrine?" croaked one on his left. "There are some not nice people there."

"Yes, I'm headed there. The Hands of the Morri killed the bad people this morning and it's safe again."

"Really?" remarked a different raven from his other side. "That is good news. The bad people chased us off after killing the eldest."

"I am sorry for your loss. The loss of an eldest is a deep sadness. May his memory not be forgotten. Did you have an arrangement with the shrine?" Nibs asked for more clarification. If they worked with the shrine, like the flock back at the temple, then they might be willing to help.

"No. The people at the shrine care for the ravens and crows on their own, but they have made no special action to gain our favor. Must be some human god thing. We like them." The first raven spoke again.

Nibs pondered this and thought about what he had learned from the elders at the temple farther southeast. There did indeed seem to be some sort of deal or pact between the ravens and the Morri, though what it was eluded him as he never heard any stories about it. He had no idea what it could be, as it was more guesswork than anything else, but he was sure there was something. Maybe he needed to help this group connect to the Morri, or even just the Hands at the shrine? "The humans are not that bad and can be really nice."

"The eldest did like them," said another, from behind Nibs.

"I think they are good allies," replied Nibs. "Maybe you all could make friends with the group here? Think about it and I can talk to you about it later atop the shrine." By this time, they had reached the village. He did a wing over and headed down toward where he could see Fanlis set up with her desk. He flapped hard several times to slow his forward momentum, angling his flight slightly upward, and dropped down onto the desk, hopping a few times to bleed off extra momentum. Fanlis managed to pluck up her ink pot before it got knocked over. "Nibs!"

"Have information." Nibs was rather pleased by her reaction. Fanlis had moved rather quickly when she caught sight of him diving down. She glared at him, but he ignored that as he passed the information he had seen. She seemed especially keen to note they had been traveling openly and casually.

"Thank you, Nibs," said Fanlis as she stood up, setting the capped ink pot onto the table away from his feet. "You've been a great help to us. I hope Asche keeps you happy."

Nibs flapped off to scan the village until he found Asche. She was checking over her dagger as he flew up and landed on the ground.

As he walked closer, Asche spotted him and smiled weakly. "Hey, Nibs."

"Feel bad?" croaked Nibs, cocking his head to the side and trying to understand her body language.

"I screwed up last night," said Asche, returning her dagger to its sheath. "I let Flit get hurt."

Nibs flapped to gain enough momentum to rise from the ground to land on Asche and dug his claws into the reinforced padding on the shoulder of the gambeson. Nuzzling her hair with his beak, Nibs hoped this helped to calm her. Humans did get upset about some strange things and needed comfort. After sitting together a while, Nibs started getting peckish. "Hungry. Going for food."

Asche watched Nibs fly off, heading out to the fields surrounding the town. She sighed. She had not meant to screw up. Honestly, she thought she had been doing the right thing by killing that rapist, and it wasn't the fact that she killed the bastard but rather that she left Flit unprotected. Leaving her partner in the middle of a mission was the issue and not specifically what she did. Being a part of a team was taking some getting used to, as she had not been on any teams before, or had anyone really be there for her. Hearing her name, she turned and saw Flit heading toward her. "Let's go. They want us at the gates."

They headed that way, Flit in the lead at a slight jog. The town's gate was where they planned to let the slavers in, as there was a bit more room to fight if it came down to that. They hoped the show of force would cow the men. They could hear the wagons creaking and people talking loudly as the slavers neared. These people sounded like they weren't afraid of anything they could encounter as they traveled. A few of the locals who were dressed like the bandits stood atop the palisade, acting like their captors had. The slavers called out, "Oi! Let us in!"

One of the disguised locals waved in recognition, calling down, "Open the gate!"

The gate swung inward rather quickly. With a snap of the reins, the wagons started to move forward toward the group of villagers sitting in the square. Once the mules of the second wagon cleared the gate, the Hands sprung the ambush. Archers popped out of various hiding spots and targeted the slavers. The heavy and medium infantry rushed out from their hiding spots and moved in for the kill. Asche did as ordered, rushing out to grab the reins of the mule team and drag them forward. It took a few tense seconds, but the mules obeyed. The wagon's jerk caused two slavers at the bench to lose their seat and fall to the side.

The battle was over quickly. The majority of the slavers surrendered, especially after a few attempted to fight back and perished under the weapons of the Hands. As the other troops dealt with the collection of the slavers, tying them up and making sure they had no knives on them, the rangers started to inspect the wagons and their contents. This was new to Asche and she followed Flit's guidance. With the work divided between wagons, the search actually went rather quickly. Asche found a hidden panel in the footwell that had some papers inside and a heavy pouch that clinked of coin. A similar cache was found in the other wagon, as well as a few other hidey-holes with bits of wealth stashed.

Once the wagons had been thoroughly checked and were clear, Terris collected the various findings and headed over to Fanlis, who was helping process the slavers. She already had two of them moved off to the side under guard for further questioning. The rest were shuffled off to where the surviving bandits were being kept, also under heavy guard. Fanlis glanced at the papers and nodded to Terris in thanks. The sarnt waved the others over and directed them to sit on the ground. She turned to Asche and asked, "I can't remember. You read, yes?"

Asche nodded.

Terris handed bits of the paper around. "You all know what to look for—who they are, where they're from, who they work for, and such. Fanlis wants summary of what we discover to help with interrogating prisoners."

Asche read over one of the pages Terris handed her. The further along she read, the more her stomach lurched. It was a shopping list with different people types listed along with their value, more women than men were listed, and there were bonuses listed for attractiveness that did nothing to help her nausea. That led her to think about the size of the wagons and the number of people who had been captured here. It looked like some of the locals would have been disposed of as excess, as the paper mentioned. She shuddered at the callousness. When she reached an entry near the bottom it caused her eyes to widen in surprise. A note about priestesses of the Morri and members of the Hands and their potential value, listed greater than any of the others. What caught her attention was it had been written in by someone else, as the writing did not match the earlier words and numbers. They had attacked the village as a bonus to the value those at the shrine would bring.

The next sheet was a map that showed this town as well as several others as part of a loop to be raided also. There were a few notes as to the planned route and the towns to be visited. This town was their first stop from what she could gather, especially since there had been no slaves in the cages. That, taken with the shopping list, made Asche's stomach twist. Someone made a plan for how this was to go.

The third sheet was a very short letter. She scanned it quickly:

*Scarpe, git them prisstesses. They wus top order. Them Handy bitchs worth gud coin too. Snag others to fill out pay.*

After a shudder of revulsion, she showed this to Terris. With a frown, she looked at the others still going over what they had been given. There were several copies of the shopping list, a second map, and one of them had found a letter with a wax seal keeping it closed. Elles had that one and opened it carefully to preserve the seal. She said, "Some priest wants us as slaves for some reason. There is no mention of which divine they serve. I don't recognize the seal either."

Terris took the notes and headed them over to Fanlis, who scanned the specific pages carefully. As the others completed their work, Terris handed over the useful paperwork. After reading the pile of papers, Fanlis motioned Asche over and sat her down at the table. "Time to question the prisoners. I need you to write what they say as closely as possible word by word. Just number the questions if you can't write that fast, as I'll know what that means. I always ask the same questions in the same order when I am first talking with them."

Asche arranged the parchment on the field desk and dipped the pen in ink and held it carefully, waiting. The first prisoner was brought over to Fanlis and shoved roughly into a chair by one of the heavy-infantry guards. The man looked about worriedly at the various armed women around him and swallowed heavily. Fanlis stood slightly to the side of him, sounding slightly bored as she asked, "Name?"

"Wut?" Apparently, he had been too busy woolgathering to register what she said.

"What is your name?" She enunciated the words slowly.

He stopped looking around the group and looked over at Fanlis. "Tedarin."

"Where you from, Tedarin?"

"Not tellin'." The man seemed adamant in his refusal.

Fanlis smiled gently, similar to how one would smile at a little, aware they did not really know all that was going on. The look was not quite pity, but there was no question as to what Fanlis thought of the man. "Tedarin, let me explain your position, in case you missed it. You are our prisoner, clearly caught in the act of slavery, with documentation to prove it. The punishment in this kingdom for being a slaver is death, and we have been empowered by the local duke to carry out acts of high justice in specific circumstances, such as this. Now, if you answer my questions honestly, I might be able to convince my kaitan not to kill you in punishment for being a slaver. We will turn you over to the duchy's forces so they can determine your guilt rather than us. So, if you have any information of value, you will likely live. I hope our place in things is clear now. So, Tedarin...where are you from?" Fanlis just stared at the man until he looked away uncomfortably, shifting in his seat.

After a pause, Tedarin answered, "Vargris."

"Vargris? You're a long way from home, Tedarin. Work as a slaver going good for you then?"

Tedarin scowled at her, glaring at Fanlis with angry eyes. Asche wrote quickly, trying to keep the letters from getting smeared on the parchment. It would be useless otherwise, though she was not succeeding as much as she wanted. Fanlis looked Tedarin directly in the eyes, waving one of the scraps of parchment they had found. "I notice you have a very specific shopping list, including me and mine, and a collection of towns and villages to visit on this map a distance from the border. So, if you are raiding villages for servants of the Morri and others, who's your buyer?"

"I don't know. Scarpe talks to the buyers and middles. I only drive the wagons and care for the mules."

"Really now? That's all, is it? So what use are you to me? Should I just call my kaitan over?" Fanlis quirked an eyebrow at him, looking bored and dismissive.

He began to sweat, droplets forming on his forehead. He stammered out, "I know things."

"Can't imagine what." Fanlis looked down at her papers and made a mark with her stylus, seeming to already be putting the conversation behind her.

"I don't know who the buyers are, specifically, but if you want them, you need to know where the market is. I know where the market is." The words spilled out over each other, and Asche had a difficult time keeping up with him.

"You think telling us about a slaver market over the border in Two Rivers is going to save you? We've known about that one for years." Fanlis gestured to the guards who came up and grabbed him by the shoulders and started to pull him to his feet.

"Not in Two Rivers! There's one here, in this kingdom!" Tedarin blurted.

All action stopped and Fanlis gestured with a slight toss of her hand. Tedarin dropped back into the seat heavily, panting a little, eyes wide and darting this way and that. Fanlis locked eyes with him. "So you might have some value to us after all. Where is this in-kingdom market?"

"I can lead you to it." There was some shifting but mostly he looked Fanlis in the face.

"And be led into an ambush? I think not," countered Fanlis. "You're going to have to do better than that, I'm afraid. Where is it?"

"I...I canna say." It looked like admitting that hurt Tedarin somehow.

Fanlis paused, her head cocking slightly to the side as she parsed this, looking at Tedarin closely. "You cannot say?"

Tedarin trembled. "Buyer did something, said a prayer and..."

"A prayer? Do you know to who?" Fanlis was intently focused on the slaver. There were only a few options of priests who might work with slavers and dislike the Morri, but there were more options than anyone wanted.

Tedarin shook his head. "It was quiet and I wasn't one of the closer ones. He said it to the whole group before we headed out."

"And you can't tell me the name of the priest or the divine or the village you were in?"

Tedarin looked to the ground in some fear.

Fanlis stared at him a bit, clearly trying to decide if she needed more questions, and then gestured. The guards hauled him away as he squawked in fear. Fanlis flipped through the paperwork they found and made a few notes of her own on the sheets Asche had been writing on. She took the maps and handed them over to Terris. "Find where those are on our maps. That might give us a lead as to where this market is."

"You think he might be telling truth?" Terris seemed skeptical.

"Maybe. He was concerned with trying to stay alive so he had plenty of reason to tell us the truth. Let's see what some of the others have to say. I think we need to question some of the others about their travel. No need to ask about where the market is more than one other time to verify it has been blocked by a prayer, but the travel information might help lead us in the right direction. And if we're lucky, this Scarpe fellow won't be dead but amongst the prisoners." Fanlis waved Terris away as the guards brought up the next prisoners. Once he was seated roughly into the chair, she looked up at the man without smiling. "Name?"

## CHAPTER TEN

The company headed back to the temple as they wanted to pass the information to their superiors and the duke's men, as this issue clearly affected more than just shrines to the Morri. They were making good time, not really in a rush like they had been on the trip out, and the slavers and brigands enjoying the comfort of their caged wagons. Kaitan Tanrei wanted to talk to her superiors about the information they discovered about this priest, and unfortunately the only priestess who could farspeak had been killed by the attackers when they had first stormed the village. Fanlis suspected the woman had actually been targeted, which raised concerns as well. If bandits somehow had the ability to target farspeakers then they had grown very talented and far more dangerous than ever before.

Asche marched along, thinking over her first battle. It had and hadn't been like anything she ever experienced. That was painfully obvious in many respects, but she had not expected the fear, the focus, the emotions, and the sheer exhaustion that followed, nor the vomiting. Songs and stories always indicated battle was a thing heroes did, that they traveled about and found the fights that needed fighting. But this situation had not been that, not really. The runner had come to them, not the other way around. And honestly, it seemed like heroes got only part of the rewards for exerting all that effort, and facing off against death, so she positively did not want to be a hero. When she had been trapped in Oxlen, she had prayed to the triad and any other divine that would listen and wanted more out of her little life. She had been so tired of being her father's punching toy and had dreaded being a farmer in a town where no one respected him in the slightest. Now she was having trouble coping with all these things her life had not prepared her for because she had gotten her wish.

Truthfully, she was not respected here either as she was so very new, but honestly, joining the Hands had given her a clean slate and she wanted to make the most of that. Based on how she flubbed her mission of opening the gate, she was not doing her best. It grated, the whole notion of not being allowed to rescue a woman in need in the short term, when the long term would take care of it and help more people. Maybe if they had not split up, they could have covered each other's backs and she would not have been chastised. That could be the key to learning from this. She had hared off on her own and could see the problem once it was shoved into her face. Teamwork was key.

Another thing the stories left out was the thrice-bedamned exercise. To get her from being just herself and dealing with a newly transformed body, her platoon decided to really push the training. Asche had to admit the constant grind of exercise was responsible for her greater ease coming to terms with her new body, but it also brought with it a large amount of pain. She could have done with less pain, to tell the truth. She was tired and her muscles ached as a rule. At least she was becoming less terrible with her raven's head sword and other weapons, after the hours of training.

The fact she was now able to actually hit someone, once out of every eight fights, as opposed to never, was a positive development, or at least what she kept telling herself. There were nuances about sword work that kept eluding her. The way the others were able to make the sword dance astounded her, and there she was stuck with basic hack and slash. Thankfully, her knife work was adequate, according to her teachers. Sure, it worked well against the bandit who had not expected her to truly fight back, but there had been better move options she hadn't used, according to Flit, so that meant more training. By the end, she was a sweaty thing, barely able to move.

That was when Elsif showed up from where her platoon had been training with the medium infantry, who focused on pole arms like the halberd and raven's beak rather than axe and hammer. Elsif was a bit of a conundrum. Asche was quite aware she liked Elsif more than casually, at the same time, she was unsure how that would work. Elsif seemed to know what she was doing, but Asche felt awkward being solely the one flirted with rather than the one flirting. To be fair, it was not like she had a great deal of experience, since back in the village he had been one of the many suitors vying for the hand of the only attractive girl in the village, Marwyn, daughter of the village's head man. It had not gone well. And then he discovered his father hoped that a love match would develop between he and Marwyn in order to override the arranged marriage being discussed with an older farmer from another town. How was someone not falling in love with him his fault? Being blamed for losing out on adding to the family's wealth had been yet another beating she was not likely to forget.

Acting fair just never mattered to her father. In fact, any obstacle, any issue, any problem that got in the way of his plans, and her father would punish her. Things had been that way since he had stepped forward at eight and begged his father to stop beating his mother for imagined failures. Asche feared he would go back to that again, however for her own sake, she had to leave Oxlen. Now, she was getting flirted with by a girl who was more attractive than Marwyn, and the only thing that might be a downside in the eyes of the villagers was she was as tall and broad-shouldered as most any male smith. Asche liked that about Elsif, as it made her her.

With a chuckle, Elsif handed over a water skin as she drew closer. "Here, drink."

Asche did so. The stream of water flowed into her mouth with a slight leathery taste to it. It did nothing to detract from how good the cool water tasted. After she swallowed, she sighed. "Thanks."

"No problem. Terris working you hard?"

"Yeah, still getting used to this, and I screwed up and didn't cover Flit like I was supposed to," grumbled Asche, before taking another swig from the water skin.

Elsif nodded. "I guess that's a thing with all you rangers. We mostly train to work as one unit, almost never needing to fight alone. We even train with the medium infantry, so we don't panic when a pole arm comes over our shoulders or head while we're engaged. I guess what you're doing has to run differently, since you don't fight the same. The need to occasionally make a shield wall is what gets drummed into us, so we stick tight to each other."

"How did the war hammer work for you?" Asche asked, remembering Elsif's talk about that before.

She smiled, dimples forming on her cheeks. "Like a dream. The techniques we use are not as nuanced as a sword so it's a lot easier to pick it up and go. Experience enough to teach you when to use the flat and when to use the spike is the hardest bit, honestly, and a lot of that depends on what armor the other person is wearing. The flat for plate and the spike for chain. The shield is big enough that the techniques aren't that complex either, though there are several ways to hold the straps. Mostly the work with the war hammer has been getting used to the weight and working on best ways to swing it, especially when in a shield wall."

"Sounds nice. The raven's head is frustrating me. It seems so straightforward, but the others can make the blade come in at an unexpected angle for a hit or even make the blade change direction mid swing. They want me to mostly think of it as a chopper right now until I can get more familiar with it." Asche sighed in frustration.

Elsif chuckled. "Who knew there were so many subtleties in being a warrior? The songs are all, the brave and stalwart warrior picked up his mighty weapon and strode forth into battle. Nothing about the work it takes to learn how to use the weapon in the first place, or how to work as a team, any of that."

Asche perked up, since her thoughts had been drifting in that direction of late. "Yes. But who the hell wants to hear a ballad about making sure your boots are treated to best keep water out, or about the importance of setting up camp properly?"

"Or how armor chafes, or the fun of making calluses? Or even trying to take your armor off so you can use the privy."

They both laughed. "How are you holding up?" Elsif asked. "Not just the training, but getting found. Becoming the woman you were meant to be is sure to be a shock. Before the dedication, you were having a lot of trouble."

Asche nodded before she looked out into the distance but not really seeing anything. "It has been an…adjustment. Everything feels the same yet so different. Having to learn things anew in some cases has been interesting, and I'm getting ready for another round of moon days, which is a wonderous statement. I'm not freaking out as much as I expected. It's possible that, in helping me forge myself, the Morri did something to make it easier, but I have no idea what it could be. In some ways, it's…like my breathing is now easier, that a tightness I've always known is gone and I can finally breathe free. Truth be told, the training and work keep me from dwelling on it too much, which I am grateful for."

"And then I blunder in and ask all about it. Sorry." Elsif looked slightly abashed.

"No worries. I like that you're concerned about me."

Elsif's cheeks darkened a little and she cut her eyes off to the side. "Well, when I first saw you, you were bravely facing all this confusing stuff and some hostility from the others, despite what the sarnt had said. The fact you weren't running, but facing this despite being afraid, was admirable. While I wondered about the whole lost sister thing, you were just trying to get by and find out what secrets your steel held. That intrigued me."

Asche blushed a touch as well, looking down where she fiddled with the hem of her damp tunic. "And do I still intrigue you?"

With a broad grin, Elsif turned back to face her. "Yes. I want to know more about you, what has helped forge you before your arrival at the temple."

"Just that?" asked Asche, feeling there was something more in Elsif's interest.

Her cheeks darkened again with a blush and she looked away. "Well, there may be a few other things."

Asche grinned and laid a hand on Elsif's strong arm. The feel of it under her palm was enjoyable. "I feel the same."

❖

Nibs was flying around the area where they were encamped, pondering various things. He had said he would help the ravens back at that village connect with the Hands there as well as the shrine. That was all well and good, but he did not want to stay there to teach the others how to talk to humans. So, what was he going to suggest? How could he help them if they couldn't talk to the humans?

This was more serious than he wanted to be, so he flew about, pulling a few acrobatic moves that amused him, but all the while his mind worked over the problem. Maybe when they returned to the temple he could ask the elders of that flock to see if they had any ideas. They had been around the Hands far longer and might have some ideas he could suggest. And if they were lucky, he could find a raven who spoke human who could go to the shrine and teach the others. It was at least something to consider.

He wafted on the breeze and moved into the warm updrafts. Nibs let all these other thoughts go and floated along, trying to glide and drift as long as possible. Flying without effort was a skill that amused him, and when the conditions were right, he could travel a long way indeed without having to flap. When he did that, he loved looking at the landscape, the way the land rolled away from the higher hills and the faint hints of distant mountains. From this vantage point, he could make out thin whisps of smoke rising from the numerous villages and hamlets that filled the area. They looked closer together from up here than they did at ground level.

He was no eagle, who soared at this height or even higher normally, but occasionally coming up here where the air felt thinner was nice. It gave him time to listen to the wind and let his thoughts float about. He could get lost in the movement of his body, how slight changes in his feathers and wing position would alter how he stayed aloft. It was mediative and restful, and after dealing with humans and their ant-like need to keep doing things, Nibs needed the break.

Hanging out with humans all the time took some getting used to. Once they grew older, they basically stopped playing, which was odd. The Hands only "played" at night when any decent raven would find a roost and rest for the next day. Some of their "music" was pretty decent, but when he was trying to sleep? More than anything, he wished he had a small flock with him or even a partner, but that was unlikely in the near future. At least Asche was getting some companionship.

His stomach gave him a reminder he needed to eat. Maybe the cooks had something small he could have. That was at least one benefit of staying with humans, there was little chance of him going hungry or having to take the time to go out looking for food. So, they at least had some use.

❖

Nibs was sitting on the Kaitan's tent, which was as large as the shrine tent, but had less in it. Earlier he had rolled down the steep sides much to his amusement. It was more fun with snow and roofs, as he could easily get his wings under him. But the slope of the tent and the short drop was fine. He was dozing but as the talking continued he began to pay attention. Fanlis was in there with the kaitan and the other leaders of the various platoons. They were arrayed around the kaitan's desk in the center, that Nibs had seen could be extended to hold a map. Fanlis asked, "You still sure about moving slower back to the temple? We have prisoners we have to deliver."

"Yes," Tanrei said. "Going slow lets us get in more training and helps the others get back into full fitness after the winter. It also lets us complete the integration of our new troops. There has always been a change in how the new troops take to the training after their first battle of the season, and we can use this time to our advantage. I have a feeling we're going to need to be fighting fit in short order given the presence of slavers working that closely with bandits and venturing this deep in the duchy. The whole mess sits wrong with me. This is feeling more and more like we discovered a military campaign using unconventional troops than some sort of common banditry. I would rather we be ready than still getting fit when push comes to shove."

"That seems fair."

Tanrei spoke to the others. "How is the training going with each of your platoons?"

Danlies, the sarnt in command of the supply team started off. "The two new girls I got are working nicely. Some of the improvements with chow are because of cooking experience one of them had working in the kitchen at an inn while growing up. The improved food will help morale, not to mention make sure everyone has enough energy to fight. The other is rather good at her work as a chiurgeon. She helped stabilize a few of the wounded villagers who had been fading since the attack. Apparently, she had worked with her village's healer before coming to the shrine. Neither girl is worth much in a fight, but they handle their spears well enough."

"The heavy infantry greens are integrating well. Several of them are still a little shaky on the shield wall, but that does take practice to fully mesh. One of the new girls seems to have some talent for the war hammer, so she bears watching," Sarnt Canli replied. "There has been no one fussing about the marching or the work outside of the usual gripes, so that's good. The more experienced girls took them in hand pretty quick and got them sorted."

Alva, the sarnt in charge of the medium infantry, spoke up. "My new recruits are getting the hang of their weapons pretty well. Still have to run drills against mounted foes, so I guess we can do that on the road so the nobles don't get twitchy."

Fanlis nodded. "That's for the best. Our relationship with this duke is better than the last, but we don't want to remind them we know how to fight against their knights and cavalry."

"The girls assigned to the archery team are seriously green. They had seen bows before but never fired one. I've had to get out some of the really light draw bows for them to train on as they don't have the arm strength for the actual war bows yet. They can at least hit a target consistently, but we need to work on arm strength. If you think we might be heading into a very active season, then they will be one of the weaknesses to our battle plan. I'm doing all I can to train them, but their muscles have to develop and they need to stop catching the string to their forearms. I'm worried it might take more than a season for them to really get it. I understand the Morri judged their steel, but it's taking a lot of work to refine their mix." Serina, the sarnt of the archery platoon, seemed irritated with the admission.

Tanrei sighed. "Well, the division of Hands is up to the Morri and we have what she gave us. We're going to have to make it work somehow, because she has shown consistently that she knows what she is doing. Are they any good at fletching or weapon care?"

"Nope. There really isn't anything they're good at yet, at least not in this job. I'm sure they'll get there, but it may take longer than you'll be pleased with. I know how important we are to the overall battle plan and I'm trying to fix it. I hate being the hole."

"So it goes," the kaitan said philosophically. "Maybe the extra training time will help them especially."

"It can't hurt."

Kaitan Tanrei nodded with a slight. "Hrmmm. Continue the training. Up the intensity a little if you think it's warranted, especially the archers. Danlies, when we get to the shrine have your team restock us immediately with staples. We may have to turn around and head back out soon if what the rangers found is verified. Make sure we have the supplies for heavy combat and plenty of medical wraps and treatments. I'd rather we lug around extra gear that turns out not to be needed, than die for want of it out there. Dismissed."

# CHAPTER ELEVEN

Three days' more travel and the Hands returned to the temple in Turling shortly after the sun rose, having camped out just beyond sight of the city. There was still another company billeted there, but they had more room than when Asche had gone through the Rite of the Lost Sister. It was also quieter, and with fewer people, they were able to expand their training that morning to include horseback riding and how to deal with people on horseback. Tigh and Elles kept trying to talk Asche into jumping onto the back of a horse to be able to stab an attacker, but after watching them do it a few times, she decided to pass. Asche was thankful she did not fall off more than once while learning how to ride, and honestly, that once was enough. The tempo of their drills had increased, and she was exhausted all over again.

After having a good chuckle at Asche's sweaty work, Nibs flew back to the top of the temple where the elders roosted. It was a brief flight, and he came in for a landing in a cleared area. The elders were there, as expected, so was the raven who had worked with him on how to speak human. After greetings were passed, one of the elders asked, "How was your first mission with the Hands?"

Nibs bobbed a little as he thought. The short trip had been rather eventful. "Different. Not as much time to play as they needed. It seemed like humans have forgotten how important that is. And then they did things at night while I slept. Waking up alone after they had gone off was bothersome. They were where I thought they would be, but it was an annoyance."

The elders nodded. "Yes, the Hands act different than other humans. While they tend to follow a schedule when here, when they travel, things change. We think it is because they fight rather than tend fields. Remember, they aren't like us. We fight to drive off, to protect ourselves and our families, however most humans seem to fight for other reasons that are hard to decipher. We know part of that action is to protect their larger flock, but why else seems hard to understand. They are a predator after all."

Nibs considered this in relation to what he had seen. "They fought to drive different humans off of the walls of that village. I guess they were protecting their flock?"

"Likely. The Hands don't get involved in the largest of battles that tear up the land and cover it in blood, offal, and the dead. They tend to fight smaller battles, only occasionally joining with larger armies. Fighting is something inherent to their nature. Do you think you will be able to do this, to stay with your friend?"

Nibs bobbed immediately. "Yes. This is something I can do. My human may be a bit different now, but they still talk to me, play on occasion, and give me food. And there is something else that pulls me, like a scent on the wind. I want to stay with them."

The elders bobbed their heads as one. "Then let us improve your ability to talk with the humans."

A while later, Nibs decided to take a break, taking to the air. After circling the temple a few times, Nibs found an open window at the temple and landed on the windowsill where he could look in. Inside the room were several of the humans he was familiar with: the kaitan, Fanlis, a priestess with a different trim on her robe, and the high priestess of the temple, who had been there when Asche had been transformed. Fanlis spoke, obviously giving a report. "…and the map shows a defended spot near the border with Tarvalis which seems the likely spot for the major camp for these bandits and slavers. There are some indications, based off interrogation, this was an action led by one of the other faiths, based on wording and such. The one slaver who apparently knew all the stuff of value, Scarpe, was one of the few killed when we ambushed them riding into the village. If we want more proof about what is going on, then the proof is going to be found in that spot."

The high priestess nodded, looking at the map open on the table. "I will have to contact the other members of the council and the duke. This may be the start of actions against either the duchy or the kingdom, so he must be informed as well. Regardless, have your company restock in preparation of a heavier fight. Some blessed steel might be in order. Otavari, please go have the farseers pass on this information to the duke and council. Tanrei's company is also going to need a farseer assigned to it, likely permanently." When her aide left the room, the high priestess turned to face the other two. "And how is the lost sister?"

"Uhm…fine," replied Fanlis.

"I see. How did she perform in combat?"

Fanlis looked toward the kaitan for some guidance. The kaitan asked, "Why are you concerned with Asche?"

"You were there during the rite, you heard the same things I did," said the high priestess.

"True, but you are the one those words mean more to, as I have to be focused on the practical. If there is something of concern with one of my troops, I need to know," said Tanrei, her tone irritated.

The high priestess waved that off. "How did she do in combat?"

Fanlis sighed before answering. "Asche did well, except at one point where she failed to protect Flit in combat. She had wandered off and wasn't there to watch Flit's back when one of the brigands came upon her with a spear."

"And what was she doing during this time?" The high priestess leaned closer, intent on the answer.

"She went to the aid of a woman being raped and killed the man."

There was a moment of silence as the high priestess took this in. She nodded. "Good, very good."

The kaitan looked at the high priestess in surprise. "Good? There was nothing good about it. She broke training protocol and didn't protect her teammate. It was not a good thing. Both Flit and her sarnt talked to her about why you don't do that. I don't see what that has to do with anything?"

The high priestess gave the kaitan a look that Nibs could not translate, sort of a shrewd and hopeful look. "What it has to do with is that Asche was more than simply transformed to her true form, her steel was also tested in the forge, like everyone else. The words spoken indicate there is more to Asche than initially thought. Those particular words have often been spoken when a person may likely be chosen by the goddess. Asche may be forged into one of the Morri's Swords, maybe even a Hammer. It all depends, of course, on her experiences and how she reacts to them."

After sharing a look with Fanlis, the kaitan nearly whispered. "Truth?"

With a faint smile, the high priestess nodded. "Indeed. She needs to be watched, trained, and allowed to be forged in the trials being a Hand entails. How she reacts to those and how she grows will indicate if she indeed has the steel to be so forged. It has been a while since we had a Sword, let alone a Hammer of the Morri. Some of us are getting worried about their lack, as the ones we had have died, some in battle, some vanished, some in odd circumstances. Our only remaining Hammer is retired and injured. The few Swords are scattered throughout the Hands. Something is going after the chosen of the Morri, but we do not know why. To that end, we are trying to nurture and cultivate anyone who has those words spoken in their dedication. We must not fail in this."

The kaitan stood tall and bowed to the high priestess, fist on her heart. "As you say, we shall not fail the Morri, High Priestess. We shall be more aware of the forging of young Asche."

The high priestess nodded. "Good. Push, but not too hard. From reports from other kaitans, raising a Sword is more like training a skittish horse than anything else. She must be allowed to grow into herself, and that shall lead her to where she needs to be. And do not neglect Tigh during this, as the words were also spoken of her. There is something she is missing that needs to be found if she is to be chosen."

Nibs flew off at this, not having understood a good bit of what he just heard. There were a lot of sounds he registered as words and even some he knew. However, they had not made as much sense in the context of the sentences. This needed to be discussed with the elders before he did anything else with it. Humans continued their baffling behavior, leaving ravens to make sense of it.

❖

Asche assisted Lynarra with the midday rite, a bit of specific prayers and incense, which served to keep the Morri's blessing on them. Asche liked this aspect of her training, as it helped her feel more grounded and at peace. When she worked with the altar, saying the prayers, and learning the stories, time did not seem to press as hard, nor did her endless questions about herself run rampant. The rite did not take long. The incense smoke was still winding its way into the air, and she was proud to have learned most of the words by heart. The two of them headed toward the refectory once they were finished.

Elsif waved Asche over to the table she was sitting at with a few other heavies. None of the rangers were there. Asche waved back and headed that way. Lynarra split off to go sit with the others from the support platoon. She sat next to Elsif, who asked, "How was training?"

"Rough. I fell off a horse and was thankful when we went back to regular weapon practice. I'm better with the raven's head at least," said Asche as she got her first spoonful of the mutton stew, that day's meal. The broth was rich with vegetables and actual chunks of meat. There was a smell of garlic that hung in the air, which she savored. The small loaf and a soft farm cheese was a good accompaniment with the savory stew.

Elsif chuckled. "We all have to start somewhere. Sarnt Canli keeps showing us different tricks for using our shields in combat that seem useful. I can't quite get them all yet, and I'm not sure what I'm missing. I understand a shield can be both defense and offense, but fighting with it like another weapon is taking some work to get into my head. And I'm still working on doing more than just holding it out there for other people to hit."

Asche scoffed a little. "They have us working on dodging attacks rather than taking hits to better counterattack. Well, they have me doing that more than the others. They're busy throwing rocks at me."

Elsif laughed, as did some of the others at the table, then she shrugged. "Makes sense. Not the rocks, but the dodging. You rangers have lighter armor, so taking a hit means you're more likely to get hurt. If it doesn't land, it can't possibly hurt you. Seems like a sound plan. We have so much gear on that we can't move as nimbly. Are you going to get a shield?"

"Apparently, that depends on the mission. If things are going to be a straight up battle, we might get them and maybe break out some of the extra spears to give us more reach. However, if we have to be extra sneaky, we're likely to go in without armor and only carry daggers. That's what we did last time."

Elsif shuddered at that thought, looking uncomfortable at the notion. "Going into battle without armor...ouch. The emphasis on dodging makes even more sense now."

Asche snorted. "Who knew getting hit in combat was bad?"

"Asked no one ever," retorted Elsif. They both snickered at that.

It was nice to have made a friend in one of the other platoons, as each group seemed to be rather tightknit. She had been feeling a bit left out on the trip back. Some of the others in her platoon were still a bit unhappy with her failure to cover Flit. Things were warming so she had hope. Besides, Asche felt warm inside whenever she was talking with Elsif and she was okay with that development. The feeling was a lot better than the bundle of nerves she had been back in Oxlen, when she tried to connect with a girl. She was honestly interested in where this might lead, because everything felt so much better than earlier attempts at romance.

Flit entered the refectory and looked around quickly. "Ah, there ye are. Come on. We have some new exercises planned for ye. And to give ye hope, tonight we're heading down into Turling to have a few drinks and just relax. It may be the last chance for a while."

## CHAPTER TWELVE

The new exercise was evil. Asche was positive of that. She wasn't sure which terrible excuse for a human being came up with the endurance event, but they were obviously trying to crush the spirits of all involved. It was called, innocently enough, stations, and made plenty of use of the extra space they had, now that they were almost the only Hands in residence awaiting orders. Asche wanted names so she could punish the inventor, that is, when she was able to move again.

Sarnt Terris stood in front of the ranger team to explain the order of the stations, while a cadre of the resident Hand company that saw to the Temple, stood behind. "Idea behind this exercise is to see how far you can push yourself doing variety of random tasks. This simulates chaotic nature of battle where you have to do random string of things to accomplish mission. When things start, you run from here to station one. At station one, you put on armor and are told a report of troop numbers. Then you run to station two, where you move four empty hogshead barrels from one spot to other. After running to station three, you spar for a bit with different weapons each visit, before running to archery range, station four. After hitting mark, you run to stable, where you saddle horse, ride lap around temple, and then remove saddle. Then back to three and four. Once you hit mark that time, you hustle back to station one, where you take armor off after you give report. Once you make it back to start you can fall over, until it's time for you to go again. If you make mistake with report, you will have to run to station two and back to try again. Everyone will do at least three repetitions."

Asche groaned, feeling ghost aches she was positive would be real in the near future. There was no way anyone would be able to get through this mess without straining something. She was also painfully aware she had no option but to do this. She had undergone the dedication of her own free will so had agreed to this. Her gear was in a bag next to her, as they would be carrying it over to the first station. It was everything, her brigandine, coif, helmet, and weapons.

Flit was first off, and she seemed unaffected by this particular exercise. This was clearly not a one-time event. She started at a quick jog rather than a flat out run, like Asche had supposed they would be doing. Neither did Elles when it was her turn, and Tigh, who was actually grinning with anticipation, moved at a faster jog but again not a full sprint. When Terris called her name, she ran over to the first station and started with her greaves and thigh armor, buckling them into place before going with the gambeson, then the brigandine cuirass, followed by her vambrace and rerebraces covering her lower and upper arms. Then she pulled on her armored leather skirt and buckled it into place. As she was armoring up, the sarnt there said, "There are fifteen guardsmen with spears and shields and ten light cavalry coming from the northwest."

Then came the padded coif, chainmail coif, and lastly, she strapped the kettle helmet on. Once she was sure it was all in place, she put on her weapons belt with her sword and dagger, repeating the report a few times. After she was fully prepared, she took off toward the next station.

The added weight slowed her down. In truth, she had only worn her full kit a few times, so it was still new and her fingers stumbled their way through the process. The hogshead barrels were a pain to move, but she was able to shift the four in short order by tipping them onto their sides and rolling them, before standing them upright. Her breath got a lot deeper on her jog to the next spot. This was exhausting. Aware that this skill was important, she repeated the report under her breath as she went.

The spar went okay at the next station. It took a while before she made a clean hit, which allowed her to run to the archery range. Asche knew she was crap at archery, having only done it a handful of times back in her village, and then with little success. Stringing the bow was a bit tricky as she was still getting used to the motion. Amazingly, it only took her four shots to hit in the mark and Asche grinned while she dashed toward the stable. That went quickly and she started the ride, moving the horse at a canter, which was as fast as she could handle and maintain control. Asche was glad of this reprieve as she was able to catch her breath. Soon enough, she was taking the saddle off her horse and then placed it back where it started, under the careful eyes of one of the cadre.

Her breath now in pants, it was harder to keep her focus in the spar. Her mounting exhaustion meant she got hit rather solidly several times before the trainer allowed her to run on. Her earlier luck failed at this point. After twelve arrows, she was finally able to get into the mark, and then only barely. She ran to the first station and repeated the report. Getting the report correct meant she could take off her armor and drop it at her feet before stuffing it back into the bag. The last run was not very fast and after crossing the start point, she staggered a few feet before she collapsed, gasping for air, chest heaving, clothes completely soaked with sweat.

Flit came over and pulled her to her feet. "Ye need to walk some. Ye sit like that after all we did ye'll get a cramp. Not a good idea."

Asche moved a little, over toward a bucket. She grabbed it up and then began chugging water. Flit slowed her down, pulling the bucket away from her mouth. "Slow down. Ye'll get sick if ye keep like that."

Asche could only nod weakly, and after pausing, had more water from a mug Flit handed her. Her heart pounded so hard it felt like her whole body was throbbing from the force of it. As everything began to slow, Flit grinned. "Ye need to work on your bow. Ye need to shoot better."

Asche strained to glower at Flit, but only had the energy for a disbelieving stare. Flit chuckled again and refilled the mug then handed it over. "This is a good exercise. Trains ye in this life rather well. We need to do a lot and do it well. This tests our ability to push through things and remain skilled. Archery is a weakness we need to fix."

"But…not…archers…" stated Asche, between heavy breaths.

"No, it's not the main job, but we do assist them and the others. We need to know everything because we have the hardest job. Takes a while to get fully trained, but we're the best. Ye work hard, ye'll be the best too." Flit patted her on the back gently and Asche swayed unsteadily. "Come on, let's head to the range and work on your archery. We're gonna do this exercise again later. Maybe ye'll do better?"

Asche moaned unhappily, finished her water, and collected her armor. She really did not want to do this, but Flit would not be denied. And she still needed to look after her armor and sword. Thankfully, one of the cadre was looking after the horses so she would not have to head over to the stables to brush down her horse when they were done, or get it fed and watered. Honestly, taking care of her horse would be far preferable to spending time on the range working with a bow she was not good with anyway.

❖

Nibs was flying, doing nothing more than enjoying himself in the air. It was great to take a bit of a break from trying to learn the silly human language. Sure, it was impressive they could say so much with the few sounds they could manage, but it seemed so inefficient. Flying was so much easier and about the only way he could relax in dealing with all of this. Maybe flight was something he wanted to work on.

There was a trick one of the elders showed him that he wanted to practice. It was apparently both fun and good for flying in an area where there were archers. Nibs had thought the whole thing looked cool when he had seen it and wanted to give it a try for that reason. Protection from arrows was just a side benefit. He was already familiar with twisting in flight so he could usually manage to dodge things in the air.

Deciding to start giving it a try, he swooped downward and tucked his wings back against his body. Canceling his lift, Nibs plummeted toward the ground, until he snapped his wings out again, and turned back to a higher altitude. It had been a bit shaky and the move hurt the muscles of his wings, especially when his wings caught air. However, he figured that was because it was a new flight practice. The falling sensation was exciting, and he wanted to see if he could drop farther before he had to open his wings up again.

Over and over, he practiced this particular maneuver, dropping and catching, dropping and catching. One time, just to see if he could, Nibs dropped over twenty feet and caught himself, then did it again immediately, plummeting another twelve feet. That had been a rush, though he had fallen closer to the ground than he had wanted, flying slightly higher than human height. He could see why it might be a good skill in dealing with archers, as arrows were a danger all birds understood, but that wasn't as important as the absolute pleasure of a brief freefall before flying again.

After practicing for nearly an hour, even dropping down above sheep, who did not appreciate his flying prowess, Nibs felt played out. All in all, he was rather relaxed. He had a good muscle ache going on, and a good meal would make everything all right. He found some crickets, which he happily chased and crunched down. Somewhat begrudgingly, as he was enjoying his meal, he returned to the temple. The human lessons were annoying, but he understood the need. Humans were focused on all the wrong things in life, and it was plain odd. Maybe Nibs could help Asche learn that play and enjoying life were far better than fighting and working all the time. Despite it annoying him, that was the focus of the Hands, and if he wanted to help Asche then he would have to be able to better communicate with humans. Maybe when he could do so he could make it clear that humans really needed to sort out their priorities. Better birds than he had tried, but maybe the right human who would listen would be found.

❖

Asche had run stations two more times, with extra sparring and archery between runs to improve her technique and help her to go through the course faster. On the last run, her heart had beat so hard and air had been so hard to come by, that she had vomited before being able to shoot the second time. The sarnt at the range had tossed a bucket of water on her to clean her up before making her finish the course. Flit and Elsif were currently helping to hold her up as they walked around the open courtyard slowly, to keep her muscles from cramping up.

Flit smiled. "You're doing good, Asche. 'Tis a very difficult course and takes a while to build the stamina to run it well. For your first time, 'tis just fine."

Elsif nodded, as the heavies had been going through the same exercise, though without the archery. They had added climbing over a wall in full armor, to make it fair to everyone. "Oh yeah, just making it through this has to be worth something. Sarnt Canli mentioned in combat a lot of things can happen and needing to change gears and do such different tasks in short order is normal."

"That's normal?" gasped out Asche, gawking at her then over at Flit, practically begging her to counter that. This was not a normal she wanted to live.

"To be fair," said Flit, "'tis not normal for most people, even in combat. Most fights are pretty straightforward, with the other units. Because we also help with disasters and such, it is normal for Hands."

"I'm not sure that's better," Asche mumbled, but the other two were close enough to overhear.

Elsif snorted. "It is what it is. We're Hands now and this is our new normal."

"Ye need to remember, Asche, the Hands are not like a militia, army, or other mercenary company. Our task is to do what the Morri asks of us, and she is a protector, a crafter, a smith. We help everyone, such as assistance after a bad storm, extra hands with harvesting, help with bandit hunting, help with keeping peace. We act for the betterment of all, not just the nobles. The duke likes us, as we are more good than bad for his people. Other rulers think the same way, for the most part." Flit handed over a mug of water and helped Asche have some before continuing. "Militias or mercenary companies only fight or intimidate. They are rarely doing any of it for the people but for coin or for power. And from what I've seen, they don't train like we do. Honestly, even the nobles don't train like we do. The Morri was abundantly clear that we must train and train hard, because that is how you shape and temper your steel. That is how we forge ourselves."

"Forge ourselves…" There was something about that phrase in Asche's mind, something niggling in the back of her head. Learning all these disparate skills, the Rite of the Lost Sister…this was all about forging herself into something true. There had been dreams and yearning looks, going back years, and Asche was sure some of her beatings had solely been about making her into a man. Her father had certainly harped on the topic often enough. Though, given the state of things, it clearly had not worked. Before being told of the rite and what it could do, she had been resigned to those imaginings being nothing more than dreams that would never take form. The Morri had made her dream a reality. Maybe she should work harder as repayment, not that the Morri asked that of her.

Nibs found her later as she and the other rangers were sitting around having a light supper and came to rest near her feet. Asche smiled and tossed a chunk of stew meat his way, wanting to keep him from taking too much of her food. Nibs ate the chunk of beef coated in sauce, then gave a weak awk, saying, "Tired."

"You're tired or I look tired?" asked Asche, not quite following exactly, given her overall exhaustion.

Nibs cocked his head as he pondered. He hopped a little bit closer, scrutinizing Asche closely, turning his head this way and that, before bobbing slowly and pronouncing, "Both."

Asche snorted. In all honesty, he wasn't wrong. She was already looking forward to sleeping that night. "Fair enough. Working hard learning human?"

"Yes, and play. Play fun and helps."

"Play helps?" Asche thought about what Nibs had just said. She never heard that sentiment before, certainly not from her father or Father Tombol.

"Play, yes. Makes you all…Ahhhhhhhhhh…" Asche goggled a bit when Nibs made the exact sound the innkeeper's wife made when finally getting off her feet after finishing the baking around midday. Mistress Gaytha made that exact noise several times before, especially in the summer months after baking for the whole village, dropping into a chair at the big table outside holding the cooling loaves and nursing a small beer. It conveyed relaxation so very clearly, Asche could only nod in understanding.

Nibs cocked his head to the other side, saying, "Me smart bird."

"Yes, yes you are," said Asche, still trying to wrap her head around the fact that Nibs was able to make that exact sound from overhearing it a few times. "And yes, we do things to relax. Maybe not play like you do, but we do relax as we can."

Asche was surprised as a yawn stretched her mouth really wide, making the corners of her mouth tight and her jaws ache with the effort. She felt her cheeks warm after she had finished. Nibs yawned as well, opening his beak wide and turning his head back and forth, overexaggerating her own movements. He closed his beak and began to laugh, or at least what sounded like laughing to Asche. Was he mocking her? "Hey!"

Nibs cackled even more and flew up out of reach and repeated the whole thing, drawing the attention from the other rangers. Asche huffed, "Good night, Nibs. I'm heading outside."

She stomped off to the sound of the raven's laughter infectiously spreading to the other Hands.

❖

The rest of her platoon along with a few members of the heavies and support platoons gathered Asche up and headed out of the temple grounds and into Turling proper. Asche was exhausted and had no interest in doing anything right now except trying to catch up on the rest her whole body craved. She looked over at Flit. "Where are we going?"

"There's a tavern here in town run by a former Hand. It's called the Broken Barrel, as she actually broke one over the head of a bandit ten years ago. That fight was when she lost her right hand. Because of her injury she had to leave the Hands, so the temple helped her get set up with the tavern."

"She lost her hand?" gaped Asche. That kind of injury had never occurred to her.

"Yes, I mean, we are a combat-oriented group when all is said and done. It shouldn't come as a surprise that sometimes people die or get really badly injured. That's just the way things are." Flit shrugged. "I mean, I do believe I got hurt last battle, as did you."

"Yes, but losing her hand?"

Flit nodded and chuckled a little. "Yes, her company t'was holding a village against a group of brigands being led by a former knight, who had done something bad and got stripped of his title and lands. This was his form of revenge. They fought, and her company won, but t'was close. There were a lot of deaths after that battle. Thankfully, Sasha only lost her hand to a sword strike. The kaitan of their company got the knight in the end, but it was a hell of a fight."

Asche was quiet as that moved through her thoughts. She knew it was possible to get seriously hurt or to die, but this took that realization to a new level. Losing a limb, or hand, or foot, or something had not registered as a possibility. Now it was about all she could think of.

Flit jostled her. "Do not dwell on that, Asche. We're planning to relax and have fun, like Nibs was saying."

"You're agreeing with him?"

"Sure! There's nothing wrong with having fun," Flit replied. "We don't get a lot of it in the field. The music and storytelling around the fire is nice but not the same. We can't just loose ourselves to enjoyment. So, when we're in town we like to go relax. Come on."

Asche allowed Flit to drag her forward to join with the others. Evidently, she was not going to have the early night her body was craving. Tigh laughed. "Come on, Asche. You've been working hard for months. Tonight, we're going to drink, listen to some music we don't have to play, and have food they can't make in field kitchens. You've earned this."

Unsure if that was true, Asche kept pace and thought about the fact she had actually been working for months. Spring had passed by now and they were moving toward early summer. At this point, she had gone through several moon days, and her body felt more like her body than at any other point in her life. That realization was surprising. It really did feel like her life had just begun.

They made it down into town and were coming up to a building with a sign hanging in front that was an actual barrel nearly broken in two. That seemed a simple enough sign to her. Music could be heard coming out of it as well as singing, only some of which was completely off-key. Inside, the tavern was a large open room filled with people sitting at narrow tables with equally narrow benches, drinking and singing along with the troupe of musicians on a little stage up at the front. Right now, they were performing the "Ballad of the Wungadore," with the audience joining in on the chorus about how the Wungadore had killed a hundred men, or more.

One of the waitresses spotted them and led the group to an empty table closer to the door than the stage and headed off. Elles and one of the others from the supply platoon gathered the orders and headed off to the counter on one side of the room, dominated by several tun casks mounted on racks, several having marks from different brew houses. In a short while, they both returned with one of the waitresses carrying a short mountain of mugs in her hands, bracketed by Elles and the other woman. Mugs were passed quickly and a quick toast was made to the house to thank them.

This tavern felt so different from the one in Oxlen, and not just because it was twice the size, though that did not hurt. The atmosphere was far more lighthearted and everyone was having a good time. Back in Oxlen, there was little music, usually performed by some traveling minstrel or one of the locals who had an instrument and the skill to play it well. The food was usually hunter's stew, a perpetual pot of food that was constantly on the fire and fed different season's foods, changing flavors over time. Here that was not the case. The waitress brought over several chickens that had been turned over a spit, clearly basted with butter and herbs. When Asche had a bite, the meat was flavorful and the skin crisp. There were loaves of black bread, which she was familiar with, served with an herbed butter, slices of some aged cheddar, and thin slices of ham. This was better than what the refectory usually put out.

Flit looked over at her enjoying the food and the excellent rich amber lager. "Still complaining about coming out?"

After licking the savory grease off her fingers from the chicken leg she had happily devoured, Asche replied, "No. This is excellent."

Tigh chuckled. "This is what we did while you were passed out during your initial training, enjoyed the Barrel's excellent food. We've all been there, nearly broken by the exhaustion, but tonight, this is more your welcome to the Hands."

At that, the group toasted Asche and the two new support women, raising their mugs, then tapping them on the table before quaffing them. Asche and the others followed suit. The young woman who was one of the new cooks seemed to be inspecting the food, as if she was trying to find a way to make this in the field. She was teased good-naturedly over that as the lengthy cooking process would be unlikely to happen any time they were out there.

The food was finished, and the group was rather pleased by the meal. They had gotten a second round of the amber beer as well as an apple, walnut, and cheddar tart they shared. After a quick toast to the house, again with the tap to the table with the mugs, the conversation started up again. Elles looked over at Asche. "You did good out there. I think all of us had that conversation at one point or another in our first six months."

Tigh snorted. "I never had it."

"Yeah, but you're a sword chaser and too good for the likes of us," retorted Elles.

"I'm just trying to live up to my steel," said Tigh, with her hands partially raised.

Flit and Elles snickered and Asche was at a loss. Sword chaser? What exactly did that mean? Elles continued. "You're blooded and you've screwed up. That makes you one of us, Asche. Welcome to the rangers!"

The other two also voiced their approval and a loud toast was made to her. At the same time the support team was making the same toast to their new members. Shortly, a woman missing a hand came over, dressed in familiar black and silver, followed by a waitress with a bottle and some small shiny pewter glasses on a tray. The woman grinned. "I heard that there are three new Hands here tonight who've been to the fight. As a gift, I give to ye a bottle of the water of life."

Flit and Elles grinned, and Tigh beamed at her. "Thank you for this generous gift, Sasha. Please, share a toast with us?"

Glasses were poured and the liquid looked a pale gold. Asche took her glass and gave a sniff, having never tried the drink, which was something only the elders of Oxlen ever had. The smell was spicy, warm, rich, and heavy with alcohol. It was far stronger than she ever smelled when hard cider was being made. Sasha raised her glass and said, "To the Hands!"

"The Hands!" said the rest of them. They tapped the table with their glasses and slammed them back. Asche and the two others slammed the drinks back as well. Asche gasped as the drink burned its way down her throat, making her eyes water slightly.

Flit patted her back. "Good, right?"

Her breath was ragged, as she wheezed out, "Wha?"

Sasha laughed, especially as one of the new support women had a similar reaction. "Tha first taste is aways a doozy. Enjoy."

Sasha left and drinking resumed. Another small glass of the water of life was downed and then the bottle capped. Elles looked around the room and grinned, then got up from the table and ran off. Asche followed her action with her eyes, looking over at Tigh. "Where's she going?"

Tigh looked about and then shook her head. "One of the locals Elles is sweet on just came in. We won't see her for the rest of the night." Tigh smirked at something happening behind Asche. There was a tap at her shoulder.

She turned to see a young man behind her, looking nervous. She raised an eyebrow questioningly, at a loss as to what this person could want. As he smiled at her, in what must surely be a flattering manner, what he must be about registered to Asche. Something must have shown on her face as he suddenly looked less sure about what he had been ready to say. Asche rushed her words in an attempt to shut this down. "Uhm…thank you, but no thank you. I'm here with friends."

Flit and Tigh snickered as the young man shuffled back to his friends, who were laughing and calling out to him. Asche focused on her beer, her cheeks hot, and not just from embarrassment. Part of her was flattered, but most of her remembered all the infighting back in Oxlen, when many of the young lads had been vying for the interest of the "attractive" girl their age. Being beaten for his failure had left a bitter taste in her and to see something that so closely reminded her of that experience made her uncomfortable.

Flit looked concerned. "Ye alright?"

"Bad memories."

Flit nodded. "I follow. Have another bolt of the water of life. That will settle ye."

Asche nodded, then poured a little into her glass before tossing it down quickly. She shuddered from the sensation of the drink, gasping a little at the burn. Part of her snickered. At least that was one concern out of the way. She was unlikely to be interested in men, because she knew too much about them, especially ones like her suitor. She had been too familiar with that type. After chasing that down with her beer, her head swam a little and she blinked slowly, as things were slightly out of focus. She had never had more than a singular mug of beer before and so all of this, even with the food, was making her woozy. She looked over at Flit and Tigh. "I…I think I've had enough fun."

Flit nodded. "Ye look it. Let's get ye abed."

The two of them left the tavern to start the walk back up to the temple, leaving the loud music and singing behind them. The cooler night air helped clear her head, but she was still on the dizzy side.

## CHAPTER THIRTEEN

The heat from the forge was impressive. The all-permeating heat was intense even from where Asche stood by a doorway. The bellows kept a steady pace, though Asche could not make out who or what was working them. The heat flared and subsided, along with the dull red glow, in time with the bellows. The sound of hammer on steel rang clear as Asche moved deeper into the space. The Morri had her back to Asche as the goddess was bent over a piece of steel she was working. Asche just watched, examining the forge, as there had been no time for that on her first visit to really take in the details.

The space was vast and the forge the central focus. The walls were of some sort of wood Asche had never seen before, looking dark with many tight age rings visible. By the forge, in protected spaces were mounds of a dull black layered rock. It reminded her of coal, but not quite. Likely it was coke, something the smith back in Oxlen complained about not having. There were lots of tools on display in racks made in the same kind of wood as the walls.

There was a rack that held different types and sizes of hammers. It even looked like there were a few sledgehammers with heads growing larger. There were also several types of tongs, swages, fullers, punches, chisels, drifts, bits of different size, and other customized tools she had no experience with and certainly no idea what they were called. Compared to her blacksmith back home, what she was seeing here was tidy and in order. Every tool that might be needed while working was set up in such a way as to be easy to retrieve.

The Morri moved in sure steady strokes, the hammer ringing out almost like a heartbeat. The dark-colored kerchief she wore over her hair seemed to have silver strands woven in it. Her muscular back rippled with her actions. The black leather ties for her apron were a contrast for the sweat-darkened shirt she wore. Her braies were tucked into her burn-scarred boots. The sound of hammer on steel stopped and the billet was thrust into a different section of the coals before she turned around to face Asche. The Morri cocked an eyebrow at Asche as she stood there nervously fidgeting under the gaze of the goddess. The Morri then smiled brightly. "So you're here again? Want to work on forging yourself, eh?"

Asche nodded, unsure how to respond. Talking to a goddess was not something she had been taught how to do.

"You know, not everyone comes back to the forge after the first time."

"Really?"

The Morri nodded, a grim twist to her mouth. "Yes. Most people find it easier to just go along with things as they are. It's easier to just take the judgment from some authority rather than work hard in order to become something more. Few people want the extra work to forge themselves anew. Sadly, most people are content with being just the one thing they think they are. To be fair, it isn't entirely wrong being that way, because continuing to forge yourself, to take the time to do the work to become better, to use the lessons life presents you to grow is not something everyone wants to do. It is hard work, perfecting your steel, making sure what imperfections exist are worked out. It is the work of a lifetime, to strive to become the best your steel can be with the changes you face. That you want to do so, to become your best, speaks highly of you."

Asche blushed. "Ah…well…it feels right to do so. I figured, after all you have done for me, I owed it to you."

"I did nothing special, merely helped your body find its way back to your soul. Helping the lost is the right thing to do. Besides, doing so improved your steel, as you became more true." The Morri took out the billet she had been working on, inspected it, and put it off to the side to rest. She grabbed a different one from a stand nearby and placed it into the coals to heat.

"Thank you?" It felt weak to say so little, but she at least owed that.

The Morri chuckled as she pulled the billet from the coals and looked it over, checking how it was heating. She turned it over and shoved it back in. The bellows heated the coke more. "This is part of your steel. Just need to heat it up some more before we work on it. You are made of good steel, Asche, and the limits on what can be done with that are rare. You can be forged into a tool, a shield, a sword, or even a hammer. A tool is not good for conflict, but extremely useful for the specific tasks for which it was made. Swords and shields are good for battle, as one excels at attacking while the other is good at protecting. A hammer can be many things depending on the design. It can be a tool used to forge steel, to build, to tear things down, or it can be a weapon with enough heft to do damage or deflect attacks. Properly made hammers can do many things. These are things to consider when working with your steel."

Asche looked over to the billet in the forge, its color growing from a light straw color and darkening as it heated. "Is there a lot of difference in the forging between them?"

"Hammers take a bit more work to shape and temper. The steel is usually thicker for the head and to get the temper of the hammer correct it has to be heated just so. However, a properly made hammer is more valuable than most swords or shields, because of all it can do. But swords and shields are the things most sought after, the gleam of the edge or the solidity of the wall. And making tools is the basic job of most smiths, a never-ending task at a forge, making nails, shaping shoes for horses, and the like. All these things have value and all these things can be achieved with your steel, because you are willing to do the work. Your heart can lead the way on this." The Morri pulled out the billet which was glowing an orangish red and hefted her hammer. She took a few hits on the steel, flakes coming off the billet with each hit, before she looked back up at Asche. "Shall we?"

Asche picked up a hammer and joined in.

❖

Waking up slowly, blinking at the light, head pounding even more as she flinched from the brightness, Asche muttered something rude under her breath. Flit chuckled. "Come on, lass. Time to get up and stretch. It'll help clear your head."

Asche tried to sit up and groaned as her muscles protested vehemently. Her hangover added to the muscle aches to make for a wonderful feeling. After a second try at sitting up, Flit reached down a hand to help. Once she was upright, Flit handed over the slightly steaming mug she had been carrying. "Drink up, lass. 'Tis willow bark tea. That should help with your aches. If it's still bad after stretching and more water, then the chiurgeon probably has a liniment that'll help ye."

Deep draughts of the tea warmed her, and the slightly bitter taste was masked by a bit of honey stirred in. Asche lowered the mug and sighed. "Is it always this bad?"

"Your hangover or your muscles? No. With your muscles 'tis because you're new to the exercise. By next season it'll be tough but not like this. Well…maybe the first of the season'll get ye like that." Flit beamed at her. "Ye have that to look forward to. Up we go." Flit reached down and got hold of Asche.

She groaned deeply as she lumbered to her feet. She did not want to do this again, but that was the order of the day. She quickly downed the rest of the tea and followed Flit out of the barracks and into the morning sun. The day hadn't warmed up yet, but it was far more comfortable in the sunlight than in the shade. Other members of the Hands were there, mostly new people, but there was a good portion of their company present for the morning exercise.

Sarnt Canli led the group through stretching, working the muscles in a way to help work out the kinks caused by yesterday's station exercise. Asche groaned as the muscles at first resisted the gentle movements and then began to slowly release. The stretches moved from the head to the feet, step by step, building on each other to get the kinks worked out. Asche was not sweating by the end but had to admit that she was a good bit warmer and felt better. Then there were some of the regular exercises the company did daily, but in moderation.

Terris got the members of the ranger platoon together after breakfast. "We have orders now. Kaitan and high priestess heard back from duke last night. We are tasked with finding and stopping these bandits from any more raids on villages and enslaving others. Based on map, we plan to rendezvous with another company to ensure we have plenty of people to take their stronghold. Duke Barvith does not want slave market in his territory. Today, we have no training. Get gear checked and prepped as well as rest. We move out tomorrow on horseback to make better time. Questions?"

Asche certainly had none and neither did anyone else, figuring details would come out as they proceeded with their mission. Once dismissed, Asche went and made sure her gear was clean and in order. All of her weapons were sharp and had a very light coat of oil to protect them. Her armor was also in excellent shape, especially since the sweat smell had faded over the evening, as it sat on the armor rack. Given the slight muskiness to the gambesons of the people who had served longer, she was positive it would get there soon enough. Once she packed her things, she was as ready as she could be.

She looked at her gear at the foot of her bed and stared at it, realizing she had no idea what to do at this point. Sure, she had been given free time, but honestly, it had been months since she had no draws on her time. Training had been rather intense at the beginning with the Hands and last night's drinking was not something she wanted to repeat. Sure, the use of counter beers was a time-honored tradition to help with the hangover, but that was not a habit she wanted. Maybe she should check to see if Elsif was busy, because it would be nice to just hang out with her. Something was growing between them, and she was interested in seeing where it could go.

As she started to walk from her bed, she heard Tigh call out, "Anyone have something to fix my boots?"

Asche did have such things, so she grabbed the kit she had taken when she ran from Oxlen and went over to Tigh. "What do you need?"

She held up one boot. "It looks like the back of my boot is coming open."

Asche took the boot and looked at the issue. It seemed one section of the seam had broken stitches. That was fixable easily enough. Using tweezers, she pulled out the stitching in that area and got a leather needle threaded with some sinew her father preferred for this sort of work. As she was pushing the needle through the leather, Tigh said, "That's a better fix than I was expecting. Where'd you learn how to do this?"

"My da is a shoemaker by trade, but mostly does cobbling. I learned how to cobble by repairing kids' shoes and doing some basic cordwaining, making new shoes a few times. I can make most basic shoes if I had to, but I can easily repair most anything." Asche stitched the section closed.

Once she finished, she handed the boots over. "Getting a new pair would be best, but those should hold you the rest of the season."

Tigh took the boot, inspected it, and put it on, moving her foot about. "Thank you, Asche. That really helps. It just opened up and I didn't think they would have enough time to fix this. Clearly, I was wrong."

Asche chuckled. "It wasn't that bad. Let me know if there are any more issues. I can easily get the supplies to make more repairs."

Tigh clapped her on the arm as Asche headed off. She returned her kit to her backpack and left their area. She wandered through the barracks until she got to where the heavies slept and there was Elsif, getting the last of her gear together. Asche smiled. "Finished yet?"

"Nearly. We got some new things for this. Our chain was replaced with blessed steel and the rings are fused somehow. Also, our shields were replaced with blessed steel, so they're lighter and stronger. What did you need? Want to spend our free time together?" Elsif asked this with a smile.

There was a slight warming of Asche's cheeks, but at least she did not look away. "Yes."

"Then let's go have some fun."

They headed out of the barracks and walked to the refectory. Elsif sweet-talked one of the village women that worked there out of a loaf of dark bread, a quarter wheel of cheese, a seasoned and spiced salami, some pickles, and a small skin of beer. Asche was sure it would make a decent lunch for both of them. As they walked out of the temple grounds and down into the town below, Nibs flew up and croaked out hello.

Asche smiled at him. "How is training going?"

Nibs made a groaning sound Asche was sure she had heard before, then grumbled, "Humans speak funny."

Asch turned to him, an eyebrow raised. "We speak funny?"

Nibs nodded and then cocked his head. "Ravens are sad you speak so poorly, with so few sounds."

Asche started to reply and then stopped, unsure what to say. Elsif burst out laughing. Asche glared at her before rolling her eyes. She looked at Nibs. "Thank you for your concern. We do all right with the sounds we make."

Nibs's skeptical look made Elsif guffaw. Townsfolk looked over at them, bemused at the sight of a woman arguing with a bird.

Before anyone could make any more comments, Elsif said, "Can you lead us to the creek? I figure we can hang out there and be away from the life of the Hands and out of the town."

Nibs cocked his head far over to one side and Elsif sighed. "Will some cheese work? We also have salami if you really need more."

He bobbed a few times in apparent agreement and took off. They followed behind, making sure to keep him in sight. Asche smiled at Elsif. "Thank you for distracting him. He's not as funny as he thinks he is."

"What do you mean? Nibs is hysterical. I think you just don't get his jokes."

Asche responded with a heavy sigh, wondering why she was still looking forward to lunch with Elsif. They cleared the town gates and following the route Nibs was flying. They turned off the road and moved along a much narrower trail. Walking through the trees, they tracked him, keeping their ears open for the sound of the water.

Nibs led them to a small copse of trees between fields with a clearing filled with snapdragons, sweet peas, and a few daisies dotted here and there with splashes of color; the rest of the floor of the copse was all clover. The water babbled in the creek and small rocks created tiny falls and rills. Elsif sighed happily and lay back on the clover, putting the basket to the side. She looked over to where Nibs was situated on one of the branches. "Thank you for finding a perfect spot."

Asche sat nearby back resting against a moss-covered rock. Nibs jumped from the branch he had been perched on and landed on Elsif's stomach. "Cheese."

"Can't you wait a bit?" grumbled Elsif.

Nibs bounced on her stomach and repeated, "Cheese!"

"Alright! Sheesh!" Elsif sat up, dislodging Nibs, who gave an indignant awk as he hopped closer to the stream. She tipped the basket the food was stuffed into and tore a hunk of cheese out. She held it up to show Nibs and then tossed it to the side. "Here you go. Thanks for finding this place."

Nibs took the cheese and launched into the air and headed in the direction of the temple.

Asche watched him fly off before looking over at Elsif, who watched her with eyes shining. The intensity of the gaze made her feel awkward and Asche looked back after Nibs, who was already out of sight. As she begged her warm cheeks to cool, she looked about the clearing and spotted the basket. "Uhm…so…luncheon?"

"Is that what you're actually hungry for?" asked Elsif, her voice husky. "We're here in this nice clearing, no others around us. Alone together for the first time."

Asche turned, surprised at the directness in that tone of voice, and Elsif was gazing at her with hooded eyes and a slight smile across her lips, promising mischief and pleasure. It was an attractive look and Asche's words dried up in her mouth. Elsif patted the ground next to her. "Come, sit with me."

Asche took a few tentative steps forward then sat next to Elsif on the clover, unsure why her heart was racing as if she were exercising. Feeling a touch emboldened, Asche laid her hand across Elsif's and curled her fingers between hers. Elsif beamed at this, then looked up and into Asche's eyes. "So you are interested."

"Well, yes, I am." Asche smiled at her, pushing some hair behind one ear. "But I wasn't ready to do something more than be interested before, since I was still getting used to this new me. It's been getting easier with the training and stuff. Like…I've moved into a new place and was getting used to the changes. That took a bit, but now I might be up for something more than simply talking."

"Well, a day off in the warm spring sun will certainly be lovely for that." Elsif smiled at Asche.

Asche nodded. Not wanting to be completely passive in this, she was the one who leaned over to press her lips against Elsif's. The kiss was brief and she started to pull back when she felt a hand run through her hair, pulling her tighter. Lips parted, tongues tentatively touching, Asche wanting to ensure the other was there in agreement before fully committing to the passion igniting inside.

Before running off with the Hands, before all of this, Asche had kissed a few girls and was not at a complete loss as to how this went. Things felt a little different now, softer, less firmness to her lips, but on the whole, kissing was kissing. She was perfectly content with what was occurring and wanted more. Tingles rolled up her neck and down her spine. She shivered in pleasure.

Elsif lowered herself slowly to the ground, pulling Asche with her. As they kissed, Elsif carded her fingers through Asche's hair, which had grown longer since she had changed. They were there for a while, and Asche was perfectly distracted with kisses and soft touches. She basked in the warm feeling growing in her, her body growing more sensitive with the touches. Emboldened, she moved one hand up and cupped one of Elsif's breasts. The nipple was firm under her palm. Elsif moaned softly, and as Asche squeezed slightly, both their stomachs growled, demanding fewer kisses and more lunch. They broke apart laughing, Asche far more at ease and comfortable with Elsif than she had been before.

They shared another chaste kiss and a promise-filled grin before they broke into their meal. There would be plenty of time to return to what they had been doing.

## CHAPTER FOURTEEN

The horses were saddled and wagons loaded, ready to go. After helping load one of the wagons, Asche had been called to the temple by Fanlis. When she got inside, there was the high priestess, Fanlis, and Lynarra, the supply person with the same task of helping with the travel altar, already waiting for her. Asche had been assisting Fanlis and Lynarra with setting up and taking down the altar for travel and learning the basic rites for the Morri, so she could pitch in at need. In addition, she had been present when special prayers had been offered to the Morri before battle. Who the Morri was and what she stood for was becoming clearer for her through the study. She was okay with that, as it made the dreams of visiting the forge easier to handle.

The high priestess stood behind their travel altar, Fanlis in front, with Lynarra and Asche flanking. A priestess was assisting, swinging an incense censer about, covering the wooden altar in bluish fragrant smoke. The high priestess raised her hands and intoned, "Blessed Morri, please set your touch upon this altar so as it travels forth it is safe under your care. Place your blessing on Fanlis, keeper of the altar, and her assistants, Lynarra and Asche. May their connection to you deepen and grow under your watchful eye. Help their steel as it is shaped, keeping it true and strong. Bless the company this altar guides, to strike true and work out the imperfections it finds. Let this altar be the forge of their creation."

Fanlis bowed her head, hands held wide, facing the travel altar. "Holy Morri, I take up this altar, this forge, so that my company and I can hear your voice, follow your guidance, and to ever forge ourselves anew. Help us to protect the weak, to give strength to those whose own has failed, to forge bonds between others and ourselves, to serve as your Hands in the wider world. I take up this altar and shall protect it until we can return it home to you."

Asche and Lynarra moved forward and took the two ends of the anvil-shaped altar, hefting it. This was Asche's first time involved in such a rite and she was very surprised how this clearly wooden anvil seemed to weigh almost as much as an actual one. They took tiny, shuffling steps as they stepped back from the temple's altar and set it within its travel box. Before the lid was placed on it, the high priestess handed over a small forge hammer and dagger to Fanlis, who bowed to the altar after they were in her hands. She stood back up and handed them backward, with Asche getting the hammer and Lynarra taking the dagger. They placed these in the box, to either side of the wooden anvil. The priestess swung her censer and covered everything in aromatic incense-laden smoke. Once the priestess stepped back, Asche and Lynarra placed the lid on it, connecting it to the box with simple latches.

Fanlis bowed to the high priestess. "Thank you for the renewed blessings upon our altar, Holy One. This mission is likely to be tough, as going after bandits and slavers is never pretty. To have any blessings of the Morri upon us will be most welcome."

The high priestess nodded in acceptance and smiled softly. "Thankfully, we have a farspeaker willing to travel with you. Sister Tanriel has decided to undertake this journey with you. This will allow you to contact us so we can track your progress and help coordinate with Kaitan Ginvert and her company who shall be traveling with Duke Barvith's representative. I wish you much luck on your mission, Fanlis. May the Morri guide your Hands."

The three of them bowed and replied, "Thank you, Holy One."

The box with the altar was not nearly as heavy as it had been when they had picked up the wooden anvil from the altar and it surprised Asche. Lynarra noticed her reaction and chuckled softly. "Yeah, it's real. Once the lid's on, the weight drops. I don't know if the box is magical or what, but it is interesting."

Fanlis chuckled, as she walked behind them, continuing her job of overseeing the altar. "No, that's not quite it. In the box, the altar weighs what it weighs, a simple chunk of carved wood. When it's out and in use, the weight of the Morri's gaze is upon it, and it becomes connected to her forge. That is what makes the difference."

"Really?" Asche turned her head to look at Fanlis as they moved toward the wagon.

"The touch or even the presence of any of the divines is something you can feel, even more so if you learn to become sensitive to it. It is like a weight, a pressure, or the air is thicker. High priestesses often feel the presence differently, as do many senior priests or priestess. Altars can take on weight or survive fires or other things wooden objects shouldn't be able to do. The touch of their power gets expressed in many different ways and the different divines each have their own expressions. One of the interesting features of our blessed steel is that it has to be blessed weekly or it will lose what makes it special. But, yeah, all the travel altars I've seen have been like this."

Asche rolled her shoulders. "It felt like we were lifting an actual anvil, not a wooden one."

"Yeah, that threw me as well when I first started helping with the altar years ago. In a way, the wood anvil becomes a conduit for the Morri's forge and anvil. Prayers and rites done in front of a blessed altar have more impact than otherwise. And in a pinch a regular anvil or a regular forge can work as an altar, if the blessed one has been captured and destroyed."

Asche shifted her hands on the box, setting her grip better. "So, if we're in a village with a smith and need to do a blessing or ritual and the altar is back in camp, we can just use their forge?"

"Yes. The Morri is the goddess of the forge before anything else. Women, children, crafting, and warriors were all added later as her faith spread to more people. There is something connecting those, but what I'm not exactly sure and I never asked a high priestess." Fanlis led them to the wagon where the altar was stored during travel. "It just is. Besides, who really knows the ways of the divine?"

They slid the box into place, secured it, and shut the gate. "Are the hammer and dagger normally part of the altar?" Asche asked.

"Not normally. The hammer's imagery is clear and the dagger relates to her work with us as warriors. It's sort of an extra level of blessing when going into a potentially tricky conflict."

"I guess the high priestess hopes we'll get some mystical support or something."

"That's likely. Anything dealing with bandits and slavers working together and what's more, those comments implying they're targeting the Hands and priestesses of the Morri are worrisome. Get to your horses. We're leaving soon."

Lynarra quickly headed off to the wagon she traveled in. Asche headed over to her horse being held by Flit, as they were currently arranged by platoon. The kaitan walked up in front of the formation to where her horse was, and Canli, the senior sarnt called out, "Hands, attention."

Asche straightened at attention, like she had been taught. Kaitan Tanrei looked over the assembled troops and smiled faintly before giving a slight nod. "This is likely going to be a tough mission. The target is nebulous, being the roots of the bandits and slavers, but we can track them down. Remember they are actively looking to bring us low. They have declared themselves our enemy. We are the Hands of the Morri; we are the ones who take her strength out from the temples and into the wider community. We will strive to free any they have captured and made slaves. We will make them pay for attacking this duchy and the Morri."

The senior sarnt yelled out, "Mount up."

The mass of troops put feet in stirrups and mounted their horses. The first elements headed out, the ones with the most experience in doing their job on horseback. Then the rest moved out of the walled compound of the temple and down the road back toward the shrine they had liberated.

The formation of troops riding along was initially based on platoons, and that held true as the company rode down from the temple and through the town. A united and orderly front was important for others to see. The Hands were riding quietly, focused on the task ahead. The people of the town came out to watch them leave, clustered in bunches on the side of the wide road that wound from the temple complex to the main gate. They held the quiet until they had passed the borders of the fields and moved into the woods proper.

Sarnt Canli called out, "At ease!"

The posture of the riders shifted to something more casual. Asche was glad as she was still trying to get used to the movement of horses. Apparently, the older Hands had been ahorse a time or two and were thus able to adapt quickly. Sitting back and enjoying both the ride and the weather, the Hands started talking and some people shifted position in the column in order to ride next to the people they wanted to ride with. Guards and scouts would be rotated over the course of travel, but on the whole, friends were allowed to ride together. There were groupings of pairs and other small groups, riding along in mass, still following the basics of unit movement.

Asche called out, "Tigh, Elles, why don't we do this more often?"

Tigh chuckled. "Riding horses? We can be more flexible on foot just not as fast. And the nobility get grumpy when non nobles ride horses or wear swords. They say it infringes on their rights as nobility. Many of the different faiths have dispensations for that, but honestly, would you want to upset one of the divines in a complaint over weapons?"

"Guess not." Asche was not positive if that answered the question. "So, we don't have horses because it makes nobles grumpy?"

Elles and Flit snorted at that. Tigh just beamed at Asche. "Yes, that is exactly it. They can pretend it doesn't matter about the swords and other weapons so long as they really come down hard on having horses."

"That doesn't make any kind of sense," said Asche.

Flit nodded. "With the swords, it's all about the straight blades. The raven's heads we use aren't 'real' swords to them. Mostly they're afeared of peasants and simple townsfolk rising up against them. Some of the nobles are worthless fools, believing a quirk of birth makes them better than anyone else."

"Really?" Oxlen only got visited by the ducal seneschal once a year at most, so she had little experience in dealing with them.

Elles replied, "Really. We've had to cross blades with a few of them now and again, and they complain we're not supposed to be doing what we do. It's always extra messy with nobles involved."

"How so?"

Flit turned to face Asche more directly. "Politics. The nobles all bicker and vie for power, but the power they believe in is solid as smoke. They count blood higher than skill at arms. Who is related to who is important, like you're breeding cows, not having children."

"What?" Asche gaped at the others.

Tigh chuckled and grinned over at her. "Flit's not a fan of nobles in general."

Flit grimaced but gave a nod conceding the point. "Aye. One tried to molest me sister, so I drove a hot poker into his arse. The Hands protected me and got the duke to protect me family. I have no love for them bastards."

Asche gaped and stared in surprise at her teammate, eyes wide. "Hot poker?"

"It was at hand." Flit gave an unconcerned shrug.

That cracked Tigh and Elles up. They laughed out loud while Flit just smirked. Asche found it amusing but not funny and looked over at Flit. Flit grinned. "I may have used that line a few other times."

Tigh and Elles rotated out with Fanlis and Terris, taking their turn at forward guard. Despite being in lands with no reports of any violence, they took turns at guard mainly to get Asche used to the rotation. Things were quiet on the ride, with only sounds of horses plodding on the trail and the creak and jingle of the wagons and tack as they rolled along.

Nibs had been riding on one of the wagons, letting someone else do the work for him. The upside was that they were giving him small morsels of cheese as the sat there. The downside was it was boring. It moved so slow compared to what he could be seeing if he flew.

With powerful wing flaps, he took off from the wagon and flew over the company. He spotted Asche, but with the way his wings felt, he needed to go for a flight. The muscles were a bit stiff, and he wanted to work them out, feel the wind on them. Wanting to go higher, he chose his ascent carefully, avoiding the thickest mass of branches on the way up and out.

In the blue again, he flew higher and higher, looking over the countryside, the thick mass of forest, occasional open spots of clearings, or larger ones for tiny villages. The wide-open lands around the temple were still visible and he could spot the flocks in the air over the fields. There were a few flocks around the smaller fields of the villages nearby, hunting for food.

His head was still spinning from all the information about humans he learned: weapon types, dangers during human warfare, lots of human words for variations on the same thing, human limitations, and more. Testing himself on the new words was helping him deal with the reality of what he had undertaken by following his human friend when she ran from home. Now he could understand the things Asche said, at least the words in some cases, as he had noted that words and meanings did not always align. That humans could express so much with so few sounds was impressive. The elders at the temple insisted they really were nearly as smart as ravens. Nibs had yet to be convinced.

He practiced a few of his flying tricks, as they were fun and kept him in practice. That drop for instance was such a great rush he had to remind himself it had more purpose than just enjoyment. He had also learned how to fly upside down, which was more of a controlled glide than actual flight. And then there was the summersault. That was a rush and he could think of no purpose besides playing in the air for that one, but it might allow him to get behind some other bird chasing him. He did a few of those and coasted a bit upside down.

When the company began riding in the open, Nibs circled down. While the flying had been a much needed reprieve, he had committed to Asche and the Hands. He was not a fan of the boring stuff they did, their yammering in that strange language they spoke; he was also not pleased with the fact they fought the way they did, but talking with the elders had made it clear that the Hands were friends with most ravens.

The way the elders explained it, Nibs almost thought this human divine, the Morri, cared about ravens. That a human divine might do so struck Nibs as odd, but the elders at the temple insisted there was more than the Feathered One that cared for ravens. Elders should know. He trusted them, believed them even, but that did not make his understanding of this any easier. But here he was, somewhat in service to a human divine, all to be a companion to a friend. He shook his head to clear it. That was way too serious.

After a few drops and a summersault to cheer himself up, he landed on one of the supply wagons, ruffling his feathers to settle better, then asked one of the people riding in the back, "Cheese?"

Asche had just returned from her riding lead, where Flit taught her about the job, and was still toward the front of the formation. As she had a drink from her waterskin, Elsif rode up next to her. They shared a smile as they kept riding. Asche was still getting used to the shifting of the horse's gait. Neither of them had done any riding before the Hands, and it was taking some concentration to ride well.

They had been riding alongside each other for quite a while before Asche asked a question that had been growing in her mind, "So what are we?"

"What?"

"I mean, are we a couple, just friends, what?" Asche blushed as she clarified.

"Oh…well…" Elsif paused for a moment, clearly trying to set things in words. "I want to be with you, if that's alright with you?"

"I do, I just…this is new to me," said Asche.

"Not for me," said Elsif, a slightly haunted look on her face. "The reason I left my village was I got caught with a girl in a hayloft. My da was…let's go with displeased, and her family was not very happy with the whole situation either. It looked like it was going to be messy, however, since I already planned on leaving, they asked me to leave a bit early. That was enforced with threats of violence. It was…annoying and irritating, but I made it to a nearby shrine easily enough."

"They chased you out?"

Elsif shrugged nonchalantly, but the hunch of her shoulders and the distant look on her face belied that action. "It's not like I'm planning to ever return there, so it's of no concern to me. To the dark realm with the lot of them for all I care. I wanted to be one of the Hands for quite a few years, after a company helped our town after a bad storm, and I've known I like women for years. Getting caught with someone was bound to happen at some point."

Asche was silent for a bit of the ride, heart in her throat, and then she looked up. "I…I got caught as well."

Elsif looked confused a moment and her eyes widened when things fell into place. "How did you find something to wear?"

Asche was looking at the back of her horse's head and seeing something else. "I…I took my mum's extra shift and tried it on. I was going to put on the overdress when my da walked in." She swallowed hard at the memory. "He…I…I got really beat over that and I knew things were going to get worse if I stayed. That's when I decided to take my chances with the Hands. I figured even if they didn't take me, they could at least get me out of there. I figured I might be able to travel with them to somewhere else at the very least."

Elsif chuckled, the sound humorless, bitter, and heavy. "And now look at us. You got found and I get to hit things with my hammer." She paused and looked up at the way the sun moved through the leaves and branches of the trees. "I guess you could say we're not doing so bad for a couple of troublemakers."

Asche looked off, her thoughts wandering a bit. "Not troublemakers, just people who weren't in the right place. I guess, when we found our where, things just fell into place like they should have."

"True." Before Elsif could continue, Sarnt Canli rode up alongside them from where she had been riding with the kaitan. They looked at her expectantly, though Asche was also a touch confused as to why Canli would have joined them. "Yes, Sarnt?"

"It looks like you two have gotten together, is that right?" she asked.

Asche and Elsif shared a look before Elsif turned back to her. "Yes…"

"Right," said Sarnt Canli. "Some ground rules." She pointed at them with her whole hand. "We are a fighting force, first and foremost; the mission comes first, full stop. So don't be late, and keep your head in the game, is that clear?"

"Yes, Sarnt," they both answered.

"Second, no over-the-top displays of affection when around everyone. If it is too blatant, it becomes a discipline issue. And lastly, if this relationship stops, do not make an issue out of it. Things end, move on. This is directly related to the mission coming first. Is that clear?"

"Yes, Sarnt."

"Okay, that was it." Her stern face softened and she gave them a warm smile. "You two take care of each other and this will be the last time we have to speak about this."

Canli rode forward to speak with Sarnt Terris, leaving them. They looked at each other and then sighed. Asche snickered. "That was unexpected."

"I guess, I mean we are a military order, so none of that is really unexpected," said Elsif.

"I'm sure they make it awkward to ensure people are doing things the right way. Because if things did go bad, I think they've made it quite clear it will be dealt with publicly." Asche did not want to imagine what sort of corrective behavior would come from not following those rules. It would probably be stations.

"Right, try not to have our fights where others can overhear, hell, try not to have fights." Elsif nodded.

"I can't see how that will work, Elsif, I mean…we are a military order."

Elsif leaned over and smacked Asche in the arm, and then almost overbalanced in her saddle, yelping and clutching at the saddle gullet. Asche leaned in and helped push her upright, laughing the whole time.

## CHAPTER FIFTEEN

The company made excellent time on the way back to the shrine they had liberated and the village of Gehrlen, thanks to the horses. Some of the extra troops that traveled with them planned to stay at the shrine to increase their contingent of Hands and help with rebuilding from the damage the bandits caused. The plan they had been briefed on was they would camp within the shrine's walls and head out along the route the slavers had come in on, to see if they encountered anyone else.

When Nibs reached the top of the shrine, he spotted some of the same ravens that had been there before, somewhat increased in numbers. That made sense, as the danger had passed and it would be safe to return to the more familiar roosts. He landed on the shrine, hopped over to them, and croaked out a greeting. "Greetings, elders. Did you decide if you want to help?"

The eldest bobbed his head, a few of the others joining in. "Yes, we can do that, but we are not sure how."

Nibs was pleased. He had been working on this issue since they left and had spoken with the elders back at the temple. "I can fix that. The elders of the town with vast fields, where we came from had suggestions. You wait here and I'll talk to one of the humans and see if this can get set up."

Nibs looked over the edge of the shrine and spotted Asche helping to offload the travel shrine under the watchful eye of Fanlis. Perfect, that was exactly who he needed in order to get this set up.

Nibs glided down and landed on the box of the altar. Lynarra and Asche squawked in surprise, nearly dropping the shrine. Asche glared at him. "Nibs! Don't do that!"

Nibs cocked his head at Asche, trying to understand what she was talking about. He looked down at the box, but it hadn't changed. It was still just a box. Whatever her concern was over this box was unimportant compared to what he was doing. "Need help."

"Fine. Just get off the box and I'll come help you," grumbled Asche.

Nibs looked down at the box, cocking his head to try and determine why it was important. He looked back at Asche, then bounced a few times. He stared up at her again, cocked his head the other direction, and said, "Good box."

Fanlis started laughing and slowly Lynarra and Asche joined in. Nibs laughed as well, which was a much different sound, more of a guttural krucking. He rode the box into the shrine, where the priestess stared at him in some confusion. Nibs just kept laughing. Humans were weird.

They set down the box and Nibs stood there looking at Asche. With an exasperated sigh, she asked, "What did you need?"

"Ravens here want to help," croaked Nibs.

The priestess heard this and stared at him. "They want to help?"

Nibs answered, "Yes. Not know how."

The priestess stared at him. This was obviously not something she was prepared for.

"You mean like scouting and keeping watch on the area? Stuff like that?" Asche asked.

Nibs and the priestess turned to face Asche. Her face heated and she stammered. "Well, it's how Nibs is helping the company right now."

The priestess looked thoughtful. "That...could help. We were completely caught unawares and extra eyes looking out for our protection would not go amiss. If the Hands are made aware of the sound, then they would be able to prepare for danger in enough time to make a difference. Thank you, Nibs. That is a welcomed offer."

"Maybe the Hands here will have more ideas," said Asche. "Personally, the two of us are still trying to figure it out as we go along."

"I will do that. Can you make the introductions?" The priestess addressed Nibs.

With a bob, Nibs replied and hopped closer to Asche. She held her arm out so Nibs could jump up onto her shoulder. He carded his beak through Asche's hair a moment, grooming his human. Asche smiled at the priestess and headed outside. "When we get out there are you going to get them?"

"I call."

With a nod, Asche stepped from the shrine into the sunlight. Nibs croaked loudly, with an almost whistle sound in there and a slight trill. Then there was a sound of wings. Lining the roof of the shrine were seven ravens, looking down at them intently, a few with graying feathers. Several of the Hands from the shrine stopped what they were doing to watch. Asche looked up at the ravens. "Can you understand what I am saying?"

A few cocked their heads in confusion, but the two eldest bobbed their heads. "Okay, some of you do and some don't."

The same ravens bobbed again.

"Nibs here said you want to help, is that true?"

Bobbing, and one croak.

"Great! Thank you." Asche beamed at them. "Nibs here does scouting at the moment, because that's all he volunteered for. Did you have any ideas for more?"

The ravens cocked their heads and began to make noises at each other. It wasn't just croaking but other sounds as well, an utter cacophony to the humans. They also looked at Nibs and made noises at him as well. Nibs shoved off Asche and flapped to the roof where they gathered and their voices became a murmur. Nibs turned back and said from the roof. "Search and find is easy. Watch easy during day. Pick up small things, as well. Best if shiny."

Some of the others were gaping at this, surprised not just at hearing a human voice from Nibs, but the offer itself from the ravens. To many of the listeners, the birds had become something in the background, not something to pay attention to, as they were just animals and not something that could think and communicate like themselves. This shattered that belief.

Asche looked at the priestess of the shrine. "Would that work?"

"Yes, that would work. That is extremely helpful, honestly. What do they want in return?"

Again, the ravens huddled. Nibs croaked out, "Make sure food in winter and spring, no attack, be friends, share shinies."

The priestess looked over at the head of the Hands for the shrine, a short, squat woman who looked very strong. She nodded. The priestess looked up again at Nibs. "Then we are agreed."

Nibs spoke to the ravens on the roof and then the others started croaking out something. "They have agreed. Everybody helps each other. It might be good to send someone back to the town with the vast fields down that road there. They might send a teacher to show you how to talk human."

"Thank you. That is a good idea. We are happy with this plan. It will make winters and spring much easier for the nesting." Others joined in, agreeing that it was a good deal. All the humans looked over at Nibs for an explanation. He looked down at them and said, "Happy."

Asche was thrilled the local ravens were going to help the shrine. Honestly, her life had gotten better since she had befriended Nibs. He had been her constant friend for the last few years, and she thought people on the whole needed to be friends with ravens. Discovering that the temple had a raven who was a friend to the high priestess had made her feel immensely at home and relaxed.

A few ravens still huddled on the roof, flying about enjoying their time in the air. Asche just had to smile. Watching birds of all sorts fly was wonderful, but ravens played in the air more than other birds and it added a sense of anticipation watching them soar. Nibs flew down to the commander of the shrine's Hands. "I teach warning sound. Ravens spot trouble, you hear."

Nibs made a short staccato caw over and over. Nibs looked at the commander again and then repeated the sound. The commander bowed her head to Nibs and said, "I have it, repeated caws in quick succession. Thank you for this." The woman turned to face the ravens perched on the roof of the shrine. "Thank you."

Nibs bobbed his head and flapped over to Asche, landing on her shoulder. Asche stroked his breastbone. "I help."

Asche grinned at him. "Yes, you did."

❖

The company was ready to move off in the morning, after the extra Hands had fully moved into the barracks and the gear wagon they had brought was unloaded. After the ceremony to prepare the shrine for travel was complete, Asche helped carry it out and place it in the wagon. The company mounted and rode off along the road the slavers had come in on. Elsif had been tasked as one of the guards so Asche was riding with Sarnt Terris. Realizing this might be a good moment, Asche decided to ask something that had been bothering her for a while now. "Sarnt, why have we only come across villages with a Morri shrine?"

"Well, in case of temple and last shrine, answer is simple, they predated villages. Hands kept those areas safe, as they were initially out in wilderness. Peasants flocked to those areas, as Hands kept them safe, so villages grew attached to them," said Terris. "Sometimes this attracted nobility and they built on as well, like in Turling. Also, they are places Hands can stay without paying tithe."

Asche nodded. It did make a kind of sense. "Okay, so why aren't there shrines to any other divines in this area?"

"Duke's grandfather granted this region to the Morri, as some Hands rescued him when he and his party were attacked on road. Apparently, Hands foiled assassination attempt. So, they gave us this land. On whole, Hands do very little in terms of ruling area. We aren't telling anyone who they should pray to or what to believe, but other than some followers of sacred triad, that's who we have in region. Your village, Oxlen, and their shrine predate this agreement and there was small shrine there to different gods and goddesses besides sacred triad. We guard there as a favor for duke."

That was a bit of a surprise to Asche, but then again, she realized she never really considered these questions before, being more concerned with surviving her father and keeping her head down than why things were this way. She had never worried about how the larger world worked or anything else thanks to her immediate concerns. "Do we often work for the duke?"

Terris shrugged. "Sometimes. We track down problematic bandit groups or help in natural disasters. Usually, we are left to own devices. He primarily talks with high holy one in main temple. Farspeakers there pass on her orders to different temples and out to companies, and it trickles down to us. High general of the Hands is there at main temple as well."

Asche's eyes widened in realization this was another thing she had no clue about. "I wasn't aware the Hands are that large?"

"We don't make fuss. I mean, our role is to follow orders of the Morri and that's it. You would not think there many women who want to do this, but we have plenty of followers and people eager to join, at least in this area. Other areas, not so much and we have to transfer people to those places."

"Why?"

"Some of other divines have issue with the Morri. When it was explained to me, it seemed like very odd reason for other divines to dislike the Morri and us. Apparently, she said no to some divine suitor and they got grumpy. Instead of respecting her no, he tried to make her marry him, and when that did not work…well, some men are like that. It's one of reasons shrines and temples take in women who have flown from such abuse. It's been long enough now it has become one of her aspects, protector of women. Lady Earth and Lady Moon both support her in this, as do other goddesses, so there is some bitterness between his faith and our Lady."

"Wait, so a divine is grumpy the Morri did not submit to him and now his people fight us?" Asche was incredulous. This sounded like a stupid reason to fight.

"Yep. And that god's friends support him and his people. The Lord of the Sun and a few of other male divines don't support him, so it's not like he has most powerful divines on his side. We mostly focus on avoiding them, if possible, because it is rarely worth grief. Fanlis is worried that bounties placed on priestesses and Hands means the Tyner and his version of Hands are involved in this. If so, then fight we're heading to is going to be…difficult."

"You've fought them before?" Asche was fascinated and unnerved by all of this. This aspect of life in the Hands was certainly not something she had expected, conflict arising from issues between divines.

"A couple seasons back," said Terris. "It was ugly. Three companies of Hand were dealing with army brought together by the Tyner's people. They had priest who was calling down power on us during battle. That's when we lost last Sword of the Morri."

"Swords?"

Terris chuckled. "Wow…your village really taught you shit."

Asche blushed hotly and looked down at the forest floor. "My da didn't want me spending any time with the priest. I think he didn't want me to have any out except what he demanded of me."

"Ouch." Terris flinched in sympathy. "Well, you are away from bastard now, so don't worry. You are with Hands and we support our own against all."

"So, about the Swords?" said Asche. She had heard the term a few times and wanted to know what it meant.

"Right. Swords and Hammers of the Morri are warriors blessed with her favor. Where we are her tools in world, they are her weapons. Swords are pretty much just fighters who, at very least, lead company of Hands and do missions she leads them to. Hammers are something different. Their connection to the Morri is stronger and what they do is more varied. It's been a while since we have had Hammer."

"They're holy warriors?"

"Basically. I know Tigh dreams of becoming Sword someday. She trains extra hard and takes on hardest missions in hopes her steel will be tested and she will be shown to be worthy. She is sword chaser."

Asche's eyes grew wide and she turned to look behind her in the column, toward where Tigh was riding, joking around with Elles and a few others. She caught her eye, leered at her, then winked, which made Asche turn away blushing. "So can anyone become a Sword or Hammer?"

Sarnt Terris shrugged at the question. "As far as I know, yes. If the Morri finds your steel a proper fit, she will temper you into Sword or Hammer. There may be more to it, but that's what I know. Having never been one, is all guesswork."

"Thank you, Sarnt."

Terris nodded and rode forward, leaving Asche alone with her thoughts. Were her dreams of the Morri's forge somehow connected to becoming a Sword? She wasn't sure and it felt presumptive to think that was the case. She was a nobody girl from a no place village who was still struggling to do her job correctly. Why would a lost sister like herself be blessed with more than just being found? That in and of itself was a balm to her soul that had been completely unexpected. She had not expected how it would make her feel more complete or whole. No, she was who she was and all she could do was serve the Morri to the best of her ability to repay the divine for finding her and making her whole.

## Chapter Sixteen

Asche was out front scouting with Flit. They had gotten the first rotation that day and started off right after breakfast, riding out before the others. Nibs was forward of where they were, watching the road ahead as well, so they were unlikely to ride into a surprise. Bits of morning mist clung to the ground as they rode along the road, the darker space under the trees holding more. The slow, steady plod of horses had a hypnotic effect on her. With a huge yawn, Asche shook her head to try to wake herself up more. She slept fitfully last night, and this was the cost. Flit looked over questioningly. Asche yawned again and looked over. "You ever have those dreams where you're so busy in them you wake up tired?"

Flit nodded. "Aye, they're not very good for rest."

"Yeah. I've been having these for a while now," said Asche. "I just feel tired all the time."

"Well, pinch your leg or something. We have to be alert," said Flit. "Even with Nibs watching out for us, he still can't see what's under the trees."

"I get that." The hard pinch she gave to the skin of her thumb gave her a flash of more awareness, but that faded as did the pain. Before she could yawn again, she gave herself another pinch, twisting a little to draw out more pain. If this was the best pinching would do, she needed some other option, as it was doing very little to wake her more thoroughly.

Needing better advice, she was about to say something when she heard a short, staccato caw caw caw, followed by a croak. The sound repeated. Asche's eyes went wide as she recognized the call and looked over at Flit. Flit turned her horse and started back down the road toward the rest of the company, moving from a sedate walk to a gallop in a fairly short distance.

Asche swiftly followed, bouncing uncomfortably on the horse, trying to grip tightly with her thighs but not having the exact technique to make a gallop less painful. The horse-riding lessons were working, and she was acclimating to riding, but there had not been enough time to develop the muscles needed to properly hold on. After a short while at that speed, they reached a wide curve in the road and nearly ran into the front of the column. After slowing their horses, Asche noted the other Hands were already dismounted and moving their horses into the wood line and the still lingering fog. Fanlis waved them over as a couple of the other rangers crossed the road and raced back the way they had come, armed with bows. "We heard Nibs and figured someone was heading this way."

Kaitan Tanrei was ordering platoons about, and the Hands were rushing into place, following the clipped orders. Fanlis looked at both Flit and Asche. "Grab your bows. Take your horses to where the wagons are and hustle back. We're to head up trail and shoot them in the back, driving them into the ambush."

"What if it's not the enemy?" asked Asche.

"Then we let them go by. However, from Nibs's call it's likely someone bad, as he knows friend from foe fairly well. That was the call he said the ravens back at the shrine were going to use for enemies," said Fanlis as she was moving quickly. "Not sure what the croak at the end means."

Asche snatched her bow, hustled to drop off her horse, and ran behind, trying to catch up to Flit, who had made the move look easy and practiced. When they got to their area to hide, she quickly strung her bow. Fanlis sketched their portion of the battle plan quickly and the group of them ghosted off into position. Once hidden behind bushes and trees, they waited.

Within a short while, they could begin to hear the clop of hooves, the creaking and jingling of a wagon, the faint groan of leather tack, and a deep murmuring. As the wagon neared, the murmuring resolved itself into voices, rough male, one loudly making a crude joke about his bedding prowess. Asche swallowed hard, wiping the nervous sweat from her palm, and quickly nocked an arrow. Her heart was pounding so hard, she was sure these bandits would be able to hear it. Nervously, she looked over at Flit, who was behind a nearby tree. Flit caught her eye and mimed breathing slowly and evenly.

Asche followed along, working to get her breathing back under control. Her hand felt slick, and she wiped it on her pant leg, leaving a wet handprint on her gambeson already damp from the mist. Pre-battle jitters were something she was hoping to control, as clearly her life with the Hands was going to put her in danger routinely. Slowly, the voices drew even with their position. Asche concentrated on staying still, breathing slowly and deeply, one with the tree.

The groan of wood and slight clink of the chains from the wagon nearing made her realize it was time, and with a deep breath, she was ready for action. Once the wagon was past, it would be time to rush out and fire. Asche swallowed, aware her mouth and throat felt dry, aware this was no time for the water skin. Flit told her the nerves would fade after a while and battle preparation would get easier, but Asche could not imagine how. It was not like the battles were going to get easier. She looked over at the other members of her platoon; they all seemed calm, ready, prepared. Could she actually become like them?

The wagon bumped loudly over a rock and there was cursing. She slowed her breathing more. This was not her first fight. She had fought and killed already. This was just another part of her life as one of the Hands. All she had to do this moment was breathe, remain focused, and follow the plan when Fanlis gave the signal. Mouthing the words, Asche quickly prayed, "Holy Morri, please strengthen my steel, guide my aim, and make me ready for battle. Bless me, Holy Morri, so I might be your hand in this fight."

She exhaled at the end, breath tickling her lips a touch, ribs compressing, muscles loosening. With a glance down, she verified the arrow was nocked correctly. It certainly would not do to screw up firing her bow in her first ambush. There was no doubt in her mind she would be mocked endlessly for such a mistake. A calm descended, and she nodded, ready, focused.

Fanlis whistled and the Hands burst from cover into the roadway, drawing their bows quickly and loosing arrows into the back of the formation.

Asche's arrow was released a heartbeat after the others, flying straight and true into the meaty upper part of the shoulder of the bandit driving the wagon. There was a yelp of surprise from the bandits, as the group nocked new arrows, drew, and fired again, nearly moving as one.

With a yell, the driver snapped the reins as best he could with one working arm; the horses neighed in surprise, lunging forward. The other bandits did the same, racing away from the archers. There was a third volley before the bandits reached the curve and drove headlong into the ambush.

The loud battle yell preceded the crash of everything being sprung. Shouts echoed in the lane and the sound of panicking horses added into the mix. As the rangers raced toward the ambush site, a few horses bolted past them, eyes wide with fear, empty of riders. They arrived just in time to see the last bandit cut down; the ones who had surrendered stood there with hands upraised.

Fanlis sent them off immediately to go through the bandits' things in search of papers, a map, anything that might have more information to add detail to the picture of what and who they were facing. Asche was assigned the wagon. First, they pulled everything off it and went through it with some of the supply troops who were helping with the moving. Stuffed into various sacks were foodstuffs, weapons, repair kits for both weapons and armor, and several chests with the pillaged wealth they had acquired. The supply troops inspected those and carried them to the company's wagons.

Looking for hidey-holes on the wagon, Asche worked hard with Flit's assistance. They started at the tailgate and worked their way forward, tapping the wood and listening for a hollow. The work was quick as there were no hidden spots toward the back. There was a slot under the driver's seat that was only slightly hidden, as it had a visible indentation to grab it up. It would have been tricky to find so long as you did not have to worry about being found by the bandits while you searched.

What Asche pulled free from the cubby was a map.

Asche was not familiar with maps, since she never had cause to use one before. Father Tombol had a map of what he claimed was the known world, but that was the extent of her familiarity. She understood what they were and even she could tell there were marks on this map from different people, using different markings to indicate paths and targets. Maybe this would be a huge help overall. Asche brought it over to Fanlis, who inspected it quickly and smiled. "Yes, good. Wasn't the driver one of the prisoners?"

"Yes, ma'am," replied Flit as she nodded. "But they seem more mulish than the last lot."

Fanlis nodded. Asche realized that they had a lot of the same information as before, but the biggest difference was this map. It would take time they didn't really have to figure out where the routes ended and began, as they were circle routes that crossed a few times. Fanlis got her table set up, and as she was getting ready for interrogations, Nibs swooped down and landed lightly on the table. "You question?"

"Yes?"

"They stinky and stubborn."

"Yes."

"Idea."

"You have an idea?"

Nibs nodded.

"What?"

Nibs waddled nearer and whispered in her ear. Fanlis sat back and stared at Nibs in shock for a short while. Asche could tell that what she heard was not anything she had been expecting. Fanlis said, "Are you sure? I know it preys on people's beliefs about ravens as omens of death. Is that what you want?"

Nibs again leaned in and said something to Fanlis. Thinking it over, a smile stretched across her face. "Terris."

"Yes, ma'am?" The sarnt came over and waited for orders.

Fanlis leaned forward and whispered what she wanted as Nibs flapped over to land on Asche's shoulder. Asche looked over at him, quizzically. "What are you planning?"

The only reply Nibs would give was a deep, throaty, croaking laugh.

❖

Several of the infantry troops helped prepare the spot, gathering up the bodies of the dead and dumping them into a crude pile. They had been collecting the bodies anyway to burn them, as it was not a good thing to allow decomposing bodies to lie on the roadway. There were a number of things that might hunt down the corpses to feed upon, many of which were a danger to other travelers. Once the pile was arranged, with the bloodiest bodies on top, the prisoners were brought over to the pile and pushed roughly to their knees. Fanlis sat there watching them coldly, her desk set up on the other side of the bodies from them.

The moment stretched, and the men began to fidget under her gaze. Fanlis smiled. The look was not comforting. "Now let me explain to you all your predicament. You have one chance to answer my questions or you get to join your fellows there on the pile. Thanks to questioning some of your friends a few weeks ago, I have most of the answers I need. So, does anyone want to volunteer an answer to one of the two questions I have: where is the market in this kingdom, and who is the buyer? You know the person I'm talking about, the one who is a priest for some divine?"

The prisoners shifted in place, trying to not look at each other. They tensed up and looked at the ground. No one said anything, refusing to look at Fanlis.

Fanlis sat more upright. "I see."

Fanlis put down the quill she had been poised to write with. Nibs flew down from a tree, flapping hard to slow himself to a landing on the pile of corpses, drawing all eyes to him. Spreading his wings wide, he krawed loudly in warning, glowering at the men. Nibs looked down at the bodies underneath him, inspecting them.

He pecked at one of the bodies and pulled free an eye and dropped it, making a sharp, metallic tok. "Not fresh."

The men started in surprise at hearing the raven's voice.

"I'm sorry. You want something fresher?" Fanlis said.

"Yes," croaked Nibs, turning back to the kneeling men. "Fresh. Fresh eyes."

The cackle from Nibs was high-pitched, and some of the men flinched under the sound. A few began to wriggle against their bindings, only to be stopped by getting struck with the foot of a polearm.

Fanlis looked over at the men, measuring them. She gestured over at the driver. "Canli, grab that one. The raven needs his fresh eyes."

The driver began to struggle as he was roughly dragged to his feet and hauled closer to the mound of corpses. Elsif came up and grabbed his other arm and they dragged him forward before shoving him down. Nibs hopped forward, beak getting closer to the man's face. The driver was shaking his head back and forth, eyes wide, and he began to mutter in fear. Nibs jumped onto the man's injured shoulder and croaked loudly, then snapped his jaws shut with an audible snap.

The man flinched from that and screamed out, "I'll talk, I'll talk!"

Nibs cocked his head, staring down into the man's eyes. "Fresh. Fresh eyes."

"Overdorfs! The market is in Overdorfs!" yelped the man.

"Is it? Really?" drawled out Fanlis.

Nibs leaned forward, snapping his beak two inches from the man's face.

"Yes! The Baron of Overdorfs hired men to raid connecting lands for wealth and slaves. He and the priest are friends. It's them. Them, not me!" The words stumbled out of his mouth almost faster than he could speak.

Fanlis leaned forward, eyes intent on the injured driver. "The priest? To whom?"

The man leaned back, trying to get away from Nibs, trying to make his mouth move, but nothing came out. Nibs cocked his head, staring at the man with one eye. The moment dragged out and the man hissed air in as he leaned away from the raven perched on his shoulder. Nibs snapped his head around and his beak pecked the man between the eyes hard, starting a trickle of blood, before he spread his wings and screeched, "Fresh!"

"The Tyner!" shrieked the driver, fear overcoming whatever was holding back his tongue.

Nibs pulled his head back and looked over at Fanlis. She narrowed her eyes and asked, "And the name?"

The man tried talking, but only gibberish came out. Then froth began spilling from his mouth as he began gagging on his tongue which swelled in his mouth. Nibs flapped away as the man toppled on to the mound and thrashed, trying to get free. The struggle grew weaker. The priestess traveling with them ran up and began to pray, her words racing against the curse gripping the man. The violence of his movements slowed even more and then stilled, his body sagging against the corpses.

The priestess stopped her prayer, changing instead to one for the dead. Nibs leapt off the mound and over to a tree, where he began to groom himself, working to clean the blood from his feet and feathers. Fanlis sighed, pinching the bridge of her nose. "Right. That's certainly a complication."

## CHAPTER SEVENTEEN

A small detachment of the Hand, comprised of some of the best riders, rode off toward one of the nearby villages with a ducal presence with the prisoners in the bed of their slave wagon. Kaitan Tanrei and Fanlis had clustered off with the farspeaker priestess who had traveled with them. She passed this information back to the temple and the farspeaker traveling with Kaitan Ginvert, who was with the duke's man, Lord Whiltaen. They had a destination now for the meetup and the guards would be able to catch up to them.

Asche was confused about what she had heard during the interrogation and sought out the priestess, as Fanlis was busy with the kaitan. Given her questions dealt primarily with the divines, she figured the priestess might be a better source than Fanlis for this information. "Uhm…Holy One?"

The woman was taller than her and had streaks of gray in her hair, despite looking young. "Yes? It's Asche, correct? The new lost sister in this company?"

"Yes, Holy One. I…uh…have a question, if I may?" Why she was so nervous? Asche was unsure, but it felt intrusive to interfere with whatever the priestess was doing. Father Tombol always hated interruptions to what he considered was his time.

"Certainly. What is it?"

"Who is the Tyner? I've never heard of that divine before," said Asche, slightly embarrassed for Father Tombol's failure in teaching.

The priestess waved Asche to go with her as she walked back toward the wagons. "He is not worshiped much in this region or kingdom for several reasons. The Tyner is not an evil god, per se, but he is also not altogether good, at least from our point of view. Basically, since he is a god of warriors and war, he believes the strong should rule over the weak and does not acknowledge the importance of the rule of law. Additionally, the Morri and he have a troubled history. One of the stories from the Book of the Divine talks of this discord and may be helpful.

"In the times before, the Morri was simply smith of the divine, crafting weapons and armor for all the gods and goddesses, as well as weaving cloth and making their garb. She crafted many beautiful items in that time. On the earth, the Tyner was hard at work, plying his trade, as mortals fought against each other. The Morri only had a few followers amongst the mortals, as not all smiths were working with her yet. The Tyner's followers favored their work as being superior to other smiths, as the Morri shared secrets of her craft with her followers, and money flowed into the coffers of the faith as warriors fought amongst each other for access to the superior steel.

"For a while, that was the state of things, as gangs and clans vied for power across the lands. People began to notice that the forges of the Morri were some of the only places of true safety amongst the battle-ravaged areas. Not taking sides, the priestess smiths of the forge shrines made things for whoever asked. Villages grew up around the forges, clinging onto what safety existed while the Tyner and others raged. Then, while a village of people drawn to the safety of the Morri were gathered at the forge shrine, offering their thanks to her, several priests of the Tyner and their army attacked the village. They killed their way through to the forge shrine, where they walked up to the smith, one of the priestesses of the forge, and asked to place an order for new swords.

"The priestess stood there, staring at the blood-drenched men demanding her work and the bodies of the men, women, and children strewn about they had killed merely for being in their way. Under her breath, she prayed to the Morri to stretch out her hands and use her hammer to smite these defilers of the forge shrine and its safety.

This was Luthera, the founder of the Hands and the first Hammer of the Morri. The goddess stretched out her power through Luthera and smote them, killing the priests first.

"Once finished, the Morri spoke to Luthera, and from that conversation between them, the Hands were born, to protect the people and to serve as a way for the Morri to reach out into the world she had barely interacted with. It was also when our Lady began to be connected to warriors who did not fight for glory but for their people, to women and children, to things forged out of the fires of this world. Ever since that day, the Tyner and his priests have been working against the Morri and all that is hers, to bring her back in line." The priestess concluded her tale and looked at Asche. "I hope that clarifies who the Tyner is."

Asche stood there and took it all in. The story clarified a lot about the Morri she had not been aware of or taught. Hearing about what priests of the Tyner had done turned her stomach. It made her remember a few incidents where her father had smacked a visiting trader for taking his seat at the tavern. It spoke of bullying and a sense of superiority that angered her the farther she got away from that behavior.

The strength of arms to protect those that needed protecting spoke to her. She had not exactly been weak back when she had been a lost sister, but those with greater strength had certainly lorded it over her a time or two. More than ever, she was glad to have run, glad to have been taken in by the Hands, and above all, to have been found by the Morri. The Tyner sounded like the worst sort of bully, and she had had her fill of such when growing up. "It does clarify that. Thank you, Holy One, for your time."

"You are welcome, Asche. I am happy to share the stories of the Morri. Besides, since you are working with the shrine, it would be good for you to learn more about the Morri and her ways, so you can better serve the goddess."

"I am trying. It's just that these stories were never really talked about at our village. The local priest, Father Tombol, mostly talked about the Most Holy Triad, and a few of the other divine, like the Arndor, but never mentioned the Morri or the Tyner that I recall. He also didn't try to teach anything about the divines as a whole. He just preached about the primacy of the triad and how we needed to follow them in all things."

The priestess chuckled, resting a hand on Asche's arm. "There are so many barely competent priests who head out to border towns, to help out there because they aren't skilled enough to be accepted anywhere else. The Most Holy Triad do not fuss too much over their priests and priestesses, as their stories are abundant and their faith so widespread. They are the parents of the other divines and naturally hold primacy through that. Some of their priests are not even trained and merely take over the post from a dead relative. It is the other faiths that have to work to ensure those they send out are highly qualified. They have to work harder to be heard over the voices of the triad."

Asche narrowed her eyes, cocking her head very slightly to the side. "You make it sound like the divine is battling amongst itself."

"There is some truth to that. Often, the discord in the heavens is played out here and vice versa. There are stories where battles begun here and have gone up into the heavens. That is never a good thing because then the divines begin to actively meddle. Last time that happened was over a hundred years ago, when the Tyner's priests killed a few priests and priestesses of the Mennat. In retaliation, the Mennat called forth the being known as the Wungadore to be their Mountain and smite their enemies. The hundred men or more the Wungadore slew were priests, Swords, and their Blades, similar to the Hands. The Tyner capitulated after that as the Wungadore was simply unstoppable. The Mennat's power and strength in the elements of the Earth was made clear."

The Ballad of the Wungadore was well known. Asche bowed slightly and said, "Thank you, Holy One. That helps."

The priestess blessed Asche and then headed off to find her place in a wagon. Asche wandered off, trying to make sense of it all. There was so much tied to the divines and the Morri. Learning about the Tyner only brought forth more questions. Would she ever figure this all out? Hearing a gwah, she turned to look for Nibs just as he landed on her shoulder. "Help."

Asche smiled and got Nibs to move down to her arm. "What can I help you with?"

"Between wings, itch."

Gently, Asche began to scritch the area between the wings on Nibs's back. This was something she had done before, as it was the one place that Nibs could not easily scratch. There were a few flakes of dried blood she noted and the scratching seemed to help clear the area. She worked her fingers up the back of his head, gently removing what blood remained there. Nibs was blissfully rolling his head under her fingers.

"Need ants."

Asche stared at Nibs. "Ants?"

"Good for itch."

That clarified nothing. That also brought up another issue she had. "Where did you come up with that plan, Nibs? You really freaked them out."

"Humans funny, scared over eating food." Nibs sounded so proud of himself.

The idea of Nibs happily eating eyeballs turned her stomach, but she was able to calmly say, "Well, bodies are not really food for humans."

There was a moan of pleasure from Nibs that sounded like a few of the women from her village, making Asche blush. Spotting the red cheeks, Nibs laughed at her. "Tasty."

"Ugh…gross."

He laughed harder, chirping out, "Clever bird."

"You are indeed a clever bird. And a pretty bird," said Asche, scratching his head a little more.

"Pretty bird," preened Nibs.

"Monster bird," said Asche.

Nibs shot back with a defensive, "Pretty bird."

Asche smiled at Nibs, rubbing his breastbone. "Thanks for being my friend, Nibs."

"Monster friend," chortled Nibs.

"Yes, you are my monster friend."

Nibs croaked happily as Asche shook her head, not even knowing what else to say. It was time to mount up and continue their travel to the meeting point. There would be plenty of time to think as they rode.

❖

Since they were getting closer to the town of Overdorfs, they made sure to stay in the tree line along the slopes and out of sight of any watchers. The rangers and Nibs had not spotted any in their sweeps, however Kaitan Tanrei had said she was not taking any chances. She wanted to get the Hands to the rendezvous point without the bandits spotting them. Given the potential issues they could be facing, surprise would be a great force multiplier.

Asche rode alongside Sarnt Terris, as the company moved through the trees. She kept looking out to the fields where the wagons were barely visible as they moved along the road. "Sarnt?"

"Yes?" It was clear Terris was distracted and not really paying attention to her.

"Why are we riding in the trees if the wagons are down there for anyone to see?"

Terris turned in her saddle to focus more directly on Asche. "Now that we know for sure enemy has at least one priest working for them, we are moving through trees to confound any scrying spells. If they look for us, all they will see is us moving through trees. Valley might have features that can make it easy to figure out where we are, but in here…one section of forest is very like other. They may not have any idea where we actually are. It will confuse watchers unless they have insanely good maps, and through familiarity with local forests, because we could be in most any forest in numerous kingdoms."

"That makes sense."

"Sometimes, Asche, using brains can make your fighting so much more effective. This way, no one has to expend energy trying to protect us from scrying, conserving energy for other purposes. Hand always tries to fight smarter, not harder. It's why we train. Other groups do basic drill, leaving nobility to do bulk of training. Knights actually work hard at job, but there are never enough of them to completely turn tide of battle. Peasants who get levied to fight and taught how to use spear are nothing against groups like Hands. It's not that people with spears are not dangerous, they are. We, however, are professionals, like knights, but with a lot more variety in skills."

"We don't have cavalry do we?"

"No. That would be infringing on rights of nobility, and we don't want that. We are heavy and medium infantry, archers, rangers, and other specialists as needed. For what we do, having a dedicated cavalry group not as helpful. Besides, there are ways to thwart cavalry on foot, but we try to not tell people who might have issue that we know great weakness." Terris chuckled briefly.

"A weakness? Like what?"

"It depends on nature of knights and time. If we have a decent amount of preparation, we can dig little holes and cover them up, put down trip wires, caltrops, rock piles, stuff like that, to break up battlefield. Horse hooves can be sensitive, and holes and trip wires can make them fall and possibly break legs. That robs knights of their devastating charge. We also carry specialized tips for pikes we can mount onto long poles, letting us injure horse at distance and thwart their charges. They aren't pretty, but it does job."

Asche thought about that. She had seen an injured horse once and the experience had been rather traumatic. No kind of life really prepares you for horses screaming in pain. It had been put down by the local butcher who tried to make it quick. That experience, magnified by the number of horses that could be in a charge, and it seemed terribly brutal. "That doesn't sound nice."

"War never is," Terris stated flatly. "All fights we have done since you joined have been small. More skirmishes than true battle. We are going into something that will surely be far worse. It is likely there will be proper battle for Overdorfs and that will be completely different experience. There are smells you really only encounter in war. You spend a day or several with bits of blood or gore caked onto you, food will taste odd because smell of blood and other things. Long battles tend to summon rain so you get coated in mud and more gore which seems to take forever to wash off. There are also screams of animals and men. War…battle is terrible. But remember, we do it to protect villages, towns, cities, kingdoms, people we care about. We help the Morri do what she thinks is right and trust in that. We fight to thwart those who glory in battle."

Asche sat quietly, pondering everything she had just learned. Then she turned and looked toward the barely visible wagons moving along the roadway. "Okay, but what about the wagons?"

"Oh, that's simple. Wagons break going through thick woods or get caught on roots. It easier for them to travel along road."

"Well, what if they get attacked by bandits?"

"We come riding to rescue and remember, they're armed and armored as well," said Terris with a bit of a smirk.

Again, that explanation made sense to Asche, who was trying to make sense of all the ins and outs of her new life. If the Hands were supposed to fight smart, then maybe she needed to get smarter about all of this and figure out how to do this job better, smarter. She sighed realizing what she was essentially asking for was more training. What was worse, this was her own decision.

Her head was abuzz with different ideas, and she had nothing else to occupy her mind as they rode through the trees. The ground was covered in leaves muffling the sounds of the hooves. She wanted to be able to hold her own in a fight, so that Flit was not distracted by trying to keep her alive. Honestly, right now she was nervous about combat, so that meant more weapon training. Knowing what she was doing might help with that concern. But she was already tired just thinking about what more she wanted to know.

## Chapter Eighteen

The field training continued. As they moved through the countryside toward the rendezvous point, Fanlis made sure Asche was getting all the training at sneaking and fighting she could manage, hoping to ensure Asche would not be a weak link in their group. It did not hurt that Asche had grasped this weakness on her own and asked for more weapon work. Every other team was also working their people, except for archery, who used hunting for deer and other game as a training tool.

What Asche found interesting was the exercises were either getting easier or she was getting more used to the work and the training. The fighting was becoming simpler and she had nearly hit Flit a time or two. Nearly. She was able to sneak fairly well, with only the occasional snapped twig as she moved through the woods as compared to her earlier smashing through the underbrush. And yet the training didn't stop but kept growing more complex and tougher. That had to be a good sign, right?

Elsif rode alongside her as they moved up a series of switchbacks on a steep slope, taking them to the higher summer pastures some of the local shepherds used. They still had to get higher up into the mountains near the border before reaching the planned meeting spot outside the village of Fahrlen. Thankfully, the riders who had transported the bandits to a village that could hold them had rejoined them after riding hard for several days. The full company was again together as they rode.

Elsif rolled her neck and groaned when it stretched the left side. She did this a few times but from the look on her face, she was getting little relief. "From what some of the others say, this training never really slows down. Sometimes it is less intense, other times more, but apparently, we always work to keep our skills up and learn new ones."

Asche wanted to rub Elsif's neck to help work out all that tension and have the same done to her in return. There were other parts of her that would enjoy that treatment as well, but that might get comments. "Well, that is one way to ensure we're the best company out there. From what Terris said, other mercenary groups don't work anywhere near this hard. We consistently beat them in the field because of the training."

"Really?" Elsif turned to face her.

"According to Sarnt Terris, we have better teamwork, we respond faster to new orders, have plans in place for things happening during the course of battle and practice them, things where preplanning and training can make a huge difference. More than just forming a shield wall was her comment."

Elsif nodded. "You know, a shield wall is good for some situations but not everything. It can stop a lot of things. Our weapons and the medium infantry weapons are also geared toward opening up shield walls, and we have drills for forming one, turning, and disengaging. It's really different in the mercenary units?"

Asche shrugged. "That's what she said. I have no idea, having never been in a mercenary unit."

Elsif gave her a look that made Asche smirk. "Well, I guess we're heading into a situation where it's going to be relevant. I hope our training makes a huge difference when facing those bandits at their fort."

"Yeah, that sounds almost fun," said Asche, rolling her eyes.

"Did you have anything better to do back at your village?"

"Not really. Working and getting beat up. At least here I have the chance to hit back," Asche said.

"There is that." Elsif shifted on her horse, trying to get a better seat.

"We've covered fighting in the open a lot, but we haven't really been still enough to address fighting in buildings or tight confines. I just want to make sure I know what I'm doing." Asche bit her lower lip and stared off into nowhere.

"You really are dedicated to being a Hand, aren't you?"

Asche turned to face Elsif. "Well, if I'm going to be here, I should do the best job I can."

"Given it could keep you alive, it makes sense. I mean, you are lightly armored and squishy." Elsif grinned at her.

"And you're a fricking wall," Asche said as casually as she could manage.

"True. It's kind of fun, in a 'did you see the look on their faces' kind of way. Those bandits really have good bug eyes when facing a solid woman in heavy armor." Elsif flexed her arms to make her point.

Asche laughed and shook her head. She felt soft, warm, and a little melty when she looked at Elsif. She noted the planes of Elsif's face, spending time on her soft lips and the memories of their feel. It took some effort to look away and focus on what her horse was doing, which made her seat worse instead of better. The trail was getting steeper, and she needed to focus on helping guide the horse up the hillside and around rocks and trees and manage to not slide off the saddle. Moving in a group, her horse would be fine to follow along the path made by the lead horses, but as things on the trail grew more complex, her assistance was needed more. At least that was what she had been taught.

The company stopped a few times for the lead rider to check the map and compass, to ensure they were still moving in the correct direction, as it was far easier to get turned around in a forest than in the open plains. They crested the hill and the village they had been headed toward was finally visible through the trees. They were nearly at the rendezvous spot.

As the trees thinned, it became clear the other company was there, as was a small camp flying the ducal banner. Fanlis sat up straighter on her horse in some surprise seeing this. She spotted

Nibs sitting on a branch just ahead of her and she called out, "Why didn't you tell us about them?"

"Said friends near. They friends," responded Nibs, who ruffled his feathers in some annoyance. He glared at Fanlis.

Fanlis rubbed her forehead, grumbling to herself about the intelligence of ravens and her own failing to make what she wanted to know clearer. Her smile was more of a grimace as she said, "Thank you, Nibs."

Nibs laughed at her, made an annoyed growling sound that sounded exactly like her, and then flew off, still croaking out amusement. Asche sighed. She needed a better way to tell Nibs what she wanted to know. Sometimes it seemed like he was actively trying to thwart her search for information.

Instead of entering the small, walled village, the company skirted around the outside of the area and joined the preexisting camp, set up in the village's fallow field, as there were growing crops in the other fields. The various tents were arranged in orderly fashion, and it was clear where Duke Barvith's representative was by the more ostentatious tent and the banner with gold and silver thread waving in the breeze. Tanrei sent her people off to organize their encampment and set off to liaise with the other kaitan there, or at least the other officers if the kaitan was with the duke's man.

Asche and Elsif busied themselves setting up their now shared tent. The company had no issues with who stayed in what tent or even what relationships they formed, as long as there was order. That suited them just fine. They set their tent up quickly and unrolled their bedrolls. They were about to relax for a bit when Elsif was called over by Canli. Elsif gave her a peck on the cheek and headed off to see what her sarnt wanted.

Looking around the campsite as it was getting set up, Asche noted most everyone was busy with one task or another. She and Lynarra helped set up the shrine before being released to set up their tents, so that was not an issue or a chore she was shirking. After a short while watching the bustle, she noticed Tigh doing some sword training off to the side of the encampment. The extra training would do her good and she had wanted to talk to Tigh about the whole Sword thing, since Tigh was so dedicated to becoming one.

Tigh stopped moving through one of the sword forms the Hands taught as Asche neared, raising an eyebrow questioningly. Asche shrugged. "I need to get better and you were training, so I wanted to ask if we could train together."

"Don't see why not." Tigh shrugged herself, gesturing to the open area around her with her raven's head sword. "Warm up with one of the forms and then we'll spar."

Asche did that, moving her raven head sword through the basic patterns of attack and defense she had been taught weeks ago. After riding all day, it felt good to stretch this way, and her body began to shift more smoothly. The movements were becoming more natural, easier, fluid, the sword beginning to feel like an extension of her arm. After she was more warmed up, they began sparring.

The main focus for Asche was trying to move past the forms and into being able to fight with her sword without relying on rote memorization of patterns. Sparring had shown quite clearly fights were far more fluid and you could never be positive what a person was going to do in response. This way she could learn how to be effective.

It did not take long for her to start moving better. The flow of the back and forth between them was going well. Feeling more comfortable, Asche took this chance to ask, "So, I was told you wanted to become a Sword?"

Tigh grinned and neatly disarmed Asche. Tigh chuckled as Asche grumbled her way to her sword. "Yes. I've worked with a couple of them since I've joined the Hands. They were really motivating to work with. It's been my focus for a while now."

Asche nodded and returned to the sparring, as she still had to improve and this was the only way. "So, you just train hard?"

Tigh was quiet a moment before she responded. "From what they told me, there's a calling. A moment where you're in a place and time, where everything is right and something changes. It happens to some girls their first year and to others after ten. It's a place where training, need, and desire all come together in a moment, where you stretch toward the Morri and she reaches back."

As they circled each other closely, Asche followed along with what Tigh was saying. She wondered if her experience was familiar. "Do you have dreams of the forge?"

Tigh completed a move, sliding behind Asche and bringing her blade to mark a successful strike to the back. She stepped back, to indicate a pause in the sparring. "The forge? Occasionally I do, where I am assisting her at the forge, kind of like the first time I saw her. We are usually busy working a billet of steel." Tight looked at her intently. "You too?"

"Yeah." Asche swallowed. So, it wasn't just her. But it had to mean something...right? "Is it connected to being a Sword or a Hammer?"

Tigh shrugged. "That's a priestess question, not a me question. I fight, I don't know all the secrets of the Morri."

"So, you have no opinion?"

"I don't know enough to have an opinion," said Tigh. "If it's a thing, it's not something the two Swords I knew ever mentioned to me. But it does make sense, that seeing more of the Morri would be connected. Heh...maybe we'll both end up becoming Swords. The Hands could use them."

"Could use them?" Asche was not sure why the Hands might need Swords and Hammers. This was all so new to her.

"Sure. We work for the Morri, so it helps if we have people amongst us who are close to the Morri but aren't priestesses. The priestesses work hard on the other aspects of the Morri's faith, but we're the ones who go out and do things, her tools in the greater world. In a way, it's like having a martial priestess."

"Not because they're the better fighters?"

"Well, if they're anything like the ones I knew, they're usually excellent fighters, but not always the best. There is more to all of that than being a great fighter, otherwise there would probably be more Swords and Hammers. It's like...there is a connection between them and the Morri that is...profound. And it doesn't hurt they can call forth her power like some of the priestesses can."

They began sparring again. With all the thoughts this conversation was bringing up, Asche had an even harder time concentrating on the fight. She didn't even tag Tigh in the last pass where there had been an opening she had been too slow to capitalize on. "So, what's the difference between a Sword and a Hammer?"

"One of the Swords I knew mentioned Swords were forged for battle, while Hammers were forged for themselves. I've never been able to figure out that one. I mean, I'm busy trying to forge myself into a Sword, so shouldn't that make me a Hammer?"

Asche shrugged and managed to tag Tigh on her outer forearm. Tigh beamed at her. "Oh yes, that's a good one. Let's work on that specific move a few times, to make sure you can do it at will. Taking an opponent's arm is far better than simply disarming them in a lot of cases."

After a more than few repetitions of the move, Asche felt like she might be able to work that into her fighting. She had to admit, if she could score that blow against someone as canny as Tigh, she would no doubt finish an actual fight rather easily. Before they could keep at the sparring, Fanlis came up and called out, "Asche, with me."

Asche sheathed her raven's head and thanked Tigh for the spar before hustling after Fanlis as she hurried toward the ducal encampment.

# CHAPTER NINETEEN

Asche raced forward a few steps to catch up with Fanlis. As she matched pace with her she asked, "You need me?"

Fanlis handed over her bag that Asche noted included her scribe gear. "Yes, I want you to take notes for me during the meeting. We're going to be planning our assault and need to coordinate with the duke's men."

"Do we often work with the duke?"

"Occasionally. Working with the temporal leaders at times is helpful, though they are occasionally sources of the problem we're facing, like this particular baron for instance. We do the goddess's work and they don't, though there is some crossover."

"Such as slavers?"

Fanlis nodded, a bit distracted as they neared the pavilion where the duke's commander was. "Such as slavers. You'll also need to talk about Nibs and maybe call him in when we explain how he has been rather helpful to us. They will probably not believe it when we tell them."

Asche was still unsure what all the differences were, though the fact they were not under the command of the ducal forces was interesting. Growing up, she learned the ducal forces controlled everything and it was a person's duty to obey all commands from His Grace. There was just so much about the Hands she did not know and wanted to. If she was going to do this, really commit to this new life, then she wanted to do it the best she could. Besides, the Morri had fixed a problem that had plagued Asche with no known remedy, so there was that debt Asche wanted to pay as well.

They reached the ducal camp and their camp was set up somewhat differently from the way the Hands did it. The camp was set up so everything was surrounding the central large pavilion in more of a circle, providing extra protection to the commander but not as much organization to the rest of the camp. Even the layering of the tent placement was designed to limit straight line approaches to the pavilion, except for one route. The Hands just set tents out in lines. The command tent was also in the center and maybe the same size as four regular tents put together, but approaches were far more direct.

There were two guards standing in front of the pavilion with spears, who came to attention as Fanlis approached. Fanlis and Asche headed inside where Kaitan Tanrei waited, along with the kaitan of the other company, Ginvert, and her adjutant. The others in the tent were a fancily dressed older gentleman with a well-groomed beard, and two other middle-aged men, wearing chainmail hauberks over finely made gambesons. Tanrei spotted Fanlis and nodded. "Good you're here."

Tanrei began her part of the brief. "As I mentioned, the bandits we captured in Gehrlen were working with a troop of slavers. After going through what documents they had, and interrogations, we noted they claimed there was a slaver camp here in the duchy. We had no more than that until we intercepted a different group and through interrogation discovered the baron was involved and that the place in question was likely his town, Overdorfs. There was also mention of a servant of the Tyner, which can complicate things."

The older man nodded thoughtfully. "Once the farspeaker passed on what had been discovered, we hastily assembled this force. Duke Barvith knew the Hands would go after such a den of iniquity, but if the local baron was involved, he would have to take matters into his hands as well, based on the charter. Our aim therefore is to capture the baron, alive preferably, so he can face ducal justice. To prey on the people of the duchy is unconscionable and a direct violation of the oaths of investiture."

The other kaitan spoke up at this. "I agree, Lord Whiltaen, and the Morri feels the same. However, the fact remains that the baron is in a well-positioned and walled town, he even has a small keep, plus given its placement on the border, a decent-sized garrison. That will make getting in to arrest the man tricky, as he can just turtle up, especially as we do not know what forces he has at his command."

Lord Whiltaen gestured and one of the other men unrolled a map onto the table showing a walled town and some of the land around it. "Thankfully, the baron was due for the ducal survey last year, so we have a decent idea as to what he has available in terms of layout and forces. If this has been an ongoing issue, which we believe it is, he did clear out some of the forces at his command, to be sure. As it is, we know he has access to the general levy, plus a company-sized element of formal troops under his banner. Those troops are the town's guard and a small forward unit of ducal forces, whose job it is to watch the border. There are even one or two knights who answer to him. We feel it's likely those troops have been suborned. As for the town itself, the baron had been slowly converting the walls of his keep into stone. Last year they had completed the gatehouse. The walls of the keep should be finished by the end of this season or next."

"So, company plus strength, a walled town, a small keep with mostly stone walls, and who knows how many irregular forces, plus a priest of the Tyner. This is not going to be easy," said Kaitan Tanrei as she looked over the map. "You know, from what this shows, there is also a decent cleared area about the town, except at the very back of the valley it's situated in."

One of Lord Whiltaen's men replied, "That's true. One idea we have for an approach is for one company of Hand to move through the mountainous area at their rear, while our forces come in at the front, as a sort of surprise inspection of sorts. If the other company of Hand is nearby and rush in after we have taken the first gatehouse, that might allow us to regain the ducal troops as the ducal banner will be flying, and sow a little discord amongst their forces."

The two kaitans regarded the map and pondered this. Kaitan Ginvert spoke up. "Not a bad notion, my lord. Given you have primarily a cavalry force with you, that could work, though the fighting in the town is not suited to that. I think we need to send out reconnaissance troops to get a better lay of the land as it is now. That might give us a better idea of what the actual numbers we might face are. We can move forces closer while the recon is ongoing. That way, when they return, we can move and strike fairly quickly. They can also scout out a path through the mountains for the rest of the troops. I can send one unit for my company's foray at the front gate and Tanrei can try to find a different entrance."

Fanlis looked over at Kaitan Tanrei questioningly. Tanrei held her gaze a moment before nodding. "There is some additional assistance we can bring to bear, especially in the area of reconnaissance. There is a raven who has taken a shine to one of our new recruits, my assistant here, and has been helping us with scouting. Since he can literally look down on the town from above, he might be able to give us a better idea of what we shall face inside the town, in terms of numbers and building placement."

The others seemed somewhat staggered by this notion, as they all had looks of disbelief. One of Lord Whiltaen's aides scoffed, and said, "And you can trust this bird to provide accurate information?"

"It has warned us of approaching slavers, who we were able to capture and interrogate. He has proven his use," said Tanrei, no humor at all in her tone.

"You are aware it does sound unbelievable," said Lord Whiltaen.

"Which makes it all the more likely the raven will not be noticed as it flies about, scouting the town. Honestly, who would suspect a raven of spying?" said Fanlis.

Lord Whiltaen inclined his head in acknowledgement. "A valid point. That sounds like a workable plan to be a fuller reconnaissance. Is it possible to meet this raven?"

Fanlis and Kaitan Tanrei turned to stare at Asche. Her cheeks heated a little as she stepped outside and gave a loud, sharp whistle then one that slid up and down in pitch. She had used this before, back in Oxlen, when she had seen him flying. In short order, Nibs landed on her outstretched arm and cocked his head quizzically at her.

Asche walked inside and turned to face Lord Whiltaen. "My lord, this is Nibs the raven."

Lord Whiltaen said, "I am told you can speak. Is this true?"

Nibs bobbed his head. Asche and Fanlis glared at him. This was not helping their case.

One of the aides snickered at this. "Ah yes, your famous talking crow."

Before either Asche or Fanlis could say anything, Nibs leapt from Asche's arm onto the table. He locked eyes with the aide and stomped across the table toward them. He snapped his wings wide with a rustle of sound and screamed out, "Kraaa! I not stupid crow, you turkey! Go stand in rain!"

Everyone stared, except Asche and Fanlis, who were both palming their faces. Asche was actually trying to keep from snickering. Lord Whiltaen was the first to find his voice. "Uhm… why did you call him a turkey?"

Nibs cocked his head to the side, appraising Whiltaen carefully before turning back to the aide and leaning forward menacingly. "Turkey stupid. Rain hit head, look up and drown."

The aide turned red in the face, while Whiltaen, Tanrei, and Ginvert all turned their laughs into coughs. "I think we can trust what the raven says," the other aide said.

Nibs hopped back to the other side of the desk and onto Asche's arm. While Asche escorted Nibs outside, he muttered, "Turkey."

"Thank you, Nibs. I'll see you when the meeting is over. Have Elsif get you some cheese."

Nibs perked up at this and took flight toward where their company was billeted. Asche returned to the command tent and stood by Fanlis.

Lord Whiltaen was speaking. "We need to find an appropriate meeting point for our forward movement and then send out the scouting elements. I hope one day of rest shall be enough for your troops to recover to be sent out on this."

"That should be fine, your lordship," said Tanrei. "I suggest Kaitan Ginvert's troops stay here and make sure the baron does not have scouts this far out."

Kaitan Ginvert nodded. "That's what I have them doing at the moment anyway, so it makes sense. Besides, two of your rangers are supposedly extremely good at this sort of mission, so it would make sense to use their skills."

"Good. Then we have the start of a plan. Prepare your troops. Ginvert and Tanrei, please stay so we can hammer out a forward meeting spot and discuss further tactics for the coming battle."

Fanlis and Asche left the tent, moving with purpose. Fanlis took the scribe gear from Asche with a shake of her head. "Asche, go find Terris and have her come to my tent. After that, make sure your gear is ready. This will be a difficult mission so have everything you might need. Then eat. We may not have a chance out at the field, unless the other company has some prepared food we can take."

"Yes, ma'am." Asche began to hustle back to their encampment, hoping that finding Sarnt Terris would be easy. Thankfully, it was. It did not take long to find her and pass on the message. She then began to look for Elsif. Nibs found Asche first, flaring his wings to slow down before alighting on her shoulder. She gave him a distracted smile and said, "Hey, Nibs."

"Why rushing?"

"The rangers are heading out tomorrow. You and I need to get ready. I also wanted to find Elsif."

"Elsif training. No cheese for Nibs." He sounded so deeply sad. "We go?"

"Yes. We need to scout out the bad guy's place. You'll be especially helpful," said Asche as she slowed down. If Elsif was training, maybe she should see to her own gear first. And likely get Nibs some cheese. She altered her direction to the company's wagons.

Nibs replied, "Always helpful."

Aware that ordering Nibs to do something was folly at best, she figured giving him a reason to do this would be helpful. "This time you get to figure out where the bad guys are grouped, what the inside of the town is like, and more. You'll be a hero."

Nibs cocked his head and looked questioningly at Asche. "I already hero."

"Well, more of a hero."

"How much more?" Nibs asked, head cocked to the side.

"I don't know, lots?" This conversation was making her want to pound her head into a tree.

Nibs bobbed his head, making an odd noise that made Asche stop and turn to stare at him. "You want to help, right?"

Nibs turned his head to stare at her as if she was a puzzle. "Said yes."

"That bawoop noise was an agreement?"

Nibs made a deep sigh that reminded her of the sigh of frustration Father Tombol made whenever something she had done vexed him. It was a sound she had heard more than thrice. Asche felt a bit chastised by Nibs. "Sorry."

"Not fault. Humans not smart like ravens."

Asche glared at him and huffed in annoyance. Nibs found this hilarious and chuckled a few times. They reached the wagons and she had one of the cooks hand over a piece of cheese. Nibs took it and then flew off toward the local shrine.

Asche began preparing for the upcoming mission. Getting her gear ready was simple, as she had done that before their march here. None of the actions they had done enroute had marred her gear anyway, though she did want to rub some more of the dubbin she had into her boots, to increase the waterproofing and soften the leather. Rations were all she honestly needed for the mission, but she figured Sarnt Terris would arrange that with the cooks. She got out her polishing rag and began to work the dubbin into her boots, taking care to work it nicely into the seams, where leaks would be most common.

Once that was completed, Asche found Elsif, who had just finished her training and was headed back. She smiled at Elsif but was not really feeling happiness. Elsif furrowed her brows a little and asked, "Hey, you okay? You look flustered."

"The rangers take off tomorrow to scout the town. Probably won't see you for a bit as we need to prepare the entry points and such." She rubbed the back of her neck. While this was not her first combat, this one was already looking to be a big one.

"Okay. That's annoying, but that's the job, right?" Elsif shrugged as they made their way back to the tent. "We promised to do the job, so let's do it."

"You aren't nervous?"

Elsif sat on her bedroll next to Asche. "Sure, but it's not like it's going to change things. At least I have good armor, a good weapon, and a shield. That makes me a bit more comfortable. You don't have those things, so I am worried."

Asche's eyes narrowed. "You don't think I can do it?"

Elsif held up her hands, palms out. "That's not what I said. From what we were briefed on I know you will be up on that wall, in less armor, exposed until we get up there. I…I don't want to lose you."

"I don't want to lose you either. We're still at the beginning of things and I want…more of us. I'm just…scared something might happen, to either of us."

Elsif cupped Asche's cheek. "Well then, we just need to make tonight special then, so you have plenty of motivation to return safe and sound."

They hugged and Elsif kissed the top of her head. Asche relaxed into Elsif's stronger arms and wondered at just how special it could be when surrounded by everyone else. Regardless, she was determined to make the most of this time.

They lowered onto the bedrolls and the kissing was more intense than ever before, fueled by worry, desire, need. When Elsif kissed and nipped softly at her neck, Asche had to swallow a moan, as she did not want to share this moment with the rest of the camp. Elsif was slowly working her tunic free from her belt, and she shifted her hips upward to make the task easier.

When the tunic was free, Elsif's warm hand met her flesh, light and burning. Everything they had done so far had been through clothes, and this, this touch, skin on skin, set everything tingling. As Elsif's hand slowly dragged up her side to rest on her stomach…she bit her lip to keep another moan trapped from full throated release. Asche felt her nipples tighten, and her skin grew ever more sensitive to the slightest touch. Elsif's kisses worked down her throat, to linger in the hollow of her neck. Elsif's hand moved through her hair, tightening its grip at the base of her neck, making her head tilt farther back.

Elsif shifted and captured her lips again, needier, more forceful. Asche cupped Elsif's head, drawing her closer and deepened the kiss. Their vocalized pleasure was muffled and then Elsif's hand moved again, to slide up her stomach, where it hesitated for the briefest moment at the base of her breast. The hand then began a slow progression toward the peak. It was maddening, the time it was taking and Asche arched her back, searching for more contact with Elsif's hand. The slow tracing around her nearly aching nipple made her pant. Elsif's attention traveled to her neck, where she began kissing and lightly sucking on Asche's tender skin.

At the moment of contact, when Elsif reached the peak and rolled fingers then her palm over the nipple, Asche's voice was guttural and unrestrained. Elsif whispered a shush just as she tweaked the nipple with finger and thumb. The slight pain rushed through her body in a wave making her whole body crave more. Elsif cupped her breast and strengthened her grip, intensifying the feelings Asche was having.

Asche began to drive her own kisses forward, taking the initiative, though every time Elsif's palm traveled circles over her nipple it made her nostrils widen as she breathed in sharply. Elsif began moaning as Asche began kissing her neck. When she tightened her hand on Elsif's neck, Elsif tilted her neck back, ragged stuttering breaths came out. Elsif shuddered over her.

The battle for who was driving things moved back and forth with tugs, soft bites, pinches, deep kisses, pulled tunics, warm lips on stiff peaks, and finally, Elsif slid her hand down Asche's braies and she was lost in sensation.

Far later, Asche was sitting between Elsif's legs as a fire crackled happily. Flit was playing a gittern, while Lynarra played a wooden flute. It was a lively tune and filled with life and happiness. Fanlis had told a story of the Hands earlier, about some battle or other. There was light applause when the tune finished. Elles got the others to play a specific song, while she played the bones and sang, a clear soprano voice that dueled the flute for heights. Nibs opened his eyes from a branch he was roosting on. At the chorus, he joined in with the others with a hearty wawawa!

Everyone laughed and they toasted to Nibs's musical genius. Asche grinned as she chuckled. Life really was pretty good now.

❖

When the heat and sound of the forge enveloped her, Asche was momentarily confused, and looked about to figure out where she was. She remembered falling asleep in Elsif's arms after making love again, and hadn't that been something. She had not been aware of just how much touch could feel like fire, or how pleasure could dance along her spine. The physical reactions she had before being found were so very different as to be basically incomparable. She blinked a few times, and tried to convince herself that the heat in her cheeks were due solely to the forge. She spotted the Morri by the forge, pulling on the bellows. The light from the coke was brightening and fading the light in the space. The goddess looked over her shoulder and spotted Asche. "Ah you're back."

"Yes, my lady." Asche moved forward and took over pulling the bellows. She tried to match the slow, steady pace the Morri had set. The Morri helped until it matched what she required.

"Good. Keep the heat steady. We don't want the steel to get too hot too fast." The Morri used the tongs to turn the billet of steel she was working on. Her eyes were intent on the steel, judging its color. "I can see you have learned more of the joys of your form. Good. You have questions?"

Asche's cheeks burned at the thought that the goddess knew what she had been up to before this. Direct questioning like this had not happened in the dream before. "Uhm…uh…yes, it was wonderful."

The Morri smiled at her with some mischief in her eyes that Asche could not figure out. "I've still been thinking about the Swords."

The Morri chuckled. "Of course you have. Your steel is strong enough to endure that type of forging, if that is what you want."

Asche swallowed at that statement. It was unexpected for many reasons. She desperately wanted to talk about something else, in some area she felt worthy. "Tigh commented she has been trying to become a Sword for a while now. If Swords are important to you, what is she missing? Why hasn't she been chosen?"

The Morri was quiet a moment, as she continued to work the bellows slow and steady. "You are here, with me. I am willing to answer questions for you on anything that you want, and you choose to ask about someone else?"

The heat from the coke was making her dizzy, and the smells of the forge were also not helping. "Well, maybe that will help me decide?"

The Morri chuckled. "I see." She spent a few moments observing the steel in the forge. "Tigh is awaiting the moment of her quench, where her steel moves from being forged and shaped, to where the Sword starts to take on its final characteristics. What's more, she knows it, inside. Everyone faces a moment in their life where their true steel is brought forth, where their strengths and flaws come together as their life takes on its shape. When one is called to be a Sword or a Hammer, that process takes on some additional stress."

"So, it is a moment of challenge?" Asche tried to grasp the specifics, but it was not really coming into form.

The Morri pulled free the billet and began hammering it out, thinning the steel before folding it over. "Mostly. You see, this moment varies from person to person, sometimes quite wildly. To tell you the truth, the arrival of the moment is not up to me, but rather up to the steel itself, the person. It lets me know, through little signs in the color of the steel and how it feels to me. Tigh will know what to do when that moment eventually comes for her, just as it does with all who try to refine their steel into something greater. As smith, I watch all of this development, nurturing it. I want people to truly become the best of their steel. Now, Asche, do you want to work on your steel to see where we go together?"

Asche nodded, at a loss for words.

The Morri beckoned her forward. "Then grab a hammer and join me."

## CHAPTER TWENTY

The hillside they moved up had flat rock bits jutting out creating a sort of natural set of stairs. The steps weren't even in any way, but Asche had to admit it looked odd compared to the hills near her village. Trees filled spaces where the rocks were not, making the climb difficult. Given that some of the steps were several feet in height, it was quite enough to hamper free movement along the slope. The rangers scampered up the hill, rather than simply hiking it.

This terrain was common in this region by the border, making farming and logging a good bit trickier. Fields would no doubt need to be cleared of all the rock before they could be used, and that would not be an easy task. The rocks and steps did seem more prominent along the hillsides, but there were sections of these "stairs" in fields they had spotted, creating islands in the tilled earth. In some ways it would certainly make the town safer to be ringed by such hills, as heavy infantry and cavalry would not be able to effectively move in such terrain. They were certain that was the thinking of the baron. However, this terrain was a gift to the recon troops as it provided a good deal of cover as they moved.

After stopping just under the crest, the rangers darkened their faces, ears, and hands with a mix of dirt and ash that became a paste when they added some water. Then they got out their shaggies and began to use twigs and branches from the bushes around them, making the outfits look more like their surroundings. Fanlis looked at everyone and nodded. "You all know your tasks. Let's get this done and do it right."

At the crest, they began to crouch and move, using the natural stairs and trees to completely cover their movement from the walls of the village they could just begin to see. The towers of the keep were higher still but did not have many rear-facing windows or guards upon the parapet. It was clear, even in a cursory glance, there was a decent presence of city guard on the walls. Each tower along the wall had several people in them and the walls had people patrolling. Sneaking over the walls would be difficult unless the conditions were right. Nibs landed on a branch over Asche, who was carrying a copy of the village map provided by Lord Whiltaen. She already made a notation about the towers and the guardsmen, as these details would be important for planning the specifics of their attack. Nibs croaked, getting her attention.

She looked up at him. "Are you ready?"

Nibs bobbed in agreement.

"And you remember the things Fanlis wants you to find out?" Asche really wanted Nibs to more than prove himself in this. That aide to Whiltaen had irritated her and Nibs with his doubts. She was well aware of how helpful Nibs could be, but more people needed to know about it. If his flight went well, it might make the man shut up for good.

Nibs looked down at her in a way that made her feel chided. "Know."

"Okay. Be safe. I'll be here." She watched Nibs fly off toward the village, and she kept her eyes out to see if she could spot the team moving closer on each side. Tigh and Elles were barely visible and that was only because they were hiding from viewers on the wall instead of those behind them. She refocused on what her task was. Since she could write well, and was still in training, her task was to make notes and observations. She went back to making notations on any variations between the map Lord Whiltean had and the state of the town now. She could only notice obvious things from this distance. The most important notes would come from Nibs, Tigh, and Elles.

Terris moved over to her, slowly dragging herself forward on the ground. Once alongside Asche, she reached into a satchel and pulled out a spyglass. "Here, this will help you see better while you are comparing map to what is there. You'll be alone up here while Flit, Fanlis, and I scout best routes for rest of company to move in. You should make blind if you want to be harder to spot while using glass. Remember, those on wall have same detail issue you have. Go slow and they won't register what you are doing."

Asche nodded. As Terris moved toward her left and down the slope, Asche looked about for fallen wood and brush she could use to build a blind to better blend into the terrain here. It did not take long to locate the materials needed to set up the improvised lean-to. Once finished, she crawled inside, got into a more comfortable working position, and opened the spyglass to better examine the village. The first thing she did was to watch the guard along the wall section closest to her to see if there was any reaction to her blind. Not seeing any change in the pattern of their patrols or any one peering in her direction, she felt safe enough to get back to it.

Using the spyglass, Asche spotted a few details she hadn't been able to discern earlier. It looked like parts of the baron's keep had been reinforced beyond what the map indicated. The map indicated a wooden palisade around the backside, and now there was evidence of stone walls. From what she could make out, the only thing in their favor was that the walls were incomplete. The back was protected, it had likely been the first section worked on, but the sides had unfinished spots as did the front part of the keep, from what she could tell at this angle. The village itself still had just the wooden palisade. The juncture of the walls looked rough and was a clear entry point.

As she watched those walls and the ongoing construction, it seemed as if the baron was using slaves for labor. She noted a couple of times where workers were whipped. She frowned, made a notation, and moved on. If there were slaves there, which seemed likely, she needed to find where they were being kept. She tried to examine the village, but there was no clear sign from this angle of where they were being kept. It would take eyes closer to make out any detail like that.

❖

Nibs had flown in a wide circle around the village before gliding down, noting there were only a few birds about and specifically no ravens. He spotted a trio of crows on one rooftop and groaned as he realized what he was going to have to do. Talking to crows was the worst. They were just so annoying and simple, and it was a good bet one of them would pull on his tail feathers. Crows thought this was the height of humor, and he did not want to play with them. Granted, tail pulling was funny, but not when done to him. He was actually working and wanted to get that over with before he got infected with the human love of always working. He had spotted an ant mound near where the rangers had paused before going over the crest. Rolling on that would be relaxing and would maybe wash away the stink of actually working.

He alighted on a building and looked around. There were people moving about the village, but they seemed subdued, moving with heads down and with purpose. They seemed scared, wanting to avoid notice as if a predator was in the area. When he spotted a patrol of rough-looking men, similar to the bandits the company had fought, it was clear what danger the people were reacting to. Predators were indeed about.

He moved about the village, winging from rooftop to rooftop, trying to see where the bandits were holed up. He moved about randomly, trying not to have a pattern to his searches, even going so far as to swoop down and steal food once or twice. It made him appear to simply be a regular raven. After coming up from his second snatch, a bit of hot sausage roll, a group of crows came up around him. Nibs sighed; he did not have time to deal with this.

"Hi!" called out one of the crows from his left side.

"Hi," Nibs replied after he had scarfed down the snatched treat. He wanted to keep his search going.

"Hi!" called out one of the crows from his right side.

"I said hello," replied Nibs in frustration. "What do you want?"

"Talk," said a different bird.

"We are talking," said Nibs, knowing he was not being helpful. They might be able to provide him with information he was looking for, so dealing with their inane chatter could pay off. But crows always annoyed him.

"Land and talk."

Nibs spotted a group of crows on a rooftop and circled to land nearby. His escorts landed as well, staying close and watching what he was doing. An elderly crow hopped his way. The other crows neared and that made it obvious how much larger Nibs was compared to them. He was nearly twice their height. Nibs looked at the elderly crow and asked, "Yes, elder?"

"Passing through or staying?" At least he was direct, thought Nibs.

"Passing through, mostly," replied Nibs, not wanting to lie but concerned about the possibility the crows had aligned themselves with the slavers. It was unlikely, but who knew with crows.

"Mostly?"

Instead of waiting for the crows to dance around what they wanted answers for, he went straight for something he wanted to know. "Are you friends to the humans of this village?"

The elder cocked his head, thinking before replying. "No. The human in the stone house does not like us, throws stones, shoots at us with arrows. New human with him tries to have more people shoot at us. They have even killed a few of us that way. We stay in the village or the forest mostly. They are not friends."

Nibs relaxed a bit, one of his worries eased. He might be able to get them to help, which could ensure his ridiculous human survived. He yelped as one of his tail feathers was pulled, and he spun, glaring at the crow who flapped away laughing. He was about to give chase when the elder cawed out, "Enough. Not while I am talking."

All the other crows murmured, "Yes, elder."

The elder turned back to Nibs. "You asked for reason?"

Nibs bobbed his head. "I am friends to some humans who are coming to get rid of the human in the stone house and all his friends, including the new human, the one you say has killed your people."

The group of crows cawed excitedly. The elder squawked for attention a few times before the chattering stopped. After glowering at them, the elder turned back to Nibs. "What help do you need?"

Nibs croaked happily. This certainly would make his task easier. "I need to know where the smelly and angry ones stay, if they have other humans trapped somewhere, how many there are."

One of the other crows replied excitedly, "We can land on roofs where the angry smelly humans are. That way you can see."

Another cawed out, "There is a barn where humans are kept. They aren't allowed out to do anything but work."

Nibs bobbed his head. "Good. Good. If you can go off and land on the roofs, I can do the rest."

"You will get rid of the new human?" asked another, looking around at the other crows with concern.

"Yes. The new human is enemy to my friends, as is the one who lives in the stone fort. We mean to get rid of them." Nibs was certain of that.

The elder bobbed his head. "Good. Good. Fly now and show this raven where they are. When you come to fight, how can we help?"

Nibs pondered as a group of crows began to fly off into the rest of the village. He looked around and noted one of the wall sentries was armed with a bow and would likely use it in the coming battle. That gave him a workable idea. "The ones who can shoot, when they are trying to do so into my friends, fly toward their faces. That should disrupt their shots. Otherwise, stay safe."

The elder nodded. "Spoil the shot, not take it?"

"Yes. Humans don't like things flying toward their faces. And there is no reason for any of you to get hurt. If they are focusing on my friends, they won't see you until you are flying at their face. They will flinch, ruin the shot."

"Good to know. Thank you, raven." The elder bowed his head.

"Thank you, crow elder." Nibs bowed his head, then turned at the sound of one of the crows behind him, before squawking when the elder tugged at one of his tail feathers. He spun back and glared at the elder, who was laughing and hopping away from him. Nibs huffed and took to the air, winding higher to get a better view of the village. He could spot where the crows gathered, one building near the main gate, another in the center of the town, and a third by the barn the crows had mentioned. This would be very helpful. He took the time to memorize where they were.

The barn was of some concern, as he turned to glide toward it. Nibs knew the Hands were against slavery and knowing where the slaves were could allow the Hands to do something to prevent more deaths. Drifting down more, Nibs noticed there were guard patrols around the barn, which made him think the crows were right. Thankfully, there was no one on the roof.

Nibs landed on the gable and looked around, hoping to spot some sort of entrance so he could have a better look. After some searching, Nibs noticed a gap. As he hopped closer, he could tell it was clear some other bird had used this entryway. He moved closer to the entrance and could smell owl. Nibs paused to consider that. If the owl was in there, where it likely made its roost, it would not be pleased to see him and would either attack or raise a fuss. Neither was something he could really afford.

Getting closer, Nibs could not yet tell if the owl was still inside. This was daytime, and if the owl's roost was in there, this would get awkward fast. He could smell dirty human, which was almost a sign, but some of the bandits smelled like this and they certainly had not been slaves. Nibs looked but could not see the owl. He hoped this was not a usual roost with a possible nest but rather a hunting area. Surely there would be mice rummaging through the straw. Actually, a mouse sounded good right now, but he reminded himself that he was working. He could have a snack later.

Down below, in the gloom of the poorly lit barn, there were a number of large cages with multiple people crammed in them, many of them grumbling or moaning in discomfort. There were ten cages he could see, and Nibs had no idea how many people were in them, but it was clearly a lot. The Hands would be pleased to know this, as they wanted to free all these people. He did not see anyone that struck him as being a Hand or priestess, so if they were not here, they would be kept somewhere else.

Nibs took to the air once he returned outside, glad to be rid of the stench. There was only one place left to check before he could go off and play some, the keep. This was not something Nibs was looking forward to, as there were more guards about who looked better armed and armored than the ones on the city walls. And there was that report of the new human who liked to shoot crows and ravens. But it had to be done.

He wafted over the keep, trying to see what differences he could spot without getting closer. Asche would want to know those details for her map, and he was trying to help. Realizing he needed to get closer if he was going to get the most detail possible, he spiraled down to land on the roof of one of the towers, one that was still primarily wood. This gave him a good view of the building and the courtyard of the keep. It looked well protected to Nibs, at least from ground creatures, and that meant a threat to his favorite human.

There seemed to be a weak spot where the walls switched from stone to wood. He noticed the doors of the main stone building open, and out strode a man dressed a little like the Hands, with armor and a symbol on his outer baldric that he had never seen before, two crossed swords, one gold and one red. The gold sword had a crown around the hilt, and the red one had three drips coming off it in the same red. Come to think of it, a number of the guards at the gatehouse had the same symbol on their gear. The man surveyed the courtyard and then glanced up and spotted Nibs. Nibs could feel the focus on him sharpen.

When the man turned and said something to one of the guardsmen nearby, Nibs took off into the air, flapping hard to gain both altitude and speed. He wanted to keep this threat in view to avoid surprise, which meant his path was not the most efficient. The man took a bow and arrow from the guard, nocked, drew, and fired in one smooth motion. The arrow sped straight and true toward Nibs, with the arrowhead a dull, pulsing red color.

Giving a squawk of surprise, Nibs pulled his wings in close, canceling his lift. The arrow sped right through where he had been, as he plummeted at least twenty feet. Maneuvering quickly behind the building, Nibs flapped away from the village at top speed, the muscles of his wings and back aching with the effort. He remained in cover as best he could, and he tried to not head straight back to where Asche was hidden. The arrow had missed him by less than a feather's width and that was far too close. The man with the crossed swords on his clothes was a danger and Nibs needed to share what he had learned. This was more of a threat to Asche than he had thought before.

## Chapter Twenty-One

Asche spotted Nibs drop and her heart went to her throat. It was farther than he usually fell when playing, and she began to breathe when the wings snapped open and he began weaving back and forth in the sky. She was worried. She looked at the keep with the spyglass to see if she could spot the cause of that fall and saw a well armored man rush up to the walls, bow in hand, and take another shot, but this one was nowhere near Nibs, who was gaining altitude and heading off to her right side, flapping harder than she had ever seen. She focused on this man and saw the symbol on his baldric. She'd have to ask Sarnt Terris or Fanlis, but this was likely the priest of the Tyner.

There wasn't much she could tell about the man, besides noting his dark hair, broad shoulders, and that he could handle a bow easily. Given what the Tyner was associated with, it made sense that a priest of his would have martial skills. In fact, it would be more of a surprise if they did not have those skills. She watched him glare at the retreating Nibs and then scan the area, both the hillside and near the walls. She held her breath and hoped no one was moving at that moment.

The priest turned and stormed away, shoving the bow into some guardsman's chest as he passed them. Asche let out a breath when the man was finally out of sight. She had gotten all the notes she could from her vantage point and would have to wait until Nibs or the other Hands returned to fill in additional spots. From what she could see, no troops were running about preparing for battle, nor were they coming around the walled village in a patrol. The baron seemed content to have patrols solely on the walls. That was something at least.

After a while, Nibs flew over to her from behind and hopped into the blind to stay out of sight of the keep. Asche sighed in relief, looking him over to ensure he was not injured. She skritched a spot on his head that he appreciated. "I was worried."

"I good." Nibs turned his head deeper into the skritch. "Got info."

Asche grinned at him. "Well, let me get ready so I can write it all down."

Nibs relayed all he learned from his flyovers and the crows. It was a good bit of detail and Asche dutifully wrote it all down. By the time he had finished telling Asche all of it, the other Hands had returned and were gathered at the back of the blind. The sun had crossed a good deal of the sky, but as summer was nearing, there was still plenty of daylight left. Asche wrote as fast as she could as they all relayed what they had discovered and confirmed.

There were several easy routes in, the majority of which involved the weakness Nibs had spotted. It was also noted there was no special attention given to those spots, as if the guards were unaware of the weak spot in the defense. They even noted that despite there being a ditch around the back of the keep, it was not going to be a significant enough deterrent, as the village's palisade did not have a similar trench. The baron was clearly more concerned with his own safety rather than his people's.

Fanlis and Terris both looked concerned when Nibs described the guardsmen at the gatehouse who had the same symbol on their baldrics as the priest of the Tyner. Fanlis shook her head and sighed. "It was to be expected. A priest of the Tyner would be unlikely to travel about with some of their Blades."

Asche and Nibs cocked their heads at the same time, which made several of the others snicker. "Blades?"

Fanlis nodded. "Yes. The Blades of the Tyner are similar to the Hands. They are really good warriors. Their presence makes this harder." Fanlis looked over Asche's notes and then gave a firm nod. "I think we got what we can. Nibs, thank you. Let's head back to the rendezvous and get some rest."

The platoon made their way slowly back over the hill and began to make their way through the thin woods and rocky hillside. They moved cautiously, since Nibs, having gotten the priest's attention, might have brought his attention to the area enough so that troops might get sent out. Clearing the area would make sure they were safe.

They moved faster once out of view of the highest tower of the keep, moving into a jog that would help them devour more distance. They ran like this until the sun had set and stopped when the darkness was deep enough it was no longer safe to continue. In truth, they were perhaps an hour or so from the agreed rendezvous point, but the woods were thick enough it would seriously hamper movement. Plus, they had been working all day. They opted for a cold camp, not wanting to risk a fire, and ate a cold meal of sausage, apples, and some flat breads.

Asche bundled up in her cloak, nestling into the ferns she was making her bed out of once the meal was finished. Above her, Nibs muttered as he settled himself on a branch, ruffling his feathers and changing his grip until he was comfortable. Sleep came quickly.

❖

Hiding a force the size of three companies was not a thing anyone could easily do, so there was no attempt at that sort of deception. The camp was again in a fallow field, so as not to destroy the crops the village depended on. The rangers moved out of the tree line and toward their camp, relaxing now that they were among friendlies. Fanlis, Terris, and Asche headed toward the command tent to pass along their report. Asche figured she was there because she wrote the notes and no one wanted them to read it wrong.

After their scouting report was passed and she had read her notes about the map, Asche headed out. Frankly, she was glad to be gone, as it felt odd being around all the officers. She was just a cobbler's daughter from Oxlen who barely knew what she was doing. Right now, she wanted something to eat that was more than trail rations and she wanted to see Elsif. The thought of Elsif made her smile.

As she made her way out of the camp, a few of the lord's troops made lewd remarks about her. Despite several of the other troops trying to shush the comments, her face burned, some in embarrassment and some in anger. The comments were invasive and not something she wanted to deal with as she was trying to cope with the last mission and get ready for the next. Those men seemed lackadaisical, like none of this mattered, like offending one of the Hands was of no concern. She wanted to hit them but was sure that was not something you did with allies. Sure, the sarnt had not said anything about it, but it made no sense. Why were men like that? That had been a question she had asked back before she had been found and still was no closer to an answer.

Making her way into her company's camp was a relief. There were no more idiotic men talking inappropriately. Part of her figured it was because she had been alone, and thus an easy target. This last mission had been exhausting, as they had moved as fast as could be managed both out and back. Now, she just ached and wanted to do nothing more than get some warm food and relax. Thankfully, Flit had taken her pack and dropped it at the tent she shared with Elsif. She grabbed her bowl and spoon from her pack and headed toward the smell of food cooking. The other members of her platoon were also there eating, despite the fact it was not quite mealtime.

After getting a bowl of warm stew, some bread and cheese, as well as a mug of dry cider, she headed over to the others. Not even looking up from her own bowl, Flit asked, "Any idea of what and when?"

"They kicked me out after my report." Asche shrugged and tasted some of the stew. Her eyes widened a little in surprise. "This is good."

Tigh snickered. "New girl made it. I mean truthfully, it's not really that good, but after being out on mission like that with only cold meals, something hot really does hit the spot."

The others murmured agreement as they ate. Elles stopped and had a drink of cider before commenting, "So, that's going to be a hard fight."

All of them nodded. "The patrolling around the keep seems competent, not like the bandits back at the shrine," said Asche.

Flit groaned. "Ye know…we shall be the ones to break into the keep."

Elles looked up from mopping up her stew with the bit of bread. "How do you figure?"

"Ye and Tigh are the best at sneaking 'tween both companies. Just wait."

They all shared a look then groaned, looking to Asche. "Please tell us there is an easier way into the keep than up and over the walls."

Asche nodded. She wasn't positive, but after getting the information from Nibs and the others, she had a somewhat better lay of the land. "I think so? The motte at the back means the usual points you all taught me aren't good. But you all saw, the motte only covers the back of the keep right now, not the whole village. Where the keep's new walls and village palisade meet, there is a gap according to Nibs and we can probably get in there."

They nodded and Elles grumbled. "I wonder what other jobs we'll have, besides opening up the keep."

Tigh snickered. "Something super stupid and dangerous, without a doubt. But at least we have two priestesses as backup this time. It's going to be tough enough without divine magic getting called down on our heads."

"Thanks for reminding me o'that, Tigh. I feel so much better now." Flit cursed under her breath. "We're not paid enough to fight gods."

Asche's eyes went wide. "Fighting gods?!"

Flit turned to face Asche. "Aye, 'tis happened before. On the whole, 'tis not pretty. Many people die when magic gets involved."

Asche gaped at Flit, who shook her head. "Don't worry. 'Tis very rare that the priests and priestesses get in to it like that. It's happened maybe twice in the history of the Hands."

"Ugh…this would be a terrible time for number three," said Elles. "And with it being the Morri and the Tyner…they're going to go at it with hammer and tongs."

Tigh shrugged. "All we can do is what we do, our jobs. Praying to the Morri also wouldn't hurt. I mean, an edge is an edge. And if the priestess can bless us before we head out, then we've done all we can. The rest is down to fighting our best."

Elles chuckled and shoved Tigh's shoulder. "Spoken like a true Sword wannabe."

Tigh just gave her a look, and Elles waved her off. "Fine. You'll be a Sword one day."

"Absolutely I will," said Tigh.

"The Lady said you needed to reach the moment of your quench, where your steel moves from being forged and shaped, to where the Sword takes on its final characteristics," said Asche. She was a bit distracted, as she was thinking about everything the others had said.

"I knew it!" Tigh sounded triumphant. Then reality set in. "I just wish I knew what moment that is."

Flit and Elles turned to face Asche. "Ye speak to the Morri?" said Flit.

Asche blushed, looking down at her mostly finished meal. "Well, I dream about her. I have since the first ritual. I mean, it's just a dream…right?"

Tigh shrugged. "You know, I've had those dreams as well. Intense, at the forge. Yeah, so maybe that's how she communicates to those of us who aren't her priestesses? And I've heard very few people talk about dreams like that."

Asche shrugged as well. "I guess I'll have to ask her."

Elles grinned, lifting her mug of water. "Good luck with that. Here's hoping you can manage to stay alive and get quenched."

Flit rolled her eyes. "Ye manage to make even faith sound filthy."

"It's a gift." Elles beamed at the others.

Before the conversation could continue, they spotted Kaitan Tanrei, Fanlis, and Terris heading back to camp with determined looks and moving with purpose. They all stood and took their bowls to where the dishes were being collected. The kaitan called all the troops together in an open spot in the middle of their camp.

Once everyone gathered, and Sarnt Canli nodded to the kaitan, she started to explain. "Right all, we have our specific orders. Our rangers scouted the area and a plan is being set into motion. Our primary task is the keep. Lord Whiltaen's forces will fight to open the gate to the town from the inside, letting in the other company. They will take out the bandits and slavers, securing the barn where the slaves are housed, before heading up to the keep. We will go over at the spot where the rangers spotted as a weak spot and move up from the village palisade to the keep. We need to get the keep's doors opened and hold them until Lord Whiltaen gets there. From what Nibs has said, there are Blades of the Tyner guarding the gatehouse.

"That is the primary task. Secondary to this is the capture of the baron and this priest of the Tyner, whose presence has been confirmed. But remember, that is secondary. We need to focus on getting the keep open and holding that." Fanlis unrolled a section of the map Asche had annotated and held it up while the kaitan continued. "Given that these sections of the keep's walls are being worked on and not secure, that makes our job both easier and harder. With it being a construction site, there may be footing issues and problems with getting into the gatehouse. That construction is what's allowing us entry, so I can live with some shaky footing." A few of the gathered infantry chuckled.

"Fair warning, it's possible the baron knows something's up and might get even more paranoid once Lord Whiltaen makes his presence known. We're hoping that might be the distraction we need to start working our way up and in, especially if he panics and commits troops from the keep. On each side here, where the palisade meets the keep, three ranger personnel will mount the walls, before dropping a rope ladder. That will allow us to get the infantry up and then the archers. If the entry point is secure enough, infantry can move to the gatehouse. Once there they can hopefully take out the troops inside."

Turning to face the majority of the party, Kaitan Tanrei said, "Infantry, if the rangers are visible on the wall, head there for backup. Sarnts, plan order of movement, because the hill down is a bit treacherous. There are routes marked in the usual manner you will be shown. And we plan to come in via stealth, which could be a challenge for some of you. Make sure each side has an initial team who can get close and scramble up to support the rangers. Archers, you'll guard from the outside and once the infantry forces are up, rush in so you can target anyone in the courtyard who are not Hands as well as any additional guards visible. Only once the gatehouse is fully secured can anyone go after the secondary targets. Any questions?"

Asche couldn't think of anything to ask, as the battle plan was complete from what she knew, and she was too intimidated to speak up if she had anything to say anyway. The kaitan searched everyone's faces before saying, "Right, dismissed. Tomorrow, we head out to the infiltration point the rangers established and the following morning we're going in. May the Morri bless us."

A number of others muttered, "Morri bless."

It was not difficult to find Elsif as she was looking for Asche as well. They stared into each other's eyes, Asche hoping Elsif was aware of what she felt for her. They held each other tight, hoping this would not be the last moment they had together but the battle ahead seemed dicey.

## CHAPTER TWENTY-TWO

The company moved to the spot behind the hill Fanlis had marked as the best gather point out of sight of the town. They were going to move into assault position during the cover of night and once ready, wait for Lord Whiltaen and his troops to arrive at the village and then engage the enemy. The sounds of battle tended to carry over distances, and if you were actively listening for it, there would be no mistaking it for anything else. That would be the sign to begin their attempt to climb the walls and begin to move into position.

Tigh and Elles left to ensure the route markers were still there to help guide the infantry to the scouted positions, and to further prep the hides where they were going to be spending the night. Hiding that many people close by the walls without being spotted would be tricky, so the majority were going to be moving down the hill to the access points as the battle commenced. The first wave of troops would be hidden in blinds near the walls themselves. That would allow them, if they were lucky, to get close to the walls without being spotted from above. Ladders were being prepared so waves of troops would have ways to get up and over the wall. They could not be used earlier, as they would be tricky to hide near the wall. Camouflage and the confusion of battle were two things they were counting on in order for this risky plan to work. Otherwise, they would be easy targets from the guards.

Nibs was supposed to be on overwatch, but for now he was flying into the village from a completely different direction to see if he could spot the elder he had spoken to when doing his initial flyover. Letting the crows know tomorrow was the day would help get them prepared for whatever tomorrow brought. If they could provide some distractions during the battle, it could make a difference. And from how Nibs saw it, if the crows helped, then maybe they could also get a reward. That might help keep them on the side of the Morri going forward. Crows could help as well as ravens, well, not as well, but they weren't as flighty as smaller birds.

Flying over the village, things looked unchanged, which was a comfort. Nibs knew any changes in the environment could be a sign of danger and he would not let his person get injured by a surprise he could spot. As he circled the village, looking for the elder, something caught his eye, a group of people coming in from the north. Drifting closer on the air currents, Nibs estimated it was a group of twenty slavers along with their three wagons. There even seemed to be people crammed into cages built into the wagons.

Winging his way back to the town, he spotted the elder crow and dove down to flare his wings nearby atop the building. He hopped closer and bowed slightly. "Hello, elder."

"Hi, Nibs. You're back."

Nibs bobbed his head. "I wanted to let you know the attack will be tomorrow. That way you can make sure you and yours are safe. Did you still want to help?"

The elder bobbed his head. "Yes. We'll help as you suggested. When?"

"Someone will be coming in from outside and a fight will start. Not sure how. Once the fighting starts, please help as you can, like I told you."

The elder bobbed his head in understanding. Nibs nodded. "May the Winged Mother protect you and yours."

"May the Winged Mother protect you as well, Nibs," said the elder crow. "Hopefully, tomorrow will bring an end to the stone house and their cruelty."

Nibs took back to the air. Those extra people he had spotted had not been armored and most had no weapons from what he had seen. The weapons could be somewhere else, but he had not been able to tell with his cursory glance. Best to find Asche and let her know of this development, in case it changed anything. After two more circles of the town to ensure no further surprises for tomorrow, Nibs headed back off to the north then circled back once he was over the hill and out of sight of any on the keep's walls.

He knew where the camp was going to be, as the wooded copse the rangers found earlier had been large enough to contain the portion of the company that fought, though it would be snug. Landing on a branch in the middle of camp, Nibs croaked out, turning his head to look for Asche or anyone else who might want to know what he had seen. Fanlis got there first. "Yes, Nibs?"

"Slavers entering town from north. Twenty people, bad stuff, people in cages." Nibs gave his report, unhappy with the lack of subtilities in human speech. There were so many details he could convey, but human sounds had such limitations. He had to sound like an idiot. Maybe he would get better in time?

Fanlis nodded. "Doesn't help us much and it's late enough you might not be able to find the others before the sun set completely. So, it goes. Thank you, Nibs." She handed over the remainder of a hunk of cheese she had been eating.

Nibs bobbed, taking the tasty morsel, then flapped off to where he had spotted Asche. Asche was seated on her bedroll, Elsif nearby, and both were eating their rations. One controlled fall later, and Nibs was stealing bites of meat from his person. "Nibs!"

He laughed and Asche hmphed. "Did you speak with the crows?" she asked.

Nibs bobbed his head.

"Anything new?"

"More slavers."

Asche worried. From what Nibs managed to spot, there was already more bandits and slavers in the village than they had troops. If what she had been told was true, things would come down to quality of training and equipment, but numbers were a big gap to overcome. If the bandits and slavers they had faced so far were the majority of the troops, there was little doubt they would win. However, if they had decent troops and decent equipment, maybe things would change and this assault would become iffy. From what Nibs said, only the troops in the keep had decent gear, which made their job harder, and the gatehouse was likely guarded by Blades of the Tyner, who were highly trained. Given that, Lord Whiltaen and the other company could deal with this new wrinkle, they had enough issues to deal with. "We'll be moving tonight to our places by the wall, so come find us in the morning?"

"Yes." Nibs nodded several times. "I keep you safe."

Elsif snickered at that, cutting her eyes over to him. "I thought that was my job."

Nibs joined in on the laughter between them.

❖

Moving into place in the dark was nerve-wracking. They had crawled slowly and precisely over the crest of the hill, wearing their shaggies, working to ensure there was as little sound as possible and staying low enough to look like nothing more than shifting shadows. Moving downhill while upright would create a chance of being noticed, a fact they drummed into the heads of the infantry who would follow behind. Thankfully, the phase of the moon was in their favor, giving a bit of light to see by and yet not enough for the guards on the walls to see clearly. Asche's team was stationed on the left and consisted of her, Flit, and Fanlis. The other three would be going up on the other side.

Once safe in the hides they had made, they took cat naps and rested until dawn broke over the horizon. The sky lightened slowly. Asche woke with the sun, despite the orders to sleep as long as possible. Between her treatment growing up and training with the Hands, it seemed like her body was convinced this was the natural time to wake. Fanlis noticed her stirring. "Can't rest anymore?"

"No. Too nervous." Asche's spoke softly, hoping the sound wouldn't carry.

Fanlis nodded, still scanning the walls ahead of them for any sign they had been noticed. "I get that. The worst part of some missions is the waiting, where your mind plays a lot of what-ifs.

Listening to them is a sure way to make things more difficult. You need to trust your training, follow orders, and we should be okay. Nibs did say most of the force's strength was down in the village, basically ill-equipped and poorly trained bully boys. They tend to make overconfident and stupid troops. Our primary focus is simple, get up the wall and defend the spot until backup arrives, which shouldn't be very long. Afterall, the first wave of the infantry is only ten feet uphill from us and they have the siege ladders. Then we move on to the more difficult part, taking the gatehouse. I'm of the opinion the infantry is really best at that, so we'll stay out of their way. Right now, we need to focus on one step at a time, and the next step is getting to the wall and up it. We have this."

"That's what you all told me, but it doesn't help when my mind casts over things," said Asche. "I've done everything I can to be ready for this and I'm trembling."

"Fair point. However, what you need to do is calm yourself more. You move faster when calm. Emotion tenses your muscles too much." Fanlis paused a moment. "Maybe what you need to do is pray. I always pray to the Morri before battle, even if it is brief. Just taking the moment to send a prayer up has helped me in many a battle."

Asche nodded and lowered her head. That was not the advice she had expected from her commander, but it was worth a try. Maybe with all those dreams of the forge her words would be heard? Praying softly to herself, Asche began, "Holy Morri, thank you for all you have given me. Every day I awake, found and blessed by your hand. Please help my steel be sufficient for this task, help my focus stay on task, help my teammates face their own battles and win through. Please help us find the fortitude to win this day against the Tyner and those allied with him. Please let our actions rescue those who are in captivity. So, mote it be."

There was a moment of what felt like pure silence before a tingling rolled up her spine to the back of her head and settled. Asche felt a sense of peace settle upon her as she exhaled. She could do this, could handle the battle to come. She was a Hand now and would serve the Morri as best she could.

She awoke to a tap on her shoulder and Flit looking at her. "Asche, wake. Whiltaen's here and there's movement along the walls."

Asche glanced up from where she had been dozing and looked toward their chosen entry point. There was a section of the defenses, where the motte guarding the keep raised up and stopped, failing to protect the village. It was also a spot where the old wooden palisade came against the somewhat newer stone, at a location where the palisade went up a flight of stairs to the stone walls of the keep. It was obvious where the old palisade had surrounded the entire keep and village, with the stone creating a new area of movement. Because it was incomplete, it would not assist with the defense as much as it would when finished. The gap that had been spotted was under the new stairs that would allow them out and onto the old walkway and have access to the new. If they could make it up.

She shifted some to ease out some of the aches from sleeping on the ground and tried to warm her muscles. Until the signal, they would have to remain in place, hidden by the stones, trees, and blinds they had constructed. Time crept, people moved forward, toward the gates of the village and then the main courtyard. This misdirection might help them if it did enough. Asche did not spot anyone on the walls near where they would be headed.

Noise erupted from the village and the crash of steel could be heard. A few of the better armed troops hustled down from the keep to the village palisade, moving closer to assist. After a few tense moments, the area was clear again. Nibs croaked out his signal, three very loud tok sounds, letting them know it was clear. Fanlis stood and began running toward the palisade. Asche promptly followed, remembering her part of the plan.

When they reached the wall, she and Fanlis spun and braced their shoulders against the wood, locked hands, and crouched just a little. Flit bolted forward, leapt onto their hands, and got boosted to the top of the wall. She scrambled over quickly and disappeared. Then they heard the sounds of a slight scuffle. The rope ladder she had carried up with her dropped down, and Flit waved them up.

Asche grabbed the ladder and put all her weight on it, leaning back to ensure it was as secure as they could manage. Once that was accomplished, Fanlis scrambled up the ladder as fast as she could, which wasn't that easy. Once she was over, Asche swiftly followed, watching the infantry rushing their way with the siege ladders. At the top, sections of the palisade floor were slick with blood, and there was a guard's body hanging off the inside edge. Flit's brigandine had some splashes of red on the fabric, marring the Morri's symbol. Fanlis was watching closely to determine if there was any movement their way. Asche moved toward the stairs, following her orders. A quick glance showed the infantry troops were hustling toward the wall, closer than before, but still farther than desired.

She kept low, her raven's head in hand, trying to peer over the top of the stairs without exposing her head too much. There was a guard running toward the village, spear held at the ready. There were two arrows sticking out of his armor, and he did not seem to be overly affected by their presence. Asche could tell his eyes were more fixed on the fight in the center of the village than on the stairs in front of him. With a hard swing, her raven's head cut into the side of his calf as he almost reached her.

He stumbled forward and tumbled down the stairs, dropping his spear. There were even a few wet snapping sounds. Flit slid close and jabbed her dagger home, killing the man before he could truly give voice to his pain. She glanced at Asche and tapped her kettle helmet.

Asche pulled her coif and helm up and into place. Flit shook her head as she turned away while Fanlis rolled the body off the palisade. Asche cut her eyes over to the side and noticed the first of the infantry troops had topped the ladder. She watched the top of the stairs for anyone moving their way. She spotted a few guards on their backs with multiple arrows in their bodies and faces along the stone parapet, but nothing and no one close enough to worry about. The archers outside were certainly helping with the defense of the entry point.

It was maddening how long things were taking. The problem was that rope ladders were nowhere near as stable as actual ladders and would slow things down. They had brought up two siege ladders, but it was still slow. She spotted a couple of the armored guards wearing the baron's livery heading her way as the battle sounds in the village kept increasing in violence. They were decently armored and both had spears. It was tight quarters by the stairs, and she was well aware she might not make it through this. Swords did not work well against armored foes. Quickly she muttered, "Holy Morri, guide my blade."

As the men neared, spear tips aimed right for her, Asche thought of something, a move she had tried on Tigh that might work here. With that, she brought her raven's head across her body and onto the spear shafts on her right. Neither man tried to avoid the hit on the spear shaft, so she immediately pivoted on her left foot, turning like a door. That action shoved the tips aside and down, where they moved past her torso a bit too close for comfort. Luckily, the guards had not checked their speed, fully intent on the spear's impact to do that for them, where it would transfer all that force to her.

The two guards stumbled down the stairs and fell into the two heavy infantry troops already on the way to help her. Once the men were dispatched, the two heavies moved to the top of the stairs, taking over guarding the stairs from Asche. "Thanks."

"Thanks for the gift. It was a nice surprise," said a heavy she was not familiar with who waved with her axe.

"Glad I could welcome you to the battle. We were lonely up here," said Asche, glad to be safely behind those shields. They were far better equipped for this than the rangers were for this kind of battle.

"I bet. We got this."

Asche rushed back down and over to the ladder to help pull the infantry troops over the palisade wall or lift the tied bundles of polearms for the medium infantry. So far everything was going according to the kaitan's plan. They had made it up onto the palisade and had control of the stairs leading to the new stone of the keep. She prayed their luck would continue to hold as this was technically the easy part.

## CHAPTER TWENTY-THREE

Nibs heard the sounds of people moving about as he slept. It was dark and he was annoyed these idiot humans were awake when decent birds, like him, were sleeping. When dawn came, and he awoke, there was nobody there, as the wagons stayed with the other company. He roused himself and spotted a chunk of cheese in a place he could get, plus some bread. Had someone left him breakfast? There were a few smaller songbirds, who were basically stomachs with wings, pecking a bit at the bread. Some of those finches worked fast. He croaked a warning as he flew down, and they scattered in a rush of wings.

After breakfast, he took to the sky, leaving some scattered crumbs for the smaller birds, and headed toward the village. When he managed to reach the top of the hill, he spotted a few of the Hands hiding below the crest. One of them waved. Nibs realized it was the kaitan and so circled down to a landing out of sight of the keep. "Yes?"

"Nibs, we still have some time before the other force should reach the town. Did you get the bread and cheese?"

Nibs bobbed his head.

"Good. Want to make sure you have the energy to pull this off. We're counting on you to let us know when to start moving down to the wall. Wait until Whiltaen and the others are fully engaged before you signal."

"Gwah."

"I know you know what you're doing. I tell this to all my people so they are positive of what they have to do. Come down from the north. I don't want to risk you getting spotted and draw eyes this way. It would end badly for us."

Nibs cocked his head at her and said, "North. Safe. Right."

"Everyone knows to wait for you. I guess, head over the village after you spot Whiltaen arriving. That should keep eyes off you. Keep an eye out for anyone trying to take shots at you. Good luck. May the Morri bless."

Nibs took to the air and moved around the forest so he could make his approach from the north, toward the main gate. It took a bit of time for him to reach a spot and settle. He had a clear view of the road to the village that Lord Whiltaen and the Turkey would be taking.

A short while later, the guy with the funny name and his troops started their approach to the city. His force was marching up to the village completely open, banners flying. He was working under the belief that to keep their cover, the guards would have to let him in, but that seemed sketchy. As Nibs watched, it seemed to be true. The gates opened after a short wait, and the troops moved into the village. Who knew?

That reminded him he had a job to do, so he winged over to begin circling the village until the fight started. There were people running from the keep to the village along the walls like angry ants, getting rid of some of the defenders. He had barely made one full revolution before the village center erupted into violence. Humans!

He turned and got closer to where he was supposed to be, watching the two entry points and letting the waiting people know when it was clear. More troops rushed down from the castle, down the stairs, and onto the palisade. A cheer rose up when the main gate to the town was opened and the other company of Hands rushed in to support Funny Name. It was very loud and someone had started a fire in one of the buildings the smelly ones lived in. The archers on the palisade kept getting interrupted as crows swooped into their faces, making them flail about. He was proud of those little annoyances.

It looked like the flood of troops toward the village trickled down and there was no one around the entry points. Nibs made three sharp, metallic sounding tok sounds as loudly as he could, sending his part of the signal. From the two sides, people ran to the wall to begin that part of this operation. On his right, he spotted Flit, Fanlis, and Asche mount the wall easily. Tigh had to fight a guard who was running back toward the keep. It had been a fast fight, and now Elles and Terris were atop the wall. He was going to keep an eye out in case the baron tried to escape the village by going over the wall, like he had been asked. True, there were archers out there who might take a potshot at him, but keeping a better eye on the area was what he had been asked to do.

Circling around to check on the entry points, Nibs spotted more of the infantry troops up on the wall, and that meant they would be heading toward the gate tower soon. His primary part in this mission was finished, but he wanted to keep an eye on Asche, because his human could be overly human and throw herself into danger, like some flight-mad chick plummeting from the nest. Without him, she was sure to get herself hurt.

❖

Since the infantry was up on the palisade, it was time to move toward their second objective. The infantry troops hustled up the stairs on the keep walls and headed toward the gatehouse, staying in formation. Capturing that and opening the keep's gates would ensure victory, as Lord Whiltaen's troops could charge right in and hopefully overwhelm the defense of the keep. At least, that was the plan. How it lined up with the enemy was another thing. The enemy rarely decided to follow their plan.

Since the old palisade wall was being replaced by stone, there was not an easy and direct route to the door that led inside. The stone lip by the gate where the door was stood taller than the new stone wall being laid. Wooden scaffolding was their main route over, and it was completely exposed to the interior of the keep's courtyard, which seemed to have some more guardsmen, armed with bows.

Fanlis saw this and called out, "Flit, Asche, grab the spears. Infantry, try to provide a bit of a shield wall on that side to block arrows."

Asche moved quickly down the stairs and grabbed the spears those guards had carried, then tossed one to her teammate. She and Flit hustled back as the first of the archers crested the wall, being the last to get up onto the palisade, currently being guarded by some of the medium infantry troops with their polearms. As the infantry made its way over the scaffolding, Fanlis gestured to Flit and Asche to follow her onto the actual stone wall. Once they were past the gatehouse, one of the infantry pushed at the door. "I think it's barred from the inside."

Fanlis snapped out, "Break it!"

Two of the infantry troops started to use their war hammers to pound into the door with the raven's beak pick. The blows landed solidly, digging deeply into the wood and prying out chunks with each blow. Small holes were beginning to appear as they worked, and they could see movement of shadows inside. The number of arrows that flew their way and thudded into shields dropped when their archers moved up the stairs and began targeting some of the keep's archers with suppressive fire.

As the holes got larger, they could see actual movement from the other side. They knew the guardsmen were waiting for them and were in a far better position to defend. Fanlis yelled, "Aim for the bottom."

The war hammers ripped and tore into the wood at the bottom of the door, peeling away the bottom parts of the boards. Gaps and holes were opening and Fanlis said, "Flit, Asche, get ready."

Once a wider gap was opened, Fanlis shouted, "Now!"

Asche thrust the spear into the open section of door and into the leg of at least one guardsman. She pulled it out and Fanlis directed, "Again!"

Fanlis pulled the bloody spear free and yelled, "Back to the door!"

Asche processed something she had seen on one of the guard's uniforms. "Fanlis, there was someone with a Tyner crest on their baldric, maybe more than one."

Fanlis cursed. Nibs had not been completely positive about the identification of those guards. They had hoped Nibs had been mistaken, but they had planned for him to be right. The war hammers were chewing their way through the hardwood door, each bite of the raven's beak wrenching through the wood. Yelps occurred occasionally when one of the shields did not stop an arrow and it bit into someone's armor. Thankfully, most of that conflict had descended into an archers' duel. A few strikes later and the majority of the door splintered under the assault. Flit and Asche were waved forward again, and were aiming to stab into the exposed calves and thighs of the defenders.

As the spears drove back some of the defenders, one of the infantry troops leaned in and smacked the beam holding the door up and out with the top of her war hammer. She backed away quickly after taking a glancing blow to the head from a mace. The infantry surged forward, smashing feet and using the raven's beaks to pull legs forward, where guards slipped on the blood collecting and coagulating on the stone floor. These defenders, all wearing Tyner baldrics, snarled at the Hands and firmed up their defense.

The first few infantry troops struggled to shove their way into the room. There was a flash of light from the other side of the gatehouse and a sound more felt than heard ringing through the area. Tigh surged into view and there was something noticeably different; her raven's head sword had been replaced by a weapon of far superior craftsmanship and steel. The metal practically shone in her hand. When it hit the armor of the Blades, it had a greater effect than the sword should. Something also seemed different in her eyes as she shouted, "Come on! We can take them!"

The Infantry troops piled into the building and turned the tide of battle inside the gatehouse and began forcing the defenders down the stairs. Asche stood outside and helped the troops get up to the doorway, using the extremely unstable steps made by the fallen guards' bodies. Flit was helped by Fanlis into the doorway, and Asche headed that way. There was a shout and Asche turned. Two guardsmen had gotten past the archers from the palisade stairs and were rushing her, spears at the ready. Numerous arrows were stuck in their armor hampering their movement, but they were moving well enough to charge her.

For a moment, Asche froze, surprised by the sudden appearance of these men. She had been so distracted helping the infantry troops in that she lost track of the wider battle. One of the men stumbled and fell when an arrow took him in the back of one knee. Fanlis was moving toward that one, raven's head sword at the ready. The other planted his feet, and then brought his hands up to fend off Nibs, who flew into the man's face with a loud, angry kow! The man's flailing helped snap Asche out of her frozen state and spurred her into action.

The shaft of the man's spear slammed into Nibs, flinging him sideways onto the wall with a loud squawk. Nibs slid across the rough stone, teetering on the edge. Asche snarled, using one hand to grab the spear shaft and hold it still, while her raven's head chopped down into his lightly protected knee. The man's knee gave way under the blow and he buckled, screaming in pain. The scratches on his exposed face were bleeding. Asche kicked the man's calf to the side, adding to the unnatural bend. With a grunt of effort, she brought the raven's head down sharply on the man's neck, which was only protected by a gambeson, ending his struggle in a splash of blood.

As she spun to rescue Nibs, she heard Kaitan Tanrei yell from the doorway of the guardhouse, "Grab Nibs and keep him safe!"

One of the archers made it over to Nibs and held him gently on his back in her hands. It was Lynarra, who called out, "Got him! Asche, go!"

Asche ran forward and made the short leap into the gatehouse. She was pulled in by Flit. She could hear the portcullis opening, so they clearly had gained control. A few jugs of water and some bread were being shared around by the others. Several people, including Asche, were panting from the exertion and wiping blood from their faces so it wouldn't make their eyes burn more than the sweat did. It seemed like everything hurt and she just wanted to lie down, though the smell was something she had never experienced, a mix of sewage pit and slaughterhouse.

The kaitan raised her voice so all could hear it. "Guard team, stay put. Hold team, hold the courtyard. Search team, get into the keep and find those other targets. Try not to destroy maps, books, or what have you. The baron is the priority. The priest is a close second. Information a third. Only fight if they resist. We want them alive. The Tyner might treat us like shit, but we aren't brutes. Go!"

Some shuffling occurred as people re-formed. Asche moved toward the group and Fanlis held her back a moment. "Nibs'll be fine, Asche. Focus on the job. Let our healers take care of him. We're not done yet."

Asche nodded, trying to damp down worry for her friend. They had known each other for several years now, and it hurt that he might be severely injured. She continued to move into place behind the infantry troops. The inner door opened, and the infantry surged out into the courtyard. A guardsman, leading a reinforcement group of Blades, had the door slammed into his wrist and body. The man fell yelling, and the force of their charge broke the detachment. They were cut down quickly.

As the heavy and medium infantry stormed the courtyard to clash against a shield wall, Asche noticed there was a small force of guardsmen with spears and backed by archers formed up at the top of the stairs leading into the keep. A few arrows flew over but mainly stuck into the shields of the heavy infantry up front. Then they were on them.

Axes and war hammers smashed into shields. Pole arms came over and landed blows onto helmets and through in the case of one poor baronial guardsman. The rangers came around the sides and attacked the archers, who dropped their bows and pulled out daggers. Asche came in low toward the unarmored left knee of one, and the archer frantically tried to interpose their dagger. With a turn of her wrist and a slight hip pivot, Asche changed the attack's direction and the raven's head bit into the archer's right arm which was also unarmored.

The dagger fell from their grip and they yelled, "Peace!"

Asche pulled back her killing blow, glancing toward the other members of their group. The majority of the defenders had cried for peace and dropped weapons, which were swiftly kicked away. The heavy infantry moved forward to the doors, as the medium infantry moved the defenders, both living and dead, out of the way. Sarnt Terris had the ranger group with her, scanning the area for more defenders.

The door had been barred, so those with axes and war hammers got to work on it, causing the door to splinter and shudder with each round of blows. Terris raised her voice, to be heard over the discordant noises. "Right, baron is likely moving to back of keep, hoping to go out over wall. There is no guarantee few archers out there will be enough to stop him, so we need to move toward back quickly. Pair up, infantry and recon. Search quick and yell if you find them. Rangers, grab spears. We can use them to support infantry upon entry."

Asche noted Tigh looked somehow more, with that shining raven's head in her hand and a fierce gleam in her eyes. There was detailed work along the blade that made the sword a work of art not just a tool for battle. Other people, waiting for the doors to break, kept stealing glances at her, seeming to gain resolve with her presence. It took a short while, but the door gave under the concentrated effort of four of the heavies.

Shaking her sword arm to get the blood flowing into her hand again, Asche stood to the side. Her wrist and shoulder ached from wielding the weapon. All the training they had done was not nearly the same as fighting for your life. She felt so drained, leaning heavily on the keep wall, desperately hoping for more energy. There was no more food to go around and there was no sign of water skins anywhere. As the sound of wood breaking increased, she pushed herself upright and moved back to the others, flexing her fingers to work out how sore they were. She looked back at the gatehouse, where the chiurgeons were currently stationed and dealing with the various wounded.

Once the door gave way, the four heavies who broke it moved to the side as the rest surged in. There was a small force with swords and shields, seemingly a better quality of guard than they had faced, plus they were fresh. However, they were not wearing baldrics with the crossed sword symbol of the Tyner, like the troops in the gatehouse who had fought them viciously. These seemed to be the baron's men and were not that great a challenge. The more senior of the infantry began to separate the attackers, creating openings for the rangers and the medium infantry to thrust spears over shoulders and toward faces.

No one stabbed anyone, but a few of the guards flinched as steel sought their faces. Two of the heavies stepped into the gap and brought their weapons over to the sides, hoping to tag the guardsmen on either side. This unexpected action caught them on the shoulders and neck, dropping them and widening the opening. The rest of the infantry rushed forward into the growing gap.

There was shouting from behind and Asche took a quick glance and spotted Lord Whiltaen's men and a few Hands coming into the courtyard at a run. She held onto the spear and moved to follow a heavy who looked like Elsif and who was moving down a side corridor, as a few others moved into the great room or down a different corridor. The hallway led to a staircase leading both up and down. Elsif paused briefly and headed up, shield at the ready. Asche followed.

Up a level, a hallway stretched off along the front of the keep, with a few doors opposite them and in the middle a gap where another hallway connected. They checked the nearest door. It opened, but it was an empty guest room. Asche noticed a more ornate door at the end of the hall. She pointed forward with the spear. "That's likely it."

The ornate door was not guarded, which struck Asche as odd. Even more so, when they tried it, the door opened inward. They moved inside, Elsif followed by Asche. Elsif cocked her head to the left, as if she heard something. Sensing movement, Asche jerked her head back as a mace came around and slammed into the back of Elsif's helmet.

Elsif went flying forward a few feet before dropping to the floor, kettle helm torn from her head. With a groan, Elsif wobblily tried to push herself upright, but the armored figure who had been hiding behind the door spoke a few words, and with a surge of something in the air, Elsif stilled.

Asche backpedaled to her right, trying to keep the spear between herself and this new and more dangerous attacker. The man wore a chest plate with the image of two crossed swords, one gold and one red embossed on it. The gold sword had a crown around the hilt and the red one had three drips coming off it that reminded her of blood. Under the plate, he was wearing a chain hauberk that looked well-made and fitted to him. The man's shield was steel, with the same heraldic image on it as his chest plate, held competently, ready to block any move she made. He seemed more amused than concerned as he regarded her. He chuckled darkly as he shifted to stand between her and the door. "Well now…look what I've caught."

## CHAPTER TWENTY-FOUR

S eeing little other choice, Asche decided to take the battle to him, thrusting her spear forward. The man caught the thrust on his shield, angled it wide, and brought his mace around. The metal head of the mace broke through the shaft easily with a loud crack. He stood there, a barbute helmet on his head, visor up, mace and shield at the ready, allowing Asche time to draw her raven's head. "Do continue, little Hand. I'm enjoying this warmup before what is sure to be the main event. I felt a Sword get called while I was here, and I would dearly love to test my mettle versus another Sword. It will be interesting to see how it plays out."

Asche swallowed dryly. This was a Sword of the Tyner and not a priest? Fuck!

She tightened her grip on her sword, circling to her right and hoping to check on Elsif, who was unmoving, a dent in the steel of the kettle helm. Asche could see a trickle of blood from her nose, but that was it. The Sword of the Tyner turned with her a smirk across his face, as Asche kept the raven's head sword focused on the centerline of his body. "My, it seems like you Hands are getting younger and younger as the years go by, so few of your veterans making it. Alas, so very sad. You and your pathetic goddess just wasting away. Why, given all of that, it's almost as if someone is hunting you…"

Asche struggled to regain calm. Maybe if she got really lucky, Tigh would show up and save them from this Sword. Barring that miracle, it was up to her to save them both and she had no idea how to fight someone so much better equipped and trained. There was no quick way to get Elsif's shield free, and facing someone with one was outside her ability. There was nothing near at hand to throw at him. She would have to get very, very lucky if she and Elsif were going to survive. Under her breath, while watching the man's every move, she muttered, "Blessed Morri, please help me figure out a way to get us out of this alive."

The man laughed at hearing her mutter a prayer. He spun the mace easily and worked his wrist and shoulder, keeping them loose and ready. "What's that, little girl? You need to speak up when talking to your betters. Maybe you can be trained. Mayhap I'll keep you as my own. Looking up at me with those pretty eyes. You'll make a lovely bedwarmer and I could always do with another."

Asche growled and swung high, hoping to do to him what she had done to a guard earlier, redirect it low. He caught her blade on his shield, chuckling, and pushed it out and away, thwarting her move. Asche turned the blade and shot out low, hoping to catch calf rather than knee. The mace head slammed into the flat of the sword, a corona of light blazing about it as it hit. The steel of her raven's head could not withstand the strike. The blade broke in half and clattered on the stone floor.

Asche's eyes went wide and her mouth dropped open as she held the handle and blinked at the cleanly broken blade.

The Sword of the Tyner stepped forward, tapping her once solidly in the chest with the head of his mace. The tap hurt, even through her brigandine and gambeson. "Now that there are no more distractions, I think you both will be coming with me."

"No!" She took a few steps, looking desperately for some route for escape.

He stood there looking at her as if she were incompetent. "So, you would rather die? That's certainly all right by me. I've had a great deal of practice killing Hands and have no problem doing a little more. My lord is rather pleased whenever I do so. And we must never let the divines down, must we?"

"Why the fuck are you doing this?" spat Asche, anger keeping the wave of fear at bay for the moment. Her mouth was dry, heart in her throat.

"Your Lady needs to learn her place, which is at his side. She plays at being a warrior goddess when the Tyner already has the job filled. She apes her betters and needs to be slapped down. Removing her priestesses and Hands seems like a simple enough way to achieve that aim. You and yours will either die or spend the rest of your life making amends for having the effrontery to pretend to be warriors." He rolled the mace in a circle again, dropping his shield arm from the ready position. It was clear that she posed him no threat.

Asche kept glancing down the hallway, hoping for signs of rescue, but there was no movement. If the rest of the people were dealing with the baron and his people, then she and Elsif might not be noticed missing for a while. And who knew when the other troops would storm in and make for this floor. The man continued talking. "So, which is it going to be, girl, death or slave?"

"That's a crap choice," said Asche, anger stronger than fear.

"And? I have given you the options that exist." He was unnervingly calm, and Asche understood why. He wore plate armor and held a mace and shield, while she had her gambeson and brigandine and naught else.

Time. She needed time more than anything. Every moment she was able to stall was another moment closer to someone finding them. What could she do to stretch it? "How do you plan on getting out of here with us? The village and the keep have been conquered. There is no escape."

"Out the window and down a rope." He said it as if that was the most obvious thing in the world. He yawned slightly, eyes never leaving hers.

She clenched her hands, wishing she had a weapon. His smug face was demanding punches. "I'll run."

"Ah, ah, ah…no, you won't, little Hand. First, you will swear an oath of loyalty to the Tyner as I pray, or I shall simply kill you and take your friend to do with as I please. Which is it, girl?"

More troops had come into the courtyard of the keep when they entered. Surely some of them would have come this way…right? She was grasping at nonexistent straws but desperate for some way to save them both. It was painful, but she had to admit, there was no easy rescue, no one to help them in that moment. Elsif was injured, the back of her helmet dented from the mace, bleeding. Asche was unarmed, but there was no damn way she would yield to this ass. She was their only salvation.

Maybe she needed to keep playing for time. If the man really was this much of an ass, and full of himself, even more than her father had been, he wouldn't expect her to keep fighting and would love to hear the sound of his own voice gloating as she capitulated. She took a step back, this act of fear only partially a ploy. She noted Elsif's weapon. Elsif had dropped it when she was hit the second time and it had slid ahead of her just a bit. That was the only choice, a weapon she had never even held before. She thanked all the divines she had done all the repair work her father had demanded, so she had a slight clue how one might use a hammer.

When her nervous shifting got her close to the weapon, Asche swallowed heavily and lowered herself to her knee, going from glaring at him to looking down at the floor. Silently, she prayed, "Holy Morri, help!"

The man moved closer, slightly to her left. She could work with that when she found her opening. His voice was thick with mock approval. "That's what I like to see, a girl who knows her place. You will swear the vow I tell you, as I call upon the might of my lord, and the Tyner will make you mine. Then my will is yours. Maybe I'll have you hunt down your sisters for me. That has always been fun."

"Wha…what must I do?" Her voice shook with real fear. If this didn't work, they were doomed. She did not want to spend the remainder of her life serving this ass. She slid her hand slowly down her leg toward the floor.

"Repeat these words, I and then your name, daughter of the Morri…" he intoned, watching her as he spoke.

"I, Asche, daughter of the Morri..." She brushed her fingers along the rug. She was over halfway there; she just needed an opening.

"...vow on my sacred heart..." There was a cruel smirk on his face when he said that.

Asche realized this vow would be powerful enough to consume her if she followed it. Father Tombol had stressed vowing on one's scared heart was the strongest of oaths, capable of binding one to the divine. She swallowed heavily, pausing. This...this was stupid and there was no way she could beat a Sword with a weapon she knew very little about. There was still no movement in the hallway.

The Sword raised his mace and shield, growling at her in a clear threat and taking a step closer to her. With another dry swallow, she said, "...vow on my sacred heart..."

"...to loyally serve the Tyner and his sons until the end of days." There was a weight of finality to that. She could hear his grip tighten on the leather cording of his mace, but his position relaxed just slightly. Then she heard him begin to mutter a prayer to the Tyner, the thing that would enforce these spoken words and make mere words unbreakable chains. This was it.

"...to loyally serve the Morri!" With a shout, Asche closed her hand on Elsif's hammer and she swung as hard as she could at the Sword's ankle, that he had so kindly put closer to her. Then the world flashed.

❖

The heat of the forge smacked her with such heavy force Asche shuddered. She looked around and spotted the Morri brushing a piece of finished work with her back to Asche. It seemed like the goddess was intent on placing the finishing touches on whatever she was doing. "Ah good, you took me up on the offer."

"Wha?" Words failed Asche. Things had been so dire and now she was here, in the safety of the forge.

"I told you to take up a hammer and join me. I was speaking literally, but you missed it. And to make that Sword of the Tyner formalize a vow on your sacred heart to me, only made the whole thing sweeter." The Morri chuckled, doing something else to the piece she was working on. She glanced over her shoulder and winked. "I knew you had good steel and only needed the correct work to bring out its full strength. And here you are."

"B…but…" What was even going on here?

"Being one of my Hands is not a safe choice. You did not waver or bend, fighting on even after that raven you keep company with was injured. Then, in a hopeless situation, you still showed that strength, that determination. And you worked to find a possible way out. But our moment here is coming to an end, young Asche. Take up your weapon and fight for your freedom." The Morri turned and handed Asche a beautifully crafted war hammer.

The weapon was all metal, a wavy pattern of light and dark through it, like ripples in a steel pond. The grip was tightly woven leather, a strap through a ring in the bottom to help keep it in hand. There was a guard above the grip designed like a flower petal. The shaft was about three feet long and twisted with a branch motif, cut branch ends, with a design of vines climbing up it worked into the metal. Where the shaft joined the head was another petal, facing down. The head had a short, twisted spike on top, and the head of the hammer had the center flat with four separate squares raised above it. Vines also covered that, merging with the patterned steel. The part that stunned her more than the rest, was the raven's beak hook that looked nearly lifelike in its detail. Asche reached out with a trembling hand and took hold.

❖

The war hammer sped through the air and smashed into the Sword's ankle. While his boots were armored, there was no way they were as strong as the metal chest plate he wore. Upon impact, there was a slight flash and a sound akin to a wet branch snapping. The Sword had begun stumbling back from the flash and the blow to the ankle spun him about and dropped him to the floor. He bellowed in pain.

Asche could see that he had bit his lip when he spat out a gobbet of blood from where he lay. "A fucking Hammer? You're a fucking Hammer? Thrice-bedamned slut!"

Asche bounded to her feet and came in with a blow toward his head, screaming out her anger. The head of the war hammer began to glow a dull red. Despite being on the ground, he was able to interpose his shield between them. The blow was loud and powerful, booming against his shield. He slid back slightly from the force and there was another wet snap under the other sounds.

Finally, Asche could hear the sounds of people yelling and rushing their way down the corridor. The Sword rolled onto his good leg and swung his mace at her. She tried to block the attack with the metal shaft of her new war hammer but was too slow. The blow slid under her war hammer and caught her in the ribs, and she tumbled up and away before slamming onto her back against a low table.

He hopped toward her awkwardly, eyes burning with focus and hatred. He slammed the visor down on his helmet as he growled at her. She flailed her legs with a pained gasp, trying to ward him off. It was so hard to breathe. "You fucking bitch! At least before they stop me, I'll have killed the newest Hammer!"

He brought his mace up overhead and then swiftly down. The head glowed a sickly color and buzzed the air. Asche saw a slight opening where his shield no longer properly covered him. She wrenched her body to the side and swung the raven's beak of her war hammer through the man's helmet and into the side of his head.

The mace dropped from his lifeless fingers and fell heavily onto her stomach, knocking the wind out of her even through the brigandine. His body fell to the side, barely off her. The weight of his body tugged the war hammer from her grasp as she gasped for air.

Tigh was first in the room and she ran over to the body. She yanked it off Asche and tossed it to the side with more strength than Asche remembered her having. Tigh's eyes went wide when she spotted the metal hammer sticking out of the man's helm. Asche grimaced as someone else helped her into a sitting position. Air was slightly easier to come by as they raised her arms above her head.

Her desperate gasps changed to merely gasps as she could take in more air. Tigh reached down to the body and pulled the weapon free. "This yours?"

Asche grinned before wincing and nodded slightly.

Tigh handed over the war hammer with a slight bow. "Then, well met, Hammer of the Morri."

"Well met, Sword of the Morri."

Tigh smirked before bellowing, "Let's get her to the chiurgeon!"

## Chapter Twenty-five

Asche leaned heavily against Tigh as she hobbled out of the keep. She had one arm across Tigh's shoulder and the other on her head, her coif and helm down. This made it easier to breathe. Elsif was on a litter being carried by some of Whiltaen's men. The circular stairs were uncomfortable and each step jarred her ribs. She hissed in pain a few times. Once down, they walked out of the keep and saw as Lord Whiltaen walked up to the baron, clapped in irons and struggling against armsmen holding his upper arms.

The baron shook off the armsmen, glared at Lord Whiltaen, and barked, "What is the meaning of this, Whiltaen?"

"You're under arrest by orders of his grace, Duke Barvith of Tivas, for running a slave market, aiding bandits, and anything else we happen to discover while we go through your papers and the rest of the keep. Bandits under your employ raided various towns and villages for slaves. The duke is looking forward to speaking with you at some length on this issue." Lord Whiltaen loomed close with his horse and stared down at the man, almost daring him to do something else. He seemed to be taking great pleasure in telling all this to him.

"You can't prove that!" spat the baron, though his eyes held more fear than anger.

"So, you are saying the slave pens in that barn the locals say you built aren't yours?" asked Whiltaen, a faint smile on his lips.

The baron's face turned crimson, and he looked like he was getting ready to spit something out. Whiltaen continued. "Or is your defense that your brother talked you into it?"

Pursing his lips together until they were nearly white, the baron turned away from Whiltaen. The armsmen grabbed the baron and dragged him off at a gesture by Lord Whiltaen. Tigh and Asche moved on, the brief show over. There was no doubt it would be repeated as more was discovered. Once they reached the triage area where most of the injured were lying or sitting, Tigh helped lower Asche to the ground. She hissed loudly on the way down, panting some from the pain. The Sword chided her. "Keep your arms up so you can breathe easier. I'll grab one of the healers."

As Tigh headed off, Asche placed her new war hammer on her lap. She stared at it in disbelief. This weapon represented the Morri's favor, represented being more than a poor abused boy who ran away from home, joined the Hands, became the person out of his dreams, and now this…Asche had a hard time wrapping her head about it. It was early summer, heading toward midsummer, and the weight of her change sat in her lap. It was a stunningly beautiful weapon that her eyes could not help but be drawn to.

The Morri said Hammers were more than weapons, they were tools for building, for breaking, for changing things. They were her way to make even more changes to the world. Asche had no idea what any of that meant. But the Morri also said the quench would set the steel and then the specific work of shaping and forming would begin. The war hammer in her lap was beautiful, a work of art. Was this how the Morri saw her? Yet if the shaping and forming had more to do with herself, then maybe she shouldn't fret over it all, but rather, discover what that meant.

She looked over to where they lowered Elsif, a short distance away. She was still unmoving, but there was a steady rise and fall of her chest, so she was at least alive. The chiurgeon headed over to Elsif and began to check her, peeling back her eyelids, checking her breathing. The chiurgeon waved over the priestess to look at her. They conferred a bit before the priestess laid her hands on Elsif's head and began to pray. There was a slight blink of color and a silent rush of sound that Asche hoped was real, else she was seeing things.

Sarnt Terris came over and sat next to her, distracting Asche from the healing. "You did good job, Asche, remained focused on mission. Flit said you did well. I don't know what will change with that, exactly." Terris gestured toward the hammer with a toss of her head. "But you do still need to work on your stamina and your fighting."

Asche chuckled, agreeing with all of those points, as she had been thinking them herself. "Thank you, Sarnt. I have no idea what this means long or short term, but hopefully, Fanlis or the kaitan can give me some guidance."

"True enough. You and Tigh...who could have imagined? And you become Hammer? The Morri knows what she's about and it's up to us to catch up. Regardless, platoon has your back. We always have your back."

Asche smiled and nodded. She then looked back over at Elsif. She was moving a bit more, which was encouraging. Maybe she was going to be all right after all. Terris gently patted her shoulder. "She'll be fine. From what Tigh said, she likely has concussion. Lots of heavies get those from time to time. Elsif has hard head, and had her helmet and coif on, so hopefully nothing got knocked loose in there."

Asche chuckled and winced, her ribs protesting the action. The priestess stepped away from Elsif and came over to her, smiling. "Let me take a look at you."

Terris stood and headed off, leaving Asche with the priestess. "You take care, Asche. I have to go look after others."

The priestess closed her eyes and said a short prayer under her breath, then ran her hands gingerly down Asche's side. The slight pressure hurt and made Asche wince, as a good-sized area was damaged. The priestess opened her eyes and looked at her. "I need to look at the area closer to get a better idea of what can be done."

With assistance, Asche was able to get her slightly dented brigandine off, before removing the gambeson with nothing more than grimaces and a few gasps. Once her armor was set to the side, the priestess pulled up her tunic, exposing her side. Twisting slightly, to get a look, Asche spotted a rather large already coloring bruise along her ribs. The priestess touched the area with delicate fingers. "I believe you have several cracked ribs, if not outright broken. There are other scrapes and small injuries, but those should heal fine on their own. We will need to bind your ribs to ease the pain and help you breathe, and I will pray over your wound."

"Thank you." Asche was sincerely grateful for the healing. There had been too many times while growing up she had not been allowed any treatment after getting injured, and Father Tombol was not the best of healers. Thankfully, none of those injuries had been critical or crippling.

As the priestess was digging into her satchel for what she needed, she said, "Thank you, Hammer. Your presence here makes all of us feel better."

Asche had no idea how to reply, as nothing in her life had prepared her for such a sentiment, so she stayed quiet as a bandage was wrapped tightly about her torso, from under her breasts down to her hips. Once the bandage had been tied off, she noted that while uncomfortable, it was better than it had been. She was able to breathe without pain flaring through her with each inhalation, so it was an improvement.

After her ribs were bound, the priestess laid hands on the most injured area and closed her eyes, starting to pray. Again, there was the light and the silent rush of sound she was connecting to the presence of prayers the divines were answering. Once over, the pain in her ribs eased some.

The priestess stood and smiled. "The ribs were indeed broken but now they have been mended. In a little over half a moon it should be fully healed. You will need to be bandaged for at least a week to help your breathing. Please try to not make it worse."

As the healer walked off, Asche awkwardly got to her feet and looked about for Fanlis. She wanted to know where Nibs was, because she didn't see him among the other wounded the chiurgeons and healers were treating. Maybe Fanlis could explain why some people were treating her like she was special, something to be revered. She was still just her, albeit with a fancy hammer.

She spotted Fanlis and the kaitan by the gatehouse talking with someone. It was awkward, but she tucked the war hammer through her belt, on the opposite side of her busted ribs. The head poked into her uncomfortably as she moved. Surely there had to be a better way to transport this. Maybe the infantry people had something that would work since many of them used war hammers. She recalled they had rings attached to their belts holding their weapons.

When she was halfway there, there was a shout from the keep doors, and a group of soldiers and Hands, came out helping some really disheveled looking women. A few of them were being carried on stretchers. She drifted that way to see what was going on.

Kaitan Ginvert listened to what the various troopers were saying. "Wait! One at a time. You there."

The man she had pointed to started to explain. "Lord Whiltaen sent us to check on the dungeon, to see if there was anyone there. When we reached the bottom, we found all these women, shackled, a few with gags in their mouths. A few had clear signs of being mistreated. But this was after we fought some o' those guys with the crossed swords on their baldrics. Yeah, and so we got keys from one of the dead and got 'em out."

Ginvert went over to one of the women on a stretcher. "I'm sorry, but I don't recognize you."

"Sister Elanieh. I was the priestess to one of the outlying villages. Over the winter, he had troops come and capture me and my protectors. The Sword of Tyner mocked us, kept trying to get us to swear oaths to serve him. A few of the youngest did, afraid for their lives and hoping their sacrifice would keep the rest safe. Their broken bodies were shown to us before disposal." The priestess spotted the war hammer at Asche's side. She began to laugh before it dissolved into a cough. "His stupid plan failed. It's a goodness to see you, Blessed Hammer."

Kaitan Ginvert nodded grimly. "Take them to the chiurgeons and get them some food and drink. I'll inform Lord Whiltaen of this as another thing for the baron to answer for."

Asche felt her cheeks warm from what the injured priestess had said. All of this was confusing and she needed answers. She turned to where Fanlis and Kaitan Tanrei were still standing by the open door of the guardhouse.

They spotted her and paused their conversation as she neared, turning to face her. Fanlis asked, "Yes, Asche? Was there something you needed?"

"I was wondering where Nibs is." she said.

The kaitan smiled. "Never fear, Asche. We have the baron's falconer looking after him under Lynarra's watchful eye. None of our chiurgeons were comfortable with bird anatomy and did not want to make anything worse. The priestess managed to put Nibs to sleep and kept him safe as the end of battle came. Once it was over, she started the search for the falconer."

"Nibs is in good hands right now," said Fanlis. "The falconer has a good reputation and has helped several injured birds recover. Lord Whiltaen spoke for him. Plus, the priestess said a healing prayer over him."

Asche felt a tension release and breathed a little easier. "Good. I was so scared when he got hit."

The kaitan reached over and grasped Asche's shoulder. "Nibs is one of us, Asche. Time and again he has proven his usefulness. There is no way we would leave him untended if there was any way to help. We always take care of our own. And Tigh told us about the end of your fight, good work stopping the priest of the Tyner."

"He wasn't a priest," replied Asche. "He was a Sword."

"What?"

"Yeah. The man bragged about killing Swords and Hammers, capturing and enslaving members of the Hands. He used a vow on your sacred heart to do that, backed by a prayer to the Tyner. He was reprehensible. He tried to get me to bind myself to him so I could help him escape with Elsif." Asche shuddered at how close things had been. If Elsif's hammer had not been right there, if the Morri had not empowered her, if there had not been that opening, she would have died or worse. The reality of the or worse was settling on her and she shuddered in disgust and fear.

Fanlis took her arm and moved her over to a wooden bench against the gatehouse wall. Asche sat, breath coming in pants, and the fear she felt, trapped in the room rose back up to fully engulf her. It felt like her whole body was trembling. The little hairs on the back of her neck were standing up and she pressed her back against the wall. She felt weak and was sure she wouldn't be able to stand.

Fanlis turned Asche's head to make her look at her. "It's okay, Asche. Breathe. You're fine and you both made it out. Just breathe. It's okay. We were told Elsif has a concussion and was under an entrapment prayer. The priestess fixed all she could and Elsif's going to be fine, Nibs is going to be fine, and you're going to be fine. You did good."

"S...ome Hammer I am. I was terrified." Shame welled up in her and a tear trickled down her face followed by another, then more.

Kaitan Tanrei crouched down in front of Asche, so she could look in her eyes. "Tigh told us your sword and the spear you grabbed had been broken. Is this true?"

"Yes." She tried to look away, but Tanrei drove on.

"And he admitted to being a Sword of the Tyner, with better armor and weapons?"

"Yes." Asche's voice was almost a whisper.

"And your lover had been knocked unconscious?"

Asche was wondering where all this was going. "Yes."

"How is that anything but terrifying. You were trapped in a situation no one wants to be in, unarmed against a superior foe. No, thank you. In that situation, you being scared is natural and wise."

Asche looked up at Kaitan Tanrei. "Wise? Really?"

"Yes. Fear is there to try to help you deal with more than you can handle. It tries to make sure you are not doing something outside of your abilities. That was a lot for you to handle. That would be a lot for me to handle. So yes, being scared was wise. It's being aware of the entirety of the danger. It's nothing to be ashamed of. It made you cautious and think of a way out, not try to force things into a situation where you would have died and Elsif would have been taken. You did everything right and the Morri blessed you for it." She gave Asche a pat on the knee.

"I don't feel like I did things right. But thank you." Asche held up the war hammer. "I don't even know what this means."

The kaitan stood and adjusted the sword on her hip. "One thing it means, we are likely going to be ordered to the mother temple when this is over so you and Tigh can get the training you deserve. We go with you because we are your company. I'm not sure what will change, as I've never worked with a Hammer before, but I have had a Sword in my command. You're going to learn and train, then we're likely to keep doing the will of the Morri."

That seemed less unrestrained and more down to earth. Down to earth was good right now. "That sounds workable."

"Don't worry, Asche, you're not in this alone. But first I need to report all of this through the farspeaker and find out what they want us to do. Right now, you rest, as I am sure no decision will be made until at least tomorrow. Rest. That's an order."

Tanrei gripped her shoulder in comfort and headed off toward where Lord Whiltaen stood with his advisors. Fanlis patted her on the thigh. "Let's go find that falconer. I'm also worried about Nibs. He was really brave when he spoiled that attack on you. We should check on him."

Asche stood and asked nervously, "I didn't want to mention this with the kaitan here, but why are people staring at me like I'm something special? I'm just Asche."

"When you were dedicated, the Morri passed along what you needed to be trained in. There was a lot. We normally do not have a new girl working with the shrine, but the Morri asked for that specifically. A lot of us didn't know if that meant anything special or not. Several people thought it did, including the high priestess in Turling. Also, and I'm sure it won't help, but you would have been stared at if you had become a Sword."

"What?" Asche stopped and turned to face Fanlis.

"Oh yes. You have to remember Swords and Hammers are a sign of special grace from the Morri. They have been touched by the divine in a special way, different from priestesses. You and Tigh, more than anyone here, represent her will in action. But you are also Asche, and always will be. I hope they can teach you how to deal with people who will see you as if you're some divine sent to us. You are that, but you also aren't."

Asche sighed and continued walking. "That remarkably doesn't help."

Fanlis chuckled as the two of them headed toward the side of the courtyard where there was a stable. Between the castle and the stable was the mews. Fanlis knocked on the door and a gruff voice called out, "Enter!"

Inside were several hooded falcons on perches, with cages against the walls. Lynara was there by the door and left when Asche and Fanlis entered. The falconer sat at a desk, looking at what he was doing, which was some fiddly work his body blocked from their view. "What?"

Fanlis spoke up. "We're here to check on the raven, Nibs. How is he?"

"When he was hit, one of his wing bones snapped. It was a clean break thankfully, and I was able to set it easily enough. I splinted his wing and braced it against his body. The raven should not be allowed to use its wings for at least three weeks, to give it time to heal." While his voice was gruff, his tone implied care.

Asche looked surprised at this. Nibs was always so independent about his eating and his activities, she had no idea how this would change things. "So what are we supposed to do?"

"Feed him, mostly meat, mice are good, they also like eggs and frogs. Keep him comfortable and safe. There is a concoction I give the falcons when they're hurt that should help the raven as well. Similar body mass. Make sure he takes that. After that…" He shrugged. "His wings will be weak and it might take a bit before he can fly again, but he should heal just fine."

"But he should be able to fly again?" Asche was very focused on this point.

"Yes. It was a simple injury and an easy fix. Rest is what he needs more than anything. In three weeks, remove the bindings and that's it. He'll be able to fly again or he won't."

"Thank you." Asche smiled at that, at least one of her worries taken care of.

The man grunted and finished securing the bandage on Nibs. Asche gently picked up her friend, noting he was still asleep. "I guess we need to get the priestess to remove the sleep."

Fanlis said, "Thank you, sir. I will pay you when I come back to get the concoction for the pain. Our healer might want to know the mix, to ensure we have plenty. This is quite appreciated."

The man shook his head. "All this fuss over a raven. A hawk or falcon I'd understand, but a raven?"

Asche looked over at the man with some confusion. "He's my friend."

The man smiled faintly. "Aye, that's fair."

They left the mews and found the priestess, still working amongst the wounded. She stood and chanted, hands moving over Nibs. It was a brief moment before the prayer had been broken and Nibs began to stir. He croaked in discomfort and Asche quickly chimed in, "Careful, Nibs. Your wing is broken. Try not to move it."

Nibs looked over at Asche and Fanlis before turning his head to get a good look at the bandages wrapped about him. He had come out of the spell quickly. "No fly?"

"No flying until it's healed."

Nibs pondered this. It would be inconvenient, but could be done. Not flying would make getting food, slicing, and such a bit more awkward, but there were humans that could help as needed. Being trapped on the ground sounded like a nightmare, despite it being something all his human friends did. He would be practically a human! That made Nibs chuckle a bit. "Down."

Asche carefully put him on the ground and Nibs took a few wobbly steps before he steadied. While not good, this did have some potential. He took several steps, wobbling his head side to side, then stopped. The women stared at him before he kept walking. "Look, I human. Dur dur dur. I human!"

Asche groaned at the joke and hid her face in a hand. Nibs cackled happily, repeating the walk and the words. Fanlis joined in on the laughter, drawing questioning eyes their way. Maybe he could handle some time like this. While it certainly was not comfortable, it would give him plenty of time to make more human jokes. "This human need food!"

"Do you want to be carried or walk?"

"Walk. Dur dur dur, I human." Nibs croaked happily and looked around at all the wounded in the courtyard.

"It's not funny, Nibs."

"Yes. Funny. Dur dur dur." Nibs walked after Fanlis, waggling his head, hoping they could find him something to eat. "We win?"

"Yes, we won," replied Fanlis. "Asche also got hurt and has bandages around her ribs."

Nibs cocked his head up and to the side to better see Asche. Spotting the tightness of her face when she breathed in, Nibs noted she was hurt. It made him a bit sad he had not been able to take care of his human, but he had dived into someone's face to keep her safe. It was so very human to charge right back into danger just after someone had saved them.

"Thank you for protecting me, Nibs," said Asche, her voice tight with emotion.

"All good. Just two injured humans looking for food." He cackled a little as he followed Fanlis in the direction of something to eat, waggling his head and making silly sounds as he moved through people. They were stared at by everyone but he didn't care. Life was good.

# About the Author

Heather K O'Malley is a fifty-plus-year-old transgender lesbian who has been writing stories since fifth grade, lots of stories. Along the way she joined the Army, got injured, traveled the world, learned a number of languages, failed epically, found true love, went to a lot of schools, got a master's in English, was an activist, taught, learned several martial arts, figured out how to cook, tried most everything, and became a proud grandmother. It has been exhausting.

# Books Available from Bold Strokes Books

**Hands of the Morri** by Heather K O'Malley. Discovering she is a Lost Sister and growing acquainted with her new body, Asche learns how to be a warrior and commune with the Goddess the Hands serve, the Morri. (978-1-63679-465-5)

**I Know About You** by Erin Kaste. With her stalker inching closer to the truth, Cary Smith is forced to face the past she's tried desperately to forget. (978-1-63679-513-3)

**Mate of Her Own** by Elena Abbott. When Heather McKenna finally confronts the family who cursed her, her werewolf is shocked to discover her one true mate, and that's only the beginning. (978-1-63679-481-5)

**Pumpkin Spice** by Tagan Shepard. For Nicki, new love is making this pumpkin spice season sweeter than expected. (978-1-63679-388-7)

**Rivals for Love** by Ali Vali. Brooks Boseman's brother Curtis is getting married, and Brooks needs to be at the engagement party. Only she can't possibly go, not with Curtis set to marry the secret love of her youth, Fallon Goodwin. (978-1-63679-384-9)

**Sweat Equity** by Aurora Rey. When cheesemaker Sy Travino takes a job in rural Vermont and hires contractor Maddie Barrow to rehab a house she buys sight unseen, they both wind up with a lot more than they bargained for. (978-1-63679-487-7)

**Taking the Plunge** by Amanda Radley. When Regina Avery meets model Grace Holland—the most beautiful woman she's ever seen—she doesn't have a clue how to flirt, date, or hold on to a relationship. But Regina must take the plunge with Grace and hope she manages to swim. (978-1-63679-400-6)

**We Met in a Bar** by Claire Forsythe. Wealthy nightclub owner Erica turns undercover bartender on a mission to catch a thief where she meets no-strings, no-commitments Charlie, who couldn't be further from Erica's type. Right? (978-1-63679-521-8)

**Western Blue** by Suzie Clarke. Step back in time to this historic western filled with heroism, loyalty, friendship, and love. The odds are against this unlikely group—but never underestimate women who have nothing to lose. (978-1-63679-095-4)

**Windswept** by Patricia Evans. The windswept shores of the Scottish Highlands weave magic for two people convinced they'd never fall in love again. (978-1-63679-382-5)

**An Independent Woman** by Kit Meredith. Alex and Rebecca's attraction won't stop smoldering, despite their reluctance to act on it and incompatible poly relationship styles. (978-1-63679-553-9)

**Cherish** by Kris Bryant. Josie and Olivia cherish the time spent together, but when the summer ends and their temporary romance melts into the real deal, reality gets complicated. (978-1-63679-567-6)

**Cold Case Heat** by Mary P. Burns. Sydney Hansen receives a threat in a very cold murder case that sends her to the police for help where she finds more than justice with Detective Gale Sterling. (978-1-63679-374-0)

**Proximity** by Jordan Meadows. Joan really likes Ellie, but being alone with her could turn deadly unless she can keep her dangerous powers under control. (978-1-63679-476-1)

**Sweet Spot** by Kimberly Cooper Griffin. Pro surfer Shia Turning will have to take a chance if she wants to find the sweet spot. (978-1-63679-418-1)

**The Haunting of Oak Springs** by Crin Claxton. Ghosts and the past haunt the supernatural detective in a race to save the lesbians of Oak Springs farm. (978-1-63679-432-7)

**Transitory** by J.M. Redmann. The cops blow it off as a customer surprised by what was under the dress, but PI Micky Knight knows they're wrong—she either makes it her case or lets a murderer go free to kill again. (978-1-63679-251-4)

**Unexpectedly Yours** by Toni Logan. A private resort on a tropical island, a feisty old chief, and a kleptomaniac pet pig bring Suzanne and Allie together for unexpected love. (978-1-63679-160-9)

**Bones of Boothbay Harbor** by Michelle Larkin. Small-town police chief Frankie Stone and FBI Special Agent Eve Huxley must set aside their differences and combine their skills to find a killer after a burial site is discovered in Boothbay Harbor, Maine. (978-1-63679-267-5)

**Crush** by Ana Hartnett Reichardt. Josie Sanchez worked for years for the opportunity to create her own wine label, and nothing will stand in her way. Not even Mac, the owner's annoyingly beautiful niece Josie's forced to hire as her harvest intern. (978-1-63679-330-6)

**Decadence** by Ronica Black, Renee Roman, and Piper Jordan. You are cordially invited to Decadence, Las Vegas's most talked about invitation-only Masquerade Ball. Come for the entertainment and stay for the erotic indulgence. We guarantee it'll be a party that lives up to its name. (978-1-63679-361-0)

**Gimmicks and Glamour** by Lauren Melissa Ellzey. Ashly has learned to hide her Sight, but as she speeds toward high school graduation she must protect the classmates she claims to hate from an evil that no one else sees. (978-1-63679-401-3)

**Heart of Stone** by Sam Ledel. Princess Keeva Glantor meets Maeve, a gorgon forced to live alone thanks to a decades-old lie, and together the two women battle forces they formerly thought to be good in the hopes of leading lives they can finally call their own. (978-1-63679-407-5)

**Murder at the Oasis** by David S. Pederson. Palm trees, sunshine, and murder await Mason Adler and his friend Walter as they travel from Phoenix to Palm Springs for what was supposed to be a relaxing vacation but ends up being a trip of mystery and intrigue. (978-1-63679-416-7)

**Peaches and Cream** by Georgia Beers. Adley Purcell is living her dreams owning Get the Scoop ice cream shop until national dessert chain Sweet Heaven opens less than two blocks away and Adley has to compete with the far too heavenly Sabrina James. (978-1-63679-412-9)

**The Only Fish in the Sea** by Angie Williams. Will love overcome years of bitter rivalry for the daughters of two crab fishing families in this queer modern-day spin on Romeo and Juliet? (978-1-63679-444-0)

**Wildflower** by Cathleen Collins. When a plane crash leaves eleven-year-old Lily Andrews stranded in the vast wilderness of Arkansas, will she be able to overcome the odds and make it back to civilization and the one person who holds the key to her future? (978-1-63679-621-5)

**Witch Finder** by Sheri Lewis Wohl. Tamsin, the Keeper of the Book of Darkness, is in terrible danger, and as a Witch Finder, Morrigan must protect her and the secrets she guards even if it costs Morrigan her life. (978-1-63679-335-1)

**A Second Chance at Life** by Genevieve McCluer. Vampires Dinah and Rachel reconnect, but a string of vampire killings begin and evidence seems to be pointing at Dinah. They must prove her innocence while finding out if the two of them are still compatible after all these years. (978-1-63679-459-4)

**Digging for Heaven** by Jenna Jarvis. Litz lives for dragons. Kella lives to kill them. The last thing they expect is to find each other attractive. (978-1-63679-453-2)

**Forever's Promise** by Missouri Vaun. Wesley Holden migrated west disguised as a man for the hope of a better life and with no designs to take a wife, but Charlotte Rose has other ideas. (978-1-63679-221-7)

**Here For You** by D. Jackson Leigh. A horse trainer must make a difficult business decision that could save her father's ranch from foreclosure but destroy her chance to win the heart of a feisty barrel racer vying for a spot in the National Rodeo Finals. (978-1-63679-299-6)

**I Do, I Don't** by Joy Argento. Creator of the romance algorithm, Nicole Hart doesn't expect to be starring in her own reality TV dating show, and falling for the show's executive producer Annie Jackson could ruin everything. (978-1-63679-420-4)

**It's All in the Details** by Dena Blake. Makeup artist Lane Donnelly and wedding planner Helen Trent can't stand each other, but they must set aside their differences to ensure Darcy gets the wedding of her dreams, and make a few of their own dreams come true. (978-1-63679-430-3)

**Marigold** by Melissa Brayden. Marigold Lavender vows to take down Alexis Wakefield, the harsh food critic who blasts her younger sister's restaurant. If only she wasn't as sexy as she is mean. (978-1-63679-436-5)

**The Town that Built Us** by Jesse J. Thoma. When her father dies, Grace Cook returns to her hometown and tries to avoid Bonnie Whitlock, the woman who pulverized her heart, only to discover her father's estate has been left to them jointly. (978-1-63679-439-6)